Ninety-Mile Prairie

A Cracker Western
by
Lee Gramling

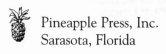

Pineapple Press, Inc.
Sarasota, Florida

Inquiries should be addressed to:

Pineapple Press, Inc.
P.O. Box 3889
Sarasota, Florida 34230
www.pineapplepress.com

Library of Congress Cataloging-in-Publication Data

Gramling, Lee.
    Ninety-Mile Prairie / Lee Gramling.— 1st ed.
        p.   cm.
    ISBN 1-56164-255-X (alk. paper) — ISBN 1-56164-257-6 (pbk. : alk. paper)
        1. Archaeologists—Fiction. 2. Florida—Fiction. 3. Cowboys—Fiction. I. Title.

PS3557.R228 N56 2002
813'.54—dc21

2002025124

First Edition
10 9 8 7 6 5 4 3 2 1

Design by Sandra Wright Designs
Printed in the United States of America

For Linton:
old friends are the
best friends.

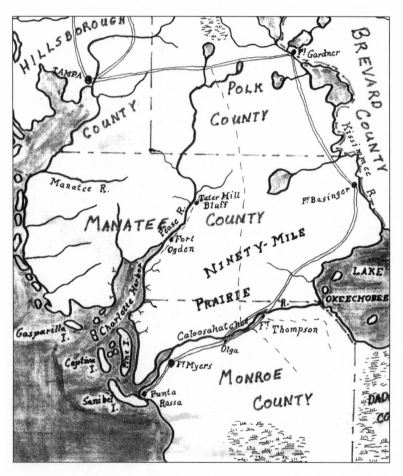

Southwest Florida, 1882

1 🌿

PEEK TILLMAN SHOOK out the short length of rope in his hand and stepped to the edge of the boggy depression. Without taking his eyes from the dark circle of water and its faint reflection of the tall cypress overhead, he nodded to his burly companion.

Cooter Wills, a dozen yards away, cupped his palms over his mouth and uttered a noise somewhere between a harsh muffled grunt and a throttled yelp. He paused, then repeated the call several more times in quick succession.

Peek kept his attention on the water. Soon a craggy brow ridge rose from the quiet surface, eight or ten inches behind the smaller island of a blunt armored snout. The alligator's appearance caused scarcely a ripple in the pool's glasslike calm.

Paying no heed to the cloud of tiny insects that flitted restlessly before his eyes, the young cow hunter stayed motionless while the prehistoric beast glided slowly toward the odd noises made by his companion. Cooter had a well-earned reputation as one of the best gator callers in all of south Florida. With luck he'd coax the dangerous reptile up onto dry land before Peek needed to make his move.

The broad, scaly back and lazily switching tail were below and abreast of him now, in water that was shallow enough to let him judge the creature's length. Nine feet, Peek guessed, maybe a tad over. Bigger than he'd have liked, but it could have been worse. He took a slow, deep breath and placed the rope between his teeth. The muscles of his body tensed as the gator threaded its way among the cypress knees that bordered the pond, waddling forward on short, stubby legs.

Once more Cooter repeated his call, and the gator continued its steady advance into a small clearing overhung by moss-draped limbs of swamp bay and black gum. Peek, behind and outside its line of vision, swiftly closed the distance between them.

Then suddenly, with the speed of a striking rattler, he sprang.

No sooner had he landed on the gator's back than there was a ferocious hiss and five feet of armored tail churned the moist earth to a gritty pulp. Peek locked his legs around the thrashing body, holding on for all he was worth while his hands sought to close around the fearsome tooth-filled jaws. The jaws opened once in a hissing roar and snapped shut with bone-crushing force. Instantly Peek clamped both hands around them, holding them together in a grip of iron.

He locked his legs more tightly around the gator's body as the powerful beast arched and twisted, striving furiously to throw its tormentor off. After a minute or two it abandoned this futile effort and began slewing sideways to regain the advantage of its own watery element. Using a momentary pause while the gator gathered its strength, Peek lifted a hand from the creature's snout to yank the bit of rope from his teeth. He whipped a half-dozen swift turns around the closed jaws and knotted the ends. Then he dug his hands and feet into the mud to keep the fierce predator from dragging him into the pool where it could continue the battle in its water-filled hole.

Cooter was beside him now, bringing a longer rope that the two cow hunters used to bind the reptile's stubby legs and thrashing body, rendering it all but helpless. When this task was done, Peek climbed slowly to his feet while his partner tied the rope to a nearby tree.

Both men stood looking down at their still-hissing captive, breathing heavily and exchanging no words. Then Peek bent to brush the worst of the mud from his homespun trousers. Finally he stretched his lanky six-foot frame and bared his teeth in a good-natured grin.

"Well," he drawled, casually skirting the hog-tied monster to recover his hat, which had fallen off during the melee. "What you think? Gator tail for supper tonight? Or do we turn this feller loose once the cows have drunk?"

It had been a long dry summer, and many of the seasonal creeks southwest of Fort Basinger couldn't be counted on to support the Rocking JG herd of long-horned cattle on their fall trek to the Gulf Coast. Deep gator holes like this one, nestled among the widely scattered cypress domes of Ninety-Mile Prairie, would likely be their only source of water now for the better part of a week.

The cattle didn't much care for the gator holes with their strong scent of musk, but it was that or go thirsty. And getting the half-wild scrub cows to water was just one of many troublesome tasks that the Florida cow hunters had to face, together with their hard-working catch dogs and tough Cracker ponies.

Cooter squatted on his heels and reached into his shirt pocket for a twist of home-cured tobacco.

"Son, you know I don't care a hoot in Hades for that stringy old lizard meat." He paused to stuff a few pieces of leaf into his sunburnt cheek. "An' I got a notion what Cookie'll say too, if you come traipsin' into camp with that critter in tow."

Peek ran his fingers through sandy-colored locks, then settled his slouch hat in place. "Shucks, Cooter, t'aint no trouble to fix. Feller back home told me all about it. Alls you got to do is cut up the tender part, right there behind the legs . . ." He pointed with a booted toe. ". . . an' then fry it up like pork chops. That gent allowed as how it was some mighty fine eatin', 'specially if they's a tad of orange marmalade to go with it. Maybe Cookie just ain't had much experience fixin' gator tail the right way. . . ."

"I reckon that's what he'll tell you, too." The older man spit a jet of tobacco juice that saturated the already damp grass at his feet. "He'll allow if you know so much about it, you can go right on ahead an' butcher it out and cook it your ownself."

With a shrug of his lean but muscular shoulders, Peek crossed the clearing to recover his cartridge belt and holster from where he'd hung them over a low-growing limb.

"Cooter, the trouble with you an' Cookie is, ain't neither one of you got a ounce of adventuresome spirit to parcel out between you. Me, I figure variety's the spice o' life, like the feller said. No matter if it's vittles, or fresh territory . . ." He paused, then went on a little self-consciously. ". . . or women, or anything else this big old world has to offer!"

Cooter responded with a sideways glance and a non-committal grunt. He let fly another stream of tobacco juice that barely missed a spider weaving its web between two possum-haw bushes.

"Why, to hear you talk," Peek went on, warming to the subject as he buckled on his six-shooter, "you'd be plumb satisfied to feed off of cornbread an' sow belly an' greens ever' natural day of your life."

"You add in a good-sized bowl of buttered grits with that," the older man stretched lazily and rose to his feet, "and you ain't far from wrong. A feller could do a heap worse."

He'd been friends with the Tillman family ever since his young companion was no higher than a saddle cinch ring and had to be lifted up to sit a horse. There always was a restless streak in the boy. Not wild exactly, just restless. It probably wouldn't be much longer before even this wide-open Florida backcountry wouldn't be enough to satisfy his craving for new adventures.

He watched thoughtfully while the younger man bent to tie the leather thongs of his holster, low down on his left thigh like some Texas gunfighter. Peek spent a lot of his spare time practicing with that six-shooter, and he was more than average fast. What's more, he generally hit whatever it was he was aiming at. A couple days ago he'd blown the head off a canebrake rattler from horseback at a distance of more than twenty feet.

But he'd never faced another man in armed combat and Cooter prayed he never would, although such encounters were at least as common on this southern frontier as they were in the West. Anyplace where the law was scarce and far between, guns were necessary for self-protection. But no man needed a reputation for being quick on the shoot, least of all some still-green young'un who hadn't lived a day of his life outside the south Florida wilderness.

The older man put such thoughts aside with a shrug, then offered his opinion on another fool notion the kid had just hinted at. "Now, far as womenfolk is concerned," he observed dryly, "since you brung up the subject . . ."

Peek favored him with a curious glance while he straightened and settled the holster more comfortably about his slim hips.

"I reckon just one of them notional critters by her lonesome ought to be enough to satisfy any sensible man's cravin' for 'variety.' More'n one is just askin' for trouble!"

The young cow hunter's grin grew broader as he came near and gave his partner a friendly nudge in the ribs. "I believe you've got to be cautious an' set in your ways, Cooter, now that you've reached your declinin' years. That wife up to Fort Drum must of flat took the wind out of your sails."

"Mebbe. But I reckon I'll keep her." The heavy-set man bent at the waist and spit again with finality. "She don't talk near as much foolishness as some a feller's liable to meet out here on Ninety-Mile Prairie."

Peek accepted his friend's remark with good-natured silence. It was no worse than he'd come to expect from the other cow hunters during this westward trek across the peninsula. Despite the fact that he'd made four earlier drives with his father and members of his family, this was his first trip on his own, as a man and for pay. And though he pulled his share of the load and a tad more besides, neither Cooter nor anybody else meant to let him forget that at the tender age of eighteen he was the "cub" of the Rocking JG crew.

He lifted his gaze toward the brightly lit prairie, only partly visible beyond the closest trees and thick foliage. After a moment he shrugged and glanced at their captive.

"Well, big feller," he said with mock resignation, "I reckon ole lawyer Cooter here's done argued you a re-prieve. I already got enough chores to keep me free from mischief, without takin' on no added cookin' duties."

He might be willing to kill an occasional gator for meat, as he would any kind of game, but neither Peek nor most other Florida natives would take the life of one of the fierce reptiles needlessly. When all the gators were gone there'd be no more gator holes, and no gator holes meant no handy places to water cattle during seasonal droughts such as this.

"You go on back an' let the rest of 'em know it's okay to bring the herd up," he said to his companion. "I'll drag this feller over yonder to that next li'l cypress dome where he can't cause no trouble."

Cooter responded with a nod and an agreeable grunt, then started for where their horses were tied a short distance away. He knew that all that was really needed was to drag the trussed-up gator deeper into the nearby woods and keep it there till the cattle had drunk. But he was willing to make some allowances for a young buck who couldn't resist having a look at whatever lay beyond the next stand of trees.

While the older man mounted and swung his horse's nose east, Peek led his own pony back to the clearing where their still-hissing prisoner was waiting. The shaggy-maned little Cracker horse snorted and tossed his head when he caught scent of the reptile, but a word from his master was enough to calm him. After all, this was hardly the first gator the Florida-bred gelding had ever had dealings with.

Peek untied the rope from the tree and climbed into the saddle. He took a few turns around the horn, leaving enough slack so the creature in tow would be a respectable distance behind them; then he clucked to his pony and urged it forward with his knees. The helpless reptile was dragged on its belly out of the hammock and across the slippery grass to the next closest cypress dome some hundred yards away.

A minute before they entered the shade of these farther trees, Peek's nose wrinkled up and he sniffed thoughtfully at the midmorning air. The gelding, sensing his master's change of mood and welcoming the opportunity for a break from his present chore, came to a stop.

Peek sampled the air again, then shook his head and bent to run his fingers through the pony's long mane. "Could of swore I smelt biscuits cookin' for half a second there." He spoke so quietly that only the horse could hear. "But that don't make the slightest kind of sense."

As far as he knew, there wasn't a settlers' cabin within thirty miles of this place. And the only cow crew that was making a drive this early was his own, still a mile or so back to the east.

Not to mention that fresh-baked biscuits were unlikely cow camp fare at any time, and surely not for the midday meal. Your average cow hunter was lucky to get a cold slab of leftover cornpone to go with his side meat and sweet potato, so long as the herd was still moving.

He sat with his brow creased in thought for a minute longer. Then the alligator twitched at the end of its tether and the Cracker pony blew and started to sidestep. Peek knew it was time he got on with the job at hand.

Still, he took a moment to slip the leather thong from the hammer of his six-shooter before urging his mount forward again. Outlaws and rustlers were common enough in the Florida wilderness, and it didn't cost a thing to be careful.

His eyes were wary as the pony moved slowly in among the shade of ancient cypresses, ringed all around with loblolly bay. The shadows were deep here, and the ground became boggy after a few dozen feet. His sure-footed gelding navigated the treacherous cluster of cypress knees without a misstep. But soon the jumble of low, knobby growths made it impossible to drag their trussed-up captive farther.

With a quiet word to his pony, Peek swung down and let the horse keep tension on the rope while he went and gingerly freed the gator. When he'd stepped aside to give it room, the big reptile lay still for a second, then turned its head to glare at Peek and utter one last angry hiss before half-waddling, half-sliding on its belly into the deeper recesses of the swamp.

Peek let out a long sigh of relief as he coiled the rope and hung it from the saddle opposite his cow whip, which was the more familiar tool of a Florida cow hunter's trade. When he'd led his pony off a short distance to avoid the cypress knees and the low-growing limbs of a gnarled old water hickory, he stepped back into the leather and they turned once more toward the open prairie.

"Come on, fella," he said gently. "Let's us get shut of this place and go find the herd."

But a bare instant before they emerged into the bright sunlight he drew rein again. Something—an unexpected sound, another odd scent, Peek couldn't say what—had caught his attention.

Anyone who lived his life in the wilderness, away from towns and the unpredictable bustle of humanity, knew the sights and sounds and smells of his native surroundings so completely that after a while he wasn't consciously aware of them. It was only when something unusual intruded on the senses—something that didn't belong—that his ears pricked up and the hairs on the back of his neck started to tingle.

And that was what Peek Tillman felt now, in the shadowed recess of a cypress hammock, miles from the closest settlement. It could be a warning of impending danger; or it might be nothing of the sort. But no one survived long in this harsh Florida backcountry who failed to pay heed to such subtle advertisements.

There was no obvious change of expression on the young man's tanned features, nor in the relaxed way he sat his horse, that might have betrayed his sudden alertness. But for several long minutes he held perfectly still, reaching out with eyes and ears and nose for any more faint clues that could give form and meaning to this unknown mystery.

The Cracker pony seemed to share his rider's wariness, frozen in place like a shaggy-maned statue, with head high and ears pricked for any hint of danger.

A gentle breeze rustled the leaves around them, cooling the sweat on Peek's forehead and neck. All the birds and insects seemed to have fallen silent too. Just one more suggestion that something—or someone—out of the ordinary was nearby.

Slowly he became aware of the small noises that had caught his attention earlier.

From somewhere, not far beyond the cluster of trees and dense growth where he waited and listened, came a faint clink of metal on metal. When he'd heard it a few more times with variations, Peek nodded his recognition. Human visitors. Only those of his own kind used metal objects.

The breeze shifted around to the north, and at last his nose caught the familiar scent of a wood fire. A moment later a horse blew and stamped, and he caught the low-pitched murmur of men's voices. The sounds seemed to come from the far side of this same cluster of woods.

"Well," Peek said quietly to no one in particular, "I s'pose we'd ought to be neighborly an' go introduce ourselves. They'll know about our outfit soon enough, onct all them cows start showin' up."

2

PEEK TOOK THE REINS in his right hand and began walking his pony slowly forward. As they emerged into the sunlight, his other hand dropped almost without thought to rest lightly on his left thigh, a comforting few inches from the butt of his Colt Peacemaker revolver.

When they were halfway 'round the cypress dome, he could see the reflection of white canvas tents. But it was several minutes longer before he was close enough to make out any details. The young cow hunter's eyes narrowed curiously as he approached and took in the layout.

There were two good-sized wall tents, almost brand-new—judging from the lack of mildew—with another broad panel of canvas spread between them to provide shade for a camp table and a half dozen folding chairs. Beyond the tents was an unhitched spring wagon, still piled high with crates and boxes of supplies.

Four big sturdy mules were staked out in the distance, and three unsaddled riding horses cropped grass on a picket rope closer by.

Just in front of the awning on the side facing Peek's approach, overheated air shimmered above the stone ring and smoke-blackened tripod of an untended cook fire. He could guess the cook was only absent temporarily, for the steaming collection of shiny, new cast-iron pots and skillets spoke of a sizable dinner almost ready for serving.

The frontier-bred cow hunter whistled softly through his teeth while he drew rein by a clump of palmettos some twenty yards away.

He'd never in his life seen such a fancy outfit as this, every bit of it shiny and new, with a mule-drawn supply wagon loaded down to the axles. But he had a pretty fair notion what it must mean.

There'd been talk about all the rich Yankees who'd been coming down to Florida since the War Between the States ended. Some meant to make their homes here and take advantage of the climate and the cheap land the state had to offer. Others had a mind to get even richer by buying up property, draining off swamps, or building railroads and hotels for the ever-increasing tourist trade.

But the greatest number were seasonal visitors, attracted for a few days or weeks by the warm weather and the novelty of an unspoiled wilderness. Many fancied themselves "sportsmen," catching fish by the dozen and then giving them away or leaving them to spoil on the banks of the rivers. Or they would blaze away with rifle and shotgun at whatever moved, most often wounding rather than killing anything they could hit. They'd grab a few pelts or a handful of feathers to show off to their friends up north, once again leaving the biggest part of their handiwork to rot.

Peek had heard tales of such foolishness from his uncle and others who traveled the northern part of the state; and though not many tourists had taken the trouble yet to venture this far south, he'd little doubt that what he saw now was one of those harebrained "sporting expeditions."

All things considered, the young cow hunter reflected sourly, he'd a lot sooner come across a marauding pack of wolves or a self-respecting rustler gang than something like this here.

But it wasn't a thing that could be helped. This was all free-range country and open to everybody. The best he figured he could do was introduce himself and explain about the herd that would be passing through in a couple of hours. Then pray that these pilgrims had enough sense to tell the difference between a long-horned steer and a deer or a panther.

The only person in view from where Peek sat his horse was a youngish man in spotless khakis and polished lace-up boots, who sat hunched over a leather-bound notebook at the far end of the long camp table. He seemed completely absorbed in whatever he was writing, so that even now he was unaware of the cow hunter's approach.

To add to Peek's growing sense of wonder at this outlandish set-up in the heart of the Florida wilderness, he saw now that the table was covered with a white linen cloth, on which were five carefully arranged place settings with neatly folded napkins, genuine china plates, and cut-glass tumblers.

Even his aristocratic aunt Polly, whose treasured collection of dishes had been rescued from her father's Georgia plantation a step ahead of Sherman's raiders, would have been hard put to match fixings like these. And Peek only saw those items grace her table at rare family gatherings such as Thanksgiving and Christmas.

He was about to walk his horse closer when he remembered himself and stopped to call out in the universal custom of the frontier: "Hello the fire! Is it all right for a rider to come in?"

The man in khaki looked up with a surprised expression on his face. He took off his reading glasses but made no immediate reply. After a moment, a second man—tall, muscular, dressed in a black broadcloth suit with a wide-brimmed dark hat—appeared at the entrance to the closest tent. Peek's eyes flicked thoughtfully to the pearl-handled revolver in its cross-draw holster beneath the new arrival's unbuttoned coat.

This man studied Peek narrowly for what might have been a slow count of ten, apparently sizing him up. Then he stepped out into the open.

"Come on ahead," he said agreeably. "Light and set!"

Peek let his pony approach the fire, and dismounted when he was a dozen feet away.

"Coffee?" the man in black asked, coming closer while Peek bent to loop his reins around some low-growing palmettos. "Or maybe somethin' a little stronger?" He grinned slyly. "As you might be able to tell, we're not exactly hurtin' here for the better things in life."

"Coffee'll do me fine." Peek glanced from the speaker to the man in khaki, who had risen now and stepped around the table to join them. "You-all are a right far piece from civilization," he observed mildly. "Come down here to do a little huntin', did you?"

He thought he saw the larger man's eyes grow cold for the barest fraction of a second. But then he shrugged and knelt to take the coffee pot from its tripod over the fire. The khaki-clad gent didn't seem to notice. He approached the cow hunter and extended a hand.

"Only after a manner of speaking," he responded with a faint but winning smile. "I'm Doctor James Westfield of Princeton University. And this is my associate, Mister Ethan Cabell."

"Pleased to make your acquaintance." Peek shook the doctor's hand and nodded at the man in black, who had taken the coffee pot to a stack of blue china cups on the near end of the table. "Peek Tillman here. I hunt cows for the Rockin' JG, over east in Brevard County."

"Won't you have a seat?" Westfield returned to his chair under the awning while Cabell handed a cup to Peek and poured two more for the doctor and himself. "It's a rare treat to have company this far from 'civilization,' as you put it. We've hardly seen anyone for more than a week."

Peek pulled out a chair and sat while Cabell brought the other two cups to that end of the table. After rummaging briefly in a nearby case of supplies the big man produced a can of condensed milk, a tin of sugar, and a half-full bottle of brandy, all of which he placed within easy reach.

"You're pretty far from home yourself," he observed casually, taking the chair across from Peek. "You travelin' out here on business, or just passin' through?"

"Little of both." Peek deliberately ignored the other's questioning gaze while he added two heaping teaspoons of sugar to his coffee and stirred it thoroughly. "We're trailin' a herd of cows through to Punta Rassa. Got in mind to water 'em over at that next cypress dome yonder, then make a few more miles before stoppin' for the night."

"Uh-huh." Cabell's face was bland as he uncorked the brandy and added a generous portion to his cup.

Peek tasted his own coffee and nodded appreciatively. "That sure does hit the spot," he said, "after a long mornin' on the range." He pushed his hat back from his forehead and eased his body into a more comfortable position. "A feller might even say," he continued with a sideways glance at Westfield, "that it's just what the doctor ordered!"

The man in khaki smiled at this mild attempt at humor, and Peek was encouraged to press his curiosity further. "I don't reckon I ever met no Princeton University doc before. What kind of doctorin' is it you do up yonder? People, or horses, or both?"

"Neither one, actually. I'm a Doctor of Philosophy. My personal specialty is primitive archaeology."

Peek frowned at the unfamiliar word. "Archy—what?"

"Archaeology," Westfield repeated, not the least disturbed by his guest's puzzled expression. "It's the study of ancient peoples and civilizations."

"Oh." The young cow hunter could recall hearing about some of those highfalutin universities now, like Harvard or William and Mary, and about people—"scholars," they were called—who spent all their lives studying and teaching instead of working for a living. It seemed like a mighty peculiar life for a full-grown man. And he'd surely never expected to meet one of them here on the Florida frontier.

"You mean you're some kind of a historian?" he asked slowly. History was one of the few subjects that had managed to capture Peek's interest during his brief years of schooling. He'd enjoyed the stories of ancient Rome and the American Revolution that the teacher had told them; and he'd even done a little reading on his own in some books of history since then.

"Yes." Westfield nodded agreeably. "In a way. But my studies are directed specifically toward those people and cultures that left no written records. Prehistoric American Indian tribes, to be exact."

Peek swallowed more coffee and scratched his ear thoughtfully. "But if those folks lived a real long time ago, and didn't leave behind no writin', then how do you . . . ?"

"There's an enormous amount to be learned from the various artifacts we discover buried in the earth. Bones, pieces of pottery, primitive tools—each has its unique story to tell. As a matter of fact . . ."

A sound at their backs caused Westfield to interrupt his explanation and turn in his chair. Peek followed his eyes . . .

And found himself gaping awkwardly at the most beautiful woman he'd ever seen in his life.

She stood just outside the entrance flap of the farthest tent. Her long golden hair cascaded loosely to her waist and framed delicately chiseled features of almost flawless perfection. She appeared to be not much older than Peek, maybe three or four years. But there was a clear-eyed reserve and self-confidence about her, which together with the severe lines of her tailored shirtwaist and long dark skirt, made her seem more sophisticated and mature than any woman in the young cow hunter's limited experience.

It didn't help to curb the hot flush he felt rising in his cheeks to notice that the lacy top of the young lady's blouse was presently unbuttoned, revealing the contours of a pale, aristocratic neck. A linen towel in her hands, which she used to pat away the few remaining drops of moisture from her forehead and chin, explained her mild state of undress.

"Dinner is just about ready, gentlemen. If you will—"

She lowered the towel and her sparkling dark eyes found Peek's for the first time.

"Oh. I didn't know we had company." There was no particular embarrassment in her manner, only the very briefest lapse of composure. "Please excuse me for a moment." She turned and disappeared once more into the tent.

All three men had risen from the table at her appearance, Peek a little more clumsily than he'd have liked. When she'd retired from view again, Ethan Cabell turned and strode off toward the open prairie. Once he was out of sight beyond the tents, two pistol shots in quick succession caused the cow hunter to jerk his head around sharply.

"It's his way of calling the others in to dinner," Westfield explained with a mild air of apology. "I had the impression it was something of a custom out here on the frontier."

"There's other ways to get folks' attention," Peek remarked dryly, "most all of which makes better sense when they's a bunch of mossy-horned cows in the neighborhood."

He finished his coffee and set the cup down carefully on its saucer. "I'd be obliged if you'd speak to Mister Cabell about that. At least for the next couple days, till our outfit's left the area."

"Of course," Westfield agreed, with a glance in the direction of his unseen associate. Then after a short hesitation: "I will certainly make it a point to mention it to him."

Something in the archaeologist's voice caused Peek to look at him curiously. He almost acted like he was a little afraid of Cabell. Yet until then it had seemed obvious that the refined and educated Princeton man was the one in charge of this party; or at least that it was his money that paid for it.

Ethan Cabell clearly wasn't the "scholarly" type; nor was he from any place up north, to judge by his speech. His broadcloth suit, though respectable enough at first glance, was actually a bit worn and frayed around the edges. Peek had had the impression that he was just some local resident, probably down on his luck, who'd hired himself out as a guide. But if that was the case, what was behind Westfield's peculiar hesitancy in dealing with him?

These thoughts were cut short by the reappearance of the young lady. Her blouse was buttoned fully now, and her hair had been hurriedly arranged in a loose bun on top of her head. Peek still thought she was the most beautiful woman he'd ever set eyes on.

The archaeologist smiled warmly as she approached and put an arm around her slim waist. "Miranda," he said, "allow me to introduce Mister Peek Tillman. Mister Tillman, my wife, Miranda."

Peek felt an odd sadness, and a lump began forming at the base of his throat. Yet he surely had no reason to imagine that any single woman of quality would be staying alone in a camp full of men.

"Pleased to make your acquaintance, ma'am," he mumbled, touching a finger to his hat while avoiding her eyes.

"It's my pleasure, Mister Tillman. Won't you join us for dinner? We have more than enough, and it's so seldom we have visitors out here in the field."

"Thanks, ma'am, I 'preciate the offer. But I'd best be gettin' on back. I been away so long now they're prob'ly thinkin' about sendin' out search parties."

"Mister Tillman is a drover," her husband explained. "He and his companions are taking a herd of cattle to market, and tonight they'll be camping a short distance west of here."

"I'm afraid it ain't a job that allows much time for social-izin'," Peek said with more regret than he might have felt under different circumstances. "We're all pretty much on the go ever' day, from can't see to can't see."

"I quite understand." Westfield nodded sympathetically. "Perhaps another time."

Miranda Westfield had moved off a few steps to exam-ine the pots at the cook fire. As Peek started around her to fetch his horse, she turned and met his eyes.

"What about in the evening?" she asked suddenly. "This evening, I mean, after your chores are done? If you're not camped too far away, mightn't you find time to come for a short visit?"

She glanced at her husband, and an unspoken commu-nication seemed to pass between them. "We've had no real company in all the weeks we've been in south Florida, and so little knowledge of the land or its people . . ." Her clear dark eyes seemed to hold Peek's in a spell. "Please come. It will be such a joy to hear fresh conversation for a change!"

Westfield nodded in answer to Peek's questioning glance. "By all means," he said warmly. "Come and spend an hour or two with us if you're able. We often sit up for a time after night falls, over coffee and brandy."

"Well . . ." Peek hesitated, weighing the cost. He'd have to hit the trail boss up for the late shift at night herd, and he'd be lucky to manage even a couple hours of sleep in between. But he reckoned he could stand it this once. After all, how many chances did a fellow like him get to spend a couple hours socializing with a genuine Doc of Philosophy from Princeton University?

And his beautiful wife.

He deliberately put aside the mild twinge of guilt brought on by that last thought and grinned at his hosts. "Okay, folks, we got ourselves a date! I'll be mighty pleased myself to hear somethin' a tad more educated than your usual cow camp gab!"

He untied the reins and swung into the saddle with a flourish, showboating just a little for the Yankee and his lady.

Like he'd told Cooter earlier, he had a mind to sample all the new experiences this life had to offer. And since he'd probably never meet up with the Westfields again after tonight, he'd just grab onto the moment and worry about the consequences tomorrow.

"I'll be seein' you!" he called out cheerfully, lifting his free hand in a parting wave. Then he lightly touched spurs to the Cracker pony's flank, and they left the camp behind at a spanking gallop.

3

WHEN HE'D ROUNDED a corner of the cypress dome and pointed his pony's nose east, Peek took a deep breath and eased the obliging animal back to a trot, then to a walk, to save it for the long afternoon ahead.

A few minutes later, he spotted two riders in the distance, heading for the Westfields' camp at a distance-eating lope. He'd little doubt these were the "others" Ethan Cabell had summoned with his ill-advised pistol shots. But they seemed hardly the type he'd expect to see in company with a Princeton University professor.

He drew back on the reins a little bit so he could study them more carefully.

Both were cold-eyed, hard-faced men, one tall and lean, the other short and heavy-set. From the battered slouch hats, scuffed boots, and patched cotton work shirts they wore, they might have been been down-at-heel cow hunters. Each was well armed, though, with a belted pistol at his hip and some kind of long-arm, either rifle or shotgun, in a boot by his saddle.

There was nothing very remarkable about their used-up clothing, and a man's physical appearance wasn't anything he could do much about. Nor were their weapons all that unusual on this harsh Florida frontier of the 1880s.

It was their horses that made Peek's brow knit in thought.

The big dun and its sorrel companion were two of the finest specimens of horseflesh he'd had occasion to set eyes on in all his eighteen years of living among horses and horsemen. Either one was worth more than any workaday cow hunter could afford on his thirty dollars a month and found.

Peek was no pilgrim, in spite of his youth. And he knew only one kind of rider who'd put such a high value on the quality of his mount, to the neglect of clothing and everything else.   A cow hunter's horse was important, so he'd be able to earn his keep. But there were those for whom a big powerful animal with speed and bottom could literally be the difference between life and death. Especially with a sheriff's posse hot on his backtrail. To the road agent or bank artist, there was nothing more vital than a good, fast horse with staying power.

Peek's brow remained furrowed as he squinted after the two riders growing smaller in the distance. He was still frowning when he lifted his Cracker pony to a trot in the opposite direction.

Now why in God's Creation would a Yankee scholar like Westfield have such men in his party?

Not that it was any of his affair, of course. Nor something he'd be likely to bring up in casual conversation. Folks on the frontier liked to keep their own counsel.

But it wouldn't be a bad idea to have all his wits about him tonight, and to be on the lookout for any stray tidbits of information. With two hard cases like that in the neighborhood, any manner of trouble was apt to be brewing. And rustling cattle was one possibility.

Before too much longer he could hear the familiar popping of cow whips in the distance, and see the faint haze of dust on the horizon that marked the slow-moving progress of the Rocking JG herd. Another half hour brought him close enough to pick out Cooter's stocky form as he rode the near flank. Peek brought his pony around in a wide half-circle to join him.

"Took you long enough," the older man said dryly, once they were riding stirrup to stirrup. "I was startin' to figure you'd got a notion to have a couple chomps on that ole lizard's tail after all." He turned his head to one side in order to eject a stream of tobacco juice. "Or mebbe t'other way round!"

"That gator an' me parted friendly," Peek informed him, "with both our tails in-tact." He paused briefly for effect, making a show of pulling his hat lower against the midday sun.

"But then afterwards I was obliged to be neighborly towards some Yankee newcomers I met along the way. We tarried over coffee an' had a right fine conversation, me an' this Princeton Doctor of Philosophy an' his wife, all about archy-ology an' the like."

Cooter rewarded his partner's cryptic announcement with a brief sideways glance. Then he clucked to his horse and trotted off to turn in a cantankerous steer that had strayed too far from the herd. For the time being, it was all the reaction the younger cow hunter was going to get.

It took six long hours to get the cattle watered at the gator holes and then trail them another mile or two west before bedding them down for the night. Everybody was bone-tired by the time the horses were finally unsaddled and Cookie started dishing up the evening's meal of hash, sweet potatoes, and cornbread.

So far Cooter hadn't said much about Peek's encounter with the Westfields, even after hearing a more complete account of it during the afternoon's ride. But when he learned at supper of his friend's plan for a nighttime visit, he finally offered an opinion:

"Son, that ain't nothin' but plain damn foolishness. Even you ought to have better sense than to go gallivantin' off in the middle of the night payin' social calls on strangers, when they's a full day's work lookin' ever'body in the face come sun-up."

"Aw heck, Cooter. It'll only be for a couple hours. An' how many chances does a backwoods cow puncher like me get to share coffee an' conversation with a genuine Doctor of Philosophy from Princeton University?"

Cooter's eyes narrowed as he regarded his young friend from under his hat brim. "An' with his good-lookin' wife?" He paused to mop his plate with one last bite of cornbread. "What it sounds like to me is, you're startin' to get a case on that there married woman."

"Pshaw!" Peek turned his head away and hoped the deepening shadows would hide the sudden rush of blood he felt coloring his cheeks. "You know I ain't the kind to be covetin' some other man's wife."

"I surely hope you ain't. That's the quickest way I know for a young buck like you to keep from ever gettin' any older."

"Besides," Peek rose to his feet and flipped out the dregs from his coffee cup with exaggerated casualness. "I reckon she's too old for me anyhow. Why, she must be ever' bit of twenty-two or twenty-three."

"Uh-huh." Cooter's tone was noncommittal, and he no longer seemed inclined to discuss the matter. He downed the last of his coffee and put the cup aside while he set about untying his bedroll from the saddle he'd been using as a backrest.

Peek glared down at him, as put out now by the older man's seeming indifference as he was by his earlier unasked-for advice. "Don't you fret over it," he said, a little bit of an edge creeping into his voice. "I'll mind my P's an' Q's just proper as you please. And after tonight, I don't expect I'll ever have occasion to meet up with any of them folks again."

Cooter still said nothing, and after a minute Peek turned and strode off to rinse and stow his dishes before resaddling his Cracker horse.

The older man watched from the corner of his eye until his partner's slender form lost itself among the shadows. Then, with a weary sigh and a shake of his head, he turned on his knees and began to spread his bedroll out for the night.

A silver-haloed three-quarter moon had risen above the flat expanse of the eastern horizon, brightening Peek's surly mood as well as his surroundings. He relaxed and let the tireless little Cracker pony set its own pace while he breathed in the cool night air and thought about his coming visit with the Westfields.

He'd known all along that his annoyance at Cooter had had more to do with the older man's correct guesses than with any moralizing he'd done. He'd tried not to admit it even to himself, but Miranda Westfield was in truth a big reason he'd accepted this late-night invitation.

She was a mighty handsome woman, and that was a fact. He couldn't seem to get the picture out of his mind, of her standing there like he'd first seen her, with her high cheekbones all pink from scrubbing and that thick mane of gold-colored hair spilling down around her shoulders.

He shook his head and took a couple deep breaths in a hopeless attempt to chase the image away. What he'd told Cooter was the truth too: He hadn't the slightest notion of setting his sights on some other man's woman, even if there'd been any signs of encouragement on her part—which there hadn't been.

It was as plain as the moon out in front of him that he'd have to forget all about Miranda Westfield, just the same as if he'd never met her. And that's what he planned to do.

Tomorrow.

Tonight . . . Well, what could be the harm in spending an hour or two just enjoying the company of a Princeton Doc of Philosophy and his fetching wife? None at all, that Peek Tillman could see.

He was so busy with his thoughts as he got near the archaeologist's camp it completely slipped his mind to announce himself as he'd done earlier in the day. That is, until he was some fifty feet from the fire and heard the sharp click of pistols being cocked in the still night air.

He'd been walking his pony forward slowly in the bright moonlight, flanked by the deeper shadows of low-growing palmetto brakes. When the sound reached his ears he drew rein quickly and sat easy in the saddle, making no move to dismount until he could be recognized.

"Hello the camp," he called out cheerfully, if belatedly. "Peek Tillman here. I'm friendly. And I'm expected."

"You just keep your hands steady up there on that saddle horn, boy. I don't know nobody by the name of Peek, and I ain't for sure they's anybody else here does either."

The voice came from the shadow of a solitary laurel oak a few yards this side of the cypress dome. As Peek turned his head in that direction, another figure loomed up from the palmettos close by and advanced with drawn pistol. Noting the cow hunter's tied-down holster, the nearer man reached out without warning to jerk the weapon roughly from its resting place.

"Hey! There ain't no call for that! I already said I was friendly!" Peek felt a sudden flush of anger as he shifted in the saddle.

"I reckon you'd best stay that way too," the man beside him answered coldly, "if you got plans to see another sunrise." He'd taken a cautious step back at Peek's sudden move, but his long pistol barrel never wavered from the young visitor's chest.

"Hey, Ethan!" the other man called out as he walked toward the fire. "You know a young cub named Peek somethin' or other?"

"Tillman," Peek said under his breath, but loud enough for the closest gunman to hear him. "You-all might want to remember it, 'case we meet up again somewheres."

After a minute the hulking form of Ethan Cabell could be seen in the flickering glow of the campfire. There was a brief exchange of words, and his slim companion lifted an arm to wave Peek and his guard on in.

Without another glance at the stocky man beside him, Peek walked his pony forward another dozen yards, dismounted, and looped his reins around the twisted branches of a convenient wax myrtle bush.

Westfield was apologetic as he greeted his guest and ushered him to the long table where his wife was seated. But he didn't seem able to find any words of criticism for Cabell and his hard-faced compatriots.

"I realize my associates' vigilance might have been accompanied by a little more tact," the archaeologist confessed with a tense smile and a show of good humor that Peek didn't find entirely convincing. "But I'm sure you of all people understand that this Florida backcountry is rife with social outcasts and those who live beyond the law. One can never be too careful about strangers, so far from towns and civil authority."

"Uh-huh." Peek took a camp chair and turned it around to sit with his arms across the back. He chose the position deliberately so he could have a clear view of his horse and the armed men in the shadows. "I reckon you're right as rain about that, Doc."

His eyes remained on Ethan Cabell while Miranda took a cup and saucer and reached for the coffee pot. The man in black was facing away from them, busy with something in front of the fire. "A feller does need to be right careful who he 'lows hisself to associate with hereabouts."

Cabell favored him with a cool glance, and for a brief instant their eyes met. Then the big man smiled and approached the table.

"I'm glad you understand our need for caution," he said pleasantly. "The doctor here's a wise man in his own field, but the Florida frontier is entirely new to him. That's why my friends and I have agreed to act as his guides and protectors while he's here doing his research. It's important work, dig-

ging up the past, and we'd want nothing unpleasant to inter-
fere with it."

"Mister Cabell is something of an amateur archaeologist
in his own right," Westfield put in, apparently glad of the
opportunity to speak on the other's behalf. "He has quite an
active interest in prehistoric Indian mounds and artifacts,
and seems well versed on the types and locations of early sites
here in the peninsula."

"It's nothing, really." The large man allowed himself a
self-depreciating shrug. "Not compared to the kind of scientific work you're engaged in. Only a hobby, but one that's fas-
cinated me since boyhood."

He turned to Peek with a mild air of conciliation. "I am
sorry for the earlier inconvenience. Quint and Butch were
simply carrying out what to them are standard nighttime pro-
cedures." He removed the cow hunter's pistol from his waistband, where he'd apparently kept it since receiving it from
the guard, and placed it on the white linen tablecloth before
them. "Here's your six-shooter back. I hope there are no hard
feelings."

Peek could see at a glance that the cylinder had been
emptied of cartridges, but—for no reason he could explain
except a sort of native cussedness—he had no intention of
reloading it in front of Ethan Cabell.

"Thanks," he said coolly, making no move to pick up
the weapon or replace it in its holster.

There had been very few people in Peek's short lifetime
he truly disliked. But this man in the broadcloth suit was

swiftly becoming one of them. He didn't believe for a second Cabell's claim to a lifelong interest in archaeology; and he found it amazing that an educated gent like Westfield would be taken in by it. Ethan Cabell was simply not to be trusted, any more than those two well-mounted owlhoots who seemed to take orders from him.

Miranda Westfield broke the awkward silence by placing a steaming cup of coffee in front of Peek and then moving a china sugar bowl and spoon beside his elbow.

"I seem to recall you take sugar in your coffee, Mister Tillman." Her words were formal, but the smile that accompanied them was so warm and appealing that Peek flushed and felt his anger starting to ebb in spite of himself. "Would you care for a glass of Burgundy to go with it? Or perhaps you'd prefer brandy?"

For the first time Peek noticed that both Westfield and his wife had long-stemmed glasses in front of them. The lady's seemed to contain wine, while the dark amber liquid by her husband must have been brandy.

His own experience with alcohol was limited, to say the least. He'd only sampled beer a time or two, and never anything that would qualify as "hard liquor." The only wine he'd ever tasted was at the family Christmas table, when a tablespoon of his father's homemade vintage was ceremoniously ladled on top of each serving of his mother's deep-dish blackberry cobbler.

"I reckon I'd take a drop of wine," he said, trying his best to sound as if such choices were an everyday occurrence.

"That is, if it's no special trouble." He decided a single glass of the stuff couldn't hurt, so long as he took care to refuse any refills.

"No trouble at all!" Westfield seemed relieved that the conversation had finally turned to more ordinary matters. "If you'll pass me that empty glass, dear." He sat down next to his wife and poured out a generous portion from the half-full bottle on the table, then handed the drink to their guest.

"Here's luck!" Peek lifted his glass in a gesture he'd seen some of the better-heeled cowmen use over dinner at the Summerlin House. The cut glass twinkled palely in the flickering firelight, looking as out of place as everything else in this outlandish tenderfoot's camp in the Florida wilderness.

When the Westfields had acknowledged his toast, Peek took a cautious sip, and then a second. Not too bad, he thought, though his father's blackberry wine might be just a tad better. But after a couple of less tentative swallows, he decided this here Burgundy was good enough so that a man could make do with it.

"Now, Mister Tillman," Miranda Westfield leaned across the table with the confidential air of a lifelong friend, while her husband refilled her glass and his, "you must tell us everything you can about the daily life of a Florida cowman." Her dark-eyed smile made Peek a little lightheaded, and, together with the wine, went a long way toward restoring his usual cheerful disposition.

4

BOTH THE LADY and her husband turned out to be interested and perceptive listeners of what, to Peek, were simply the harsh realities of working long-horned scrub cows among the hammocks and palmetto prairies of the southern peninsula. Like any cow hunter worth his salt, of course, he threw in a few carefully embellished yarns about floods and rustlers and fierce native predators to spice up the narrative.

It wasn't very long before Ethan Cabell said his good-nights and retired to his tent, taking with him a nearly full bottle of brandy and making little effort to hide his lack of interest in the topic of conversation. His two friends seemed to have made themselves scarce as well, and Peek wasted few regrets on their absence. At last he found himself able to relax and enjoy himself.

Before he knew it an hour had passed, and despite all his good intentions he'd allowed his host to refill his glass and open a second bottle of wine before he could turn their talk to the subject of greatest interest to him: Westfield's own peculiar line of work, and the archaeologist's reasons for coming to Florida.

"Miranda and I are in the process of conducting a preliminary survey of ancient Indian mounds in the region," the man from Princeton explained, "in hopes of laying the groundwork for more extensive excavations and research into early native tribes of the area."

Peek was well aware of the many Indian mounds scattered about the state, as was any Florida native who'd spent much of his life out-of-doors. But he had a few notions of his own about their possible usefulness to science.

"You mean you got a mind to dig up those places and find out what's inside 'em?" he asked after a short pause.

He tried his best to keep the skepticism from his voice, but there was good reason for it. Despite old folks' warnings about ghosts and ha'nts that were supposed to guard the ancient burial grounds, Peek and some of his boyhood chums hadn't been able to resist the lure of hidden treasures and human skeletons. One summer they'd dug into several of the larger mounds near his parents' cabin on the upper St. Johns.

The entire weeks-long project had turned out to be a lot of grimy, sweaty work for nothing. They'd found arrowheads, which could be had just for the looking along any freshwater stream in the state, together with some broken scraps of pottery and the bones of animals, but not even the faintest suggestion of human remains—no skeletons, no weapons, no jewelry. Nothing at all of any real interest or value.

When Westfield had nodded in answer to his question,

Peek went on to ask carefully, "And what exactly is it you reckon you're liable to find there?"

"A few of the mounds may be human burial sites," the other replied with a shrug. "But I'm sure the vast majority will be middens."

He smiled at the cow hunter's puzzled look, then went on to translate good-naturedly: "That's a scientific word for garbage dumps, places where the ancients disposed of refuse from their villages. Each one is an absolute treasure trove for the archaeologist—perhaps even more so than a burial mound—because of all the varied clues it yields about people's daily lives."

Still frowning with lack of understanding, Peek just stared at him and waited.

"Animal bones, and shells, and plant seeds tell us what kinds of food the people ate," Miranda explained while her husband took a sip of brandy. "Arrowheads and shards of pottery help us to classify and date the tribes that lived at a certain location, while broken tools and other artifacts give us added information about their customs and day-to-day activities."

The easy familiarity with which she spoke of her husband's specialty took Peek by surprise briefly. For some reason he hadn't expected this young and strikingly beautiful woman to be interested in rooting through long-abandoned Indian mounds. But it did make a kind of sense. Her shared enthusiasm for her husband's work would go a long way toward explaining why an obviously cultured and city-bred lady would be willing to spend weeks at a time camping out in some untrodden wilderness.

Something in his face must have betrayed his thoughts, for when he glanced in her direction he was embarrassed to see that Miranda was smiling at him with dark-eyed amusement.

"You'd be surprised how much there is to be learned," she concluded brightly, "from what others have thrown away."

Peek lowered his gaze for a moment to his empty wine glass, turning it idly between his fingers.

"I reckon maybe I see what you're drivin' at," he said finally. "It ain't really so much different from the way a tracker or a hunter reads sign in the woods. You can tell a awful lot about people or animals if you pay attention to where an' how they made their mark, or done their eatin', or from whatever odds an' ends they might of left layin' around."

"That's it exactly!" James Westfield seemed delighted with the frontiersman's comparison. "The task of the archaeologist is to read and interpret the sign from human trails that have long since grown cold!"

He noticed—but misinterpreted—Peek's fidgeting with the wine glass, and took up the bottle to pour a refill. The cow hunter opened his mouth to protest, but by then it was too late. Well, he told himself, what the heck? If the Doc and his lady could keep on drinking the stuff—which wasn't half bad once a fellow got used to it—the least he could do was relax and be sociable about it.

He took a fresh swallow and looked over the table at Westfield. "I reckon that makes sense, far as it goes," he said agreeably. "But they's another real important part to readin' sign, which is knowin' where to go huntin' for it in the first place. . . ."

He hesitated, but then decided he might as well say his piece. The Doc didn't seem the type to fight shy of the truth, even when it wasn't exactly what he wanted to hear.

"The trouble of it is," Peek went on soberly, "I don't 'call seein' hardly any of them Injun mounds away out here in the middle of this ole prairie, not no place a-tall."

Westfield nodded. "I realize that now. And I might have guessed it beforehand if I'd been familiar with the country prior to our arriving here. But maps of Florida are notoriously lacking in detail where this southern peninsula is concerned. So the only alternative was to see it for ourselves."

He shrugged and took a sip of brandy. "I've no serious complaints. As I said, this is a preliminary survey. And all it's cost us to gain first-hand knowledge is a few extra days of travel. We might have gone more seriously astray had we pushed on south from Lake Istokpoga without learning any differently. But fortunately fate intervened, in the form of Mister Cabell and his associates. . . ."

Peek kept silent and tried to shape his features into a bland expression. He had an idea that any warning from him about Cabell and the others would be worse than useless right now, coming as it did from a stranger and with no evidence to back it up but a few vague suspicions. Westfield seemed not to notice his reaction, having paused to glance at his wife before continuing.

". . . It was truly a stroke of good luck that we happened on such a man in that remote and unlikely location, one with not only a thorough knowledge of the region, but with an interest in archaeology as well. All the more so because he and his companions were willing to offer their services for a very modest fee, in addition to, as they called it, their 'keep.' They are now in the process of leading us west, to what I'm told will be much more fruitful territory."

Peek glanced at the tent where Ethan Cabell had retired with his bottle of brandy, and almost had to bite his tongue to keep his thoughts to himself. He resisted the temptation to speak, and for a brief instant believed he'd succeeded. Then he became aware of Miranda Westfield's dark eyes, watching him thoughtfully from across the table.

"I understand there are a number of Indian mounds along the banks of the Pease River," the archaeologist went on, completely absorbed now with the object of his quest. "And quite a few more in the vicinity of Charlotte Harbor and its barrier islands."

"That's true," Peek agreed. "I seen some myself there by the river, whilst we was stoppin' at Fort Ogden on my last trip through." Suddenly, when he mentioned Fort Ogden, he had an idea.

"You know," he went on conversationally, "that there Fort Ogden's where Judge Ziba King has his store an' home place, though you're liable to see his Circle O brand most anywhere 'round this end of the prairie. He's one of the biggest cowmen they is in these parts, and a mighty well-respected gent to go with it . . ."

The young cow hunter paused, as if the thought had just occurred to him. "In fact, I'll bet if you was to talk to him or some of his people about them Injun mounds, they could take you to 'em and tell you just about anything you'd want to know."

"Possibly so," Westfield said without conviction. "But I've found Mister Cabell's knowledge of the subject to be quite impressive thus far. And he is, after all, something of a fellow archaeologist."

Once again Peek had to swallow hard to keep back the answer his instincts suggested. Instead, he just shrugged and observed mildly, "Well, I don't reckon it ever hurts to hear a second opinion."

"That's true," Miranda Westfield said quickly. When Peek glanced at her, her brow was creased with what seemed to be thought. Or was it worry? "We're grateful to you, Mister Tillman, for giving us the name of one of the area's leading citizens."

She turned to her husband and laid a hand on his arm. "This Judge King could be a valuable acquaintance, dear, once we start planning more extensive expeditions to Florida."

"Of course you're right, my love." Westfield smiled and covered her hand with his own. "As usual. We'll make it a point to look the gentleman up when we are in the vicinity."

"You-all be real sure an' do that." Peek tried to make the suggestion sound more casual than he felt. The Circle O had a reputation for being a tough, stand-up outfit. And Ziba King was one of the shrewdest poker players in the state. If he saw anything even remotely suspicious about Ethan Cabell or his companions, he'd be likely to run them clean out of the country, with or without benefit of a trial.

"How far is it from where we are now to Fort Ogden?" Miranda asked, turning her eyes back to their guest.

Peek considered the question for a moment. "I expect it'll take y'all one good solid day of travel, or maybe a tad more considerin' the wagons an' ever'thing." He could easily make the journey in less time on his Cracker horse. But he'd the impression this Princeton Doc and his wife weren't much accustomed to being on the trail at first light, nor to spending long hours in the saddle either most likely.

"Very well." The archaeologist seemed to have made up his mind. "I'll mention it to Mister Cabell first thing in the morning. Then we'll resume our journey without further delay."

"Judge King's place shouldn't be no trouble to find," Peek inserted, hoping to reinforce his suggestion. "You just foller the sun west toward where it sets down, and when you're close to the river ask anybody you meet."

When he'd seen both husband and wife nod their agreement, he took a deep breath and tried to will his taut muscles to relax, letting his eyes roam briefly to the dying embers of the fire and to the moonlit prairie beyond. The frogs and insects in the nearby hammock had long since grown silent, and the only sound that came to his ears just now was the soft *hoot-hoot* of a hunting owl.

He reckoned he'd done the best he could for these folks, though it seemed mighty little when you stopped to think about it. He had a real bad feeling about leaving them in the hands of Ethan Cabell and his friends. But when he tried to put his finger on a definite reason for that, all his thinking seemed to come to a dead end.

If robbery was their plan, they'd almost surely have done it before now—as soon as they'd gotten the Westfields alone and away from the settlements, in fact. Why bother posing as guides and risk the chance of being seen together, when the easiest thing in the world would be to trail that heavily loaded wagon to some isolated place in the wilderness and then do what they pleased?

But if it wasn't robbery, what else could they want?

The same arguments applied to almost any other crime Peek could think of: murder, kidnapping, or even rape—assuming a man was willing to risk the one certain hanging offense there was on the frontier. Every one of those could have been done sooner, and with less risk, than what was going on here.

It was possible, though he didn't really believe it, that he had misjudged Cabell and his cohorts. Rooking Yankee tourists was a common enough form of larceny in Florida, and it might be that all the three men had in mind was to take advantage of the Westfields' ample supply of good food and liquor while being paid for the privilege. What to a Princeton professor was a "modest fee" could be quite a lot by local standards. And while Peek didn't entirely approve of the practice, there wasn't a lot he could do to prevent it.

"Well," he said at last, pushing his worries to the back of his mind while he unfolded his lanky body and stood up from the table, "I surely have enjoyed the comp'ny and the conversation. But I still got me a bit of a ride before I can spread my blankets for the night."

He picked up his Colt and began stripping five fresh cartridges from his belt with his free hand. "I don't reckon daylight's goin' to come any later, just to suit my social calendar."

Deliberately ignoring the curious looks of his hosts, he reloaded the pistol and gave the cylinder a spin before resetting the empty chamber under the hammer. Then he slid the weapon into its holster and looked up to meet the eyes of Miranda Westfield.

"It's been a genuine pleasure knowin' you, ma'am." He bowed slightly and took a grip on his hat brim between thumb and forefinger. Her husband rose from the table and the two men shook hands. "You too, Doc. Maybe we'll meet up again somewhere down the line."

"I would welcome it." The archaeologist offered an arm to help his wife to her feet. "The best of luck on your cattle drive!"

"And thank you so much for your advice, Mister Tillman." Peek glanced at the young woman, struck by something in the tone of her voice. It seemed almost as if her dark eyes had been reading his thoughts. He had a notion that she, at least, knew why he'd brought up the subject of Ziba King and his ranch.

He wanted to add something more, but all he could manage was, "*De nada,* ma'am, like they say down in Cuba." Then he turned and went to untie his horse.

When he'd tightened the cinch and gathered the reins, he again faced the couple, who now stood a few yards away.

"You 'member what I told you 'bout Judge King and the Circle O." He directed his words to the archaeologist in particular. "If you need any kind of help a-tall, you be sure an' give them a holler."

Westfield nodded as Peek climbed into the saddle. It seemed there was nothing else to say, so he lifted his free hand in farewell and swung his pony's head west. After a minute he brought it up to a trot.

The night air was cool, and it felt good against his cheeks as he made his way across the expanse of moonlit prairie. There might be a hint of coming rain from the smell of it. But right now it was just the pick-me-up Peek needed after all the wine he'd drunk and his troubled thoughts about the Westfields with their hard-case "guides."

When he'd put a couple hundred yards behind him, he took one last look over his shoulder at the cluster of white canvas tents against the darker backdrop of the cypress dome.

He had a sudden uncomfortable feeling that other eyes besides the Westfields' were watching him depart.

5 ⚜

JUST LIKE PEEK had expected, morning came a whole lot sooner than he would have preferred. And to make matters worse, ominous black thunderheads darkened the eastern horizon when he dragged himself from his blankets and shuffled to the chuck wagon's water barrel to slake his voracious thirst. The muggy predawn air was heavy with electricity and the scent of rain.

Anticipating the worst from the weather and its effect on their half-wild charges, the other cow hunters had gone to saddle their horses as soon as they woke, even before stopping at the fire for an eye-opening cup of coffee. Nobody wanted to be caught on the ground in the middle of a stampede. As soon as he'd swallowed two gourds of water and splashed a third on his face, Peek hurried to join them.

His stomach churned and his head felt light as he tugged his saddle to where his Cracker pony waited, head up and nostrils flared, scenting the approaching storm. His mood was as foul as the taste in his mouth, but he made himself speak gently to the tolerant animal while he tossed up the blanket and saddle, then bent to tighten the cinch. The effort seemed to help clear his head just a tiny bit.

After returning to roll his bedding and stow it with the others' under the chuck wagon's tarp, he joined the crew as they wolfed down a hasty breakfast of white bacon, cornbread, and grits. For his part, Peek decided he'd make do with just a few scalding cups of Cookie's powerful coffee. He didn't even feel up to adding sugar to it on this particular morning.

Cooter was watching him from under his hat brim, but Peek had no desire for idle chatter, and even less for questions or critiques about his previous night's outing. He squatted on his heels a short distance apart and nursed his coffee while keeping one wary eye on the low-hanging clouds.

By the time the red-orange sun finally made its grudging appearance, the entire herd of mossy-horns was on its feet, complaining and stirring about restlessly. It was going to be one hell of a job holding them together on a day like today and pushing them ten or twelve miles closer to the pens at Punta Rassa. But after a long, sour-faced inspection of the sky and a few well-chosen pronouncements from his colorful vocabulary, Ed Porter, the trail boss, passed the word to start moving 'em out.

"Them ornery knotheads is as liable to spook right here as anyplace else," he growled to no one in particular. "'Least if they take a notion to make a run for it somewheres down the trail, we'll of got 'em pointed in the right dang direction first."

It seemed a reasonable assessment under the circumstances. Besides which Porter had to be thinking that the
sooner they got this early gather to the waiting ships for
Cuba, the better the price they'd bring. Unfortunately for
him and his hard-pressed crew, Mother Nature and eight
hundred wild-eyed longhorns had different ideas.

The agitated beasts caused trouble from the start, showing a tendency to bunch and mill rather than stringing themselves out in ordinary trail-drive fashion. All morning long
small groups kept trying to break free from the main body,
only to be brought back in line by swift-darting cow dogs and
their grim-faced masters. From every side, cow whips cracked
like pistol shots in the moisture-laden air.

Still, they made better progress than expected for the
first few miles. As long as the thunderheads remained at their
backs, flickering and grumbling in the distance, the restless
steers could be kept moving in the opposite direction.
Sporadic flurries of oversized raindrops were a minor annoyance, pricking fitfully at the riders' cheeks and making them
hunch lower under their ponchos.

The work was demanding and constant, giving Peek no
time to dwell on his personal discomfort. After a few hours of
hard riding while taking in deep gulps of the brisk humid air,
he was scarcely aware of any effects from the wine and his
lack of sleep. He'd be mighty happy to crawl back into his
blankets again come sundown, but otherwise it seemed he'd
lived through the experience with no lasting complaints.

Still, with every passing minute the relentless dark

clouds kept gaining on them. And when the tempest finally struck it came down with all four feet.

Midday turned to dusk in seconds. Brilliant sheets of lightning ripped across the pitch-black sky, cracking ominously in their wake and making the cow hunters' neck hairs stand on end. Huge rolling salvos of thunder chased each other across the flat, open prairie like storm-crested waves.

With the first dazzling flash above their heads, followed almost instantly by a sharp crack and an ear-splitting boom, the skittish cattle lost what scant composure they'd managed to retain. One old brindle steer near the middle of the bunch gave a sudden high leap like a deer on the fly, and the stampede was on.

Peek and Cooter, riding a dozen yards apart on the flank swing, had been watching for such an event and were more than half expecting it. As soon as he saw the dark brown mass surge blindly forward, the older cow hunter let out a wild Texas whoop, clapped spurs to his horse, and rode with the flow. Peek's own Cracker pony was close on their heels, galloping flat out with its young rider stretched low over its neck.

There was nothing else to do. At that minute the senseless torrent of razor-sharp horns and earth-churning bodies was as uncontrollable as the raging tempest overhead—and infinitely more deadly should they be caught in its path.

Peek hung on grimly while his determined little mount lined out to keep pace with their wild-eyed charges. He tried not to think about the virgin prairie below them, where any chance encounter with a gopher hole or misplaced clump of palmettos could send horse and rider tumbling to their deaths under three hundred tons of hoof-pounding beef.

His heart was hammering and his breath came in ragged gasps. Huge drops of rain stung his face, soaking his shirtfront while the corners of his poncho flapped uselessly behind. His hat was off too now, beating a rough tattoo on his shoulders where it was kept by the rawhide strings that chafed at his neck.

He muttered a curse and blinked water from his eyes, trying to comfort himself between bone-jarring jolts with the fact that at least this had happened during daylight and in open country. A night stampede would have been ten times worse. It would have cost all of them even more hours of sleep, plus several long days of rounding up stragglers.

After four or five endless, pulse-racing miles, the unrestrained beasts finally began to tire. Once their pace slackened, Peek and Cooter managed to bring their mounts abreast of the leaders and let the cow-wise ponies start the dangerous job of hazing the spent but still cantankerous steers away from their line of travel.

Other cow hunters soon arrived and joined in the task, followed by some of the hardier dogs. Before too many more minutes they had the herd in a mill. After that it was just a matter of gradually tightening the circle until the clumsy beasts slowed to a walk and started bawling dolefully at one another.

The worst of the storm was over by now, and it was possible for a few riders and dogs to hold the tired cattle in check while their companions gave their horses a much-needed rest. The rain had turned into a mild but steady drizzle, with only occasional flashes of lightning and the low drumming of thunder far off to the west.

Peek's body sagged under the weight of near-exhaustion as he swung a leg over his saddle and dropped to the ground. The closest trees were more than a mile away, much too far to travel for whatever scant shelter they might provide. When he had ground-hitched his pony and loosened the cinch, he made one halfhearted attempt to brush water from his eyes with a sodden shirtsleeve. Then he laid his two arms across the saddle and lowered his head.

In a couple more minutes he heard Cooter's sharp "Whoa!" a dozen feet away. The older cow hunter dismounted and seemed to be rummaging in his saddlebags for something. Probably a dry twist of tobacco, Peek thought idly. He raised his head and gazed at his partner through red-bordered eyes.

"Nothin' like a li'l jog in the rain to get a feller's juices to flowin'!" the burly man remarked cheerfully as he fished an oilskin-wrapped bundle from the leather pouch and began to untie it. Peek just scowled at him and shook his head.

"You look a mite peaked, young'un. Don't reckon it could have somethin' to do with that there late-night social-izin', do you?"

Peek grunted and pulled himself up to his full six feet. "Don't you worry 'bout me. I'll stay in the saddle 'long as any man on this prairie. And I'll pull my share of the load too, come hell or high water!"

"Never figured you wouldn't." Cooter finished opening the bundle and held out its contents to his partner. "But here's a little somethin' extry to help keep your strength up till we make it to night camp."

Folded inside a clean kerchief were several thick slices of cooked bacon, a cold sweet potato, and a sizable chunk of cornpone. "Happened to notice you didn't grab nothin' from the chuck wagon 'fore we set out this mornin'."

"Thanks." Peek felt his cheeks burning because of his earlier outburst. "Go halves with you?"

"You go on ahead an' help yourself." The older man hunkered down on his heels under his poncho and began filling his cheek from a fresh tie of tobacco that he'd brought from the saddlebags. "I already et."

It was a long, wet, miserable afternoon for the Rocking JG crew as they slowly brought the exhausted herd back onto the trail and headed them southwest again. The constant drizzling rain offered no sign of letting up, even after Ed Porter finally called a halt for the cow hunters to bed themselves and their charges down for the night.

When Peek at long last managed to curl up in his blankets next to Cooter's gently snoring form under a hastily built lean-to of palmetto fans, it occurred to him that it had been almost twenty-four hours since he'd been able to spare a moment's thought for Doctor James Westfield and his beautiful wife. And a moment was all the time he could manage now, to wonder how they'd fared during the storm, before he was drawn irresistibly into a deep and dreamless sleep.

❖ ❖ ❖

Miranda Westfield gathered her skirts more tightly about her legs and shivered, as much from fear as from the torrential downpour's windborne chill, while she sat huddled under a precariously jutting corner of their overturned supply wagon.

Her fear was entirely justified, and she knew it. Searing volleys of lightning tore through the leaden sky with ominous frequency, rendering the falling drops outside her makeshift shelter a dazzling gossamer white. When she dared to count the seconds between a flash and its ear-splitting aftermath, her breath would catch at how terrifyingly close it had been. She knew well that on such a treeless expanse as this, electrical storms posed a greater threat to life and limb than all the hurricanes and cyclones for which the Florida peninsula was famous.

Gingerly avoiding any contact with the heavy wagon that might cause it to shift suddenly and crush her with its weight, she eased her slim body farther back into the angle between its sharply canted bed and the ground. If this offered only minimal protection from the lightning, at least she could hope to escape the relentless spattering of mud that leapt up from the saturated prairie to stain her cheeks and her thin cotton blouse. The hem of her long dress was already soaked. She could feel its clammy wetness pasted to the stockings above the tops of her high-laced boots.

For several long minutes she sat there without moving, hugging herself to try and stop the shivering. Then a kind of native restlessness caused her to lower her head in an effort to get a better look at her surroundings.

The men had been gone for what seemed like hours now, although it was no doubt considerably less. She'd wanted desperately for James to remain here with her, but she'd known without voicing it that such a plea would fall on deaf ears. Rounding up the runaway mules after they'd bolted and caused the accident was something he believed to be "man's work." And for all his fine qualities, James Westfield was sensitive about his masculine prerogatives—even when his lack of experience made him poorly equipped for the job, as it did now.

He was an indifferent rider at best—something that Miranda, a daughter of Hudson River gentry who'd begun riding with the hounds when she was six, had to take particular care not to comment upon. He had even less knowledge of mules, making no secret of his dislike for the big stubborn draft animals and readily accepting the fact that the feeling appeared to be mutual.

No one was in sight as she peered out from her limited vantage point across the barren, rain-drenched landscape. She found herself uttering a silent prayer for her husband's safety. There were all kinds of dangers in this unsettled wilderness. A stray bolt of lightning was just one of the more dramatic. A fall from a horse and a broken limb would be serious enough, with the closest medical doctor almost a week's ride away.

The rain seemed to be letting up a bit, and the lightning was farther off as well. For several more minutes, Miranda fought the overpowering urge to be up and doing something. She clasped her arms around her knees and made herself count slowly to a thousand. Then she counted backwards from a thousand to one.

Finally, she brushed a lock of matted hair from her forehead with an irritable swipe of her hand and turned to begin searching through the jumbled mass of goods and equipment that lay strewn about her under the wagon. Her eyes fell on a familiar cedar chest with its lid broken open, and she moved closer to examine its partly spilled contents.

A metallic glint, half buried under a small pile of kerchiefs, caught her attention. Suddenly wary, she glanced quickly to left and right while gathering the gold coins in her fingers. There was still no one in sight, and she breathed a sigh of relief.

It was little enough in value: three Spanish *reales* that they'd gotten in change for their bank draft after they bought supplies in Tampa. According to the clerk who waited on them, gold was a common form of exchange in south Florida as a result of the flourishing cattle trade with Cuba.

Still, Miranda had no intention of letting Ethan Cabell or his companions see the gold pieces, even though she'd be hard-pressed to say exactly why. All three had behaved decently enough since joining the expedition. But there was something about the big man with the pearl-handled revolver that made her uneasy. And the feeling was stronger when it came to his two friends.

In any event, she could think of no good reason to place temptation before strangers. This was the reason she and James had arranged from the outset to carry no substantial amount of cash with them.

After searching the ground without success for the small purse in which the coins had been hidden, she felt around inside the chest with her fingers, still taking care not to make any move that might shift or dislodge the ponderous weight over her head. But the purse didn't seem to be there.

That was odd. Yet with everything in such a topsy-turvy state perhaps she'd overlooked it. Surely no one would have taken the purse and left the coins behind.

As a temporary measure, she wrapped the *reales* in a spare kerchief and tied it under her blouse. It would be the safest thing in any case, since the present disastrous state of affairs meant that virtually everything they had would have to be emptied out and repacked before they could resume their journey.

With the gold concealed from view, Miranda studied the wreckage around her for another few minutes. Then she crawled to a second nearby chest and carefully removed a gray woolen blanket. Drawing its comforting warmth about her shoulders, she bent once more to peer out at the glistening prairie beyond her unwieldy shelter.

The worst of the storm had moved on now. The sky was noticeably brighter, and the rain had slackened to a gentle but steady drizzle. She found she could easily count to five or more between occasional flickers of lightning and the rumbles of thunder that followed.

Taking a firm grip on the ends of the blanket with her fingers, she drew the covering over her head and crawled clumsily out into the chilly, misting rain. Even with only this meager protection from the elements, she felt a delicious kind of freedom as she rose to her feet and took in deep breaths of the clean, moist air.

Miranda Westfield had never been one to sit idly by when there were tasks that needed to be done. And recapturing their runaway mules was only the first of many difficult chores that would be have to be accomplished before their ill-fated expedition could get under way again.

The wagon would have to be unloaded and repaired—a cursory glance revealed that one of its axles was broken, and there might be other damage as well. Then, assuming these repairs could be made with the tools and manpower at hand, everything they had brought with them would have to be laid out, dried, and repacked before they could think about continuing on to Fort Ogden.

For a long minute she stood motionless in the rain, gazing at the ruin of their wagon and collecting her thoughts. She scarcely knew where to begin.

The dark thunderheads were now far off to the west, still flickering and muttering angrily as they receded. The broad prairie seemed stark and forbidding as she turned to scan the cloud-ringed horizon. There was no sign of James or their three guides.

Strewn beyond the wreck of the wagon she could make out a littered trail of canned goods and other items that had shaken loose from its bed, starting at a point some sixty yards away where the mules had first bolted. Unable to think of anything more productive to do for the moment, she strode back to start gathering things up in her arms and returning them to the tiny patch of shelter from which she'd just emerged.

6

MIRANDA HAD MADE a half-dozen trips and was kneeling to rescue a heavy cast-iron skillet from the mud when she heard the sound of a horse behind her. Rising and turning with the skillet in her hands, she recognized the mounted figure of one of Ethan Cabell's companions, the short but muscular man known as Butch.

"Where are the others?" she asked quickly—a little too quickly, she thought as she said it, and with more of an edge to her voice than she had intended as well. There had always been something about the way this cold-eyed little man looked at her that made her uneasy.

"They'll be along directly." The burly rider swung a leg over his saddle and dropped to the ground. "We finally run them mules to earth, maybe three, four mile off. Gettin' 'em minded to stay put an' take a rope is liable to need a while longer."

"Why aren't you helping?" Once again, Miranda was aware that she'd allowed an uncharacteristic harshness to color her speech.

"I reckon three men an' horses is enough to round up four tuckered-out mules. So I offered to ride on ahead an' see that we'd got a fire an' coffee waitin'."

Butch took a step toward her and grinned. It was the kind of grin that sent chills up the young woman's spine. "Looks like I had the right idea, too," he went on contemptuously. "I notice you ain't managed to get no fire started here by your lonesome. Nor no coffee made neither."

"There's no dry wood," Miranda responded evenly, meeting the man's smirking gaze. "And in case it hasn't occurred to you, the closest trees are a mile or more away."

"Uh-huh. Well, I reckon they's somethin' under that wagon yonder that'll take a match. I'll just have a look-see in a minute or two." He let his horse's reins trail on the ground and took another catlike step toward her. "Meantime, I got a idea what'll warm us both up a heap quicker'n any fire. . . ."

She'd been expecting something of the kind, and in the same instant that Butch made his move to grab her blanket, Miranda brought the heavy skillet up and around with every ounce of strength her slender frame possessed. The ringing blow connected solidly with a muscular shoulder, but aside from knocking the heavy-set man off balance temporarily, it seemed to have no serious effect.

She took a frightened step back while Butch planted his feet and spread his arms apart to resume the assault. His grin had become a bare-toothed snarl. Harsh animal noises issued from deep in his throat.

Again the iron skillet lifted, almost of its own accord,

swinging round in a murderous backhand that smashed violently into the man's leering face. There was a sickening crunch and blood gushed from Butch's nose. He dropped to the ground on hands and knees, shaking his head from side to side as he spit out pieces of broken tooth.

"You damned li'l she-painter," he muttered, slurring the words between torn and bleeding lips. "Now you done made me mad. I'll learn you somethin' 'bout respect afore I'm . . ."

The sudden crash of a pistol shot ripped apart the moisture-laden air, interrupting Butch's threat and freezing him where he knelt. Miranda, the heavy skillet poised unsteadily by her shoulder for one last desperate blow, risked a quick glance above and beyond him. After a moment, Butch turned to follow her eyes.

He found himself staring into the black, faintly smoking maw of Ethan Cabell's .44 Colt revolver. The man in the broadcloth suit was sitting his horse a scant three feet away. An icy scowl of rage darkened his face as he drew back the hammer.

"No!—Listen, Boss, I didn't mean nothin'. You know me, just a li'l funnin'. . . ." The words tumbled from Butch's ruined lips while he strove desperately to avoid what he knew was certain death. He was practically sobbing now. "Please, Boss. I didn't . . ."

The hammer under Cabell's thumb clicked relentlessly into place.

"Mister Cabell."

Ethan Cabell's trigger finger relaxed slightly as his eyes

shifted to Miranda. He gazed at her for a long moment, then seemed to recover his composure.

"Yes, Mrs. Westfield?"

"I would be very much obliged if there were no killings in my presence today." She lowered the skillet with a sigh, and let it fall from numb and aching fingers. "Or on any other day, for that matter." As she rubbed circulation back into the trembling muscles of her arm, she looked down at her assailant.

"Despite your associate's actions, I would be content to see him disarmed and banished from our company. If he should show himself again in our vicinity, then you have my blessing to shoot him on sight."

Cabell remained motionless, his pistol unwavering from the bridge of Butch's broken nose, for what might have been a slow count of ten. Finally he uncocked the weapon.

"All right," he said to the man on the ground. "You heard the lady. Unbuckle your cartridge belt and leave it where it falls. Then get up real careful and go fetch your horse."

The stocky man did as he was told, without looking in Miranda's direction or offering any word of thanks. When he'd climbed into the saddle Cabell walked his horse alongside and reached into a coat pocket.

"I reckon you're still due some wages up till now," he said grudgingly, handing a few bills to his former associate. There was a moment when Miranda thought other low-voiced words might have passed between them, but she couldn't be sure. Then Cabell gave Butch's horse a slap on the rump and said, "Now go pull your freight!"

She stood and watched the stocky rider grow small in the distance before she finally bent to recover her blanket. As she straightened and turned to draw the soggy material around her shoulders once more, she felt an inexpressible surge of relief when she saw her husband and Quint riding toward them from the other direction with their runaway mules.

No sooner had they dismounted than Miranda was clinging to the surprised archaeologist with all her might. By that time Butch was no longer in view.

Daylight came late the next morning, with a low-hanging fog that hid the prairie's expanse behind a clinging veil of gossamer white. The rain had ended sometime after midnight but had been replaced by a heavy dew that lay upon the cow hunters' camp like a watery blanket.

When Peek opened his eyes in the predawn dark and reached for his hat, everything around him was clammy and cold to the touch. He could hear Cooter stirring nearby, fumbling with his suspenders and cursing the wetness that had soaked into his socks before he could tug on his boots.

Taking a lesson from his partner's misfortune, the younger man shook out his own boots and brought them under the covers before pulling them on. He'd kept his rolled-up pistol belt next to him while he slept, so the weapon and cartridges were mostly dry as he crawled from the lean-to and rose to belt them into place. Fully dressed now and ready to meet the graying day, he took his coffee cup and hurried to join Cooter and the others at the welcome warmth of a smoking, hissing, oversized campfire.

Most of the dead wood close by was wet, but a few of the more experienced hands had had the foresight to collect lighter knots and chunks of pitch pine at earlier stops along the way, storing these in saddlebags and under the chuck wagon's tarp against such an eventuality. The fat pine made a hot, bright blaze that helped to dry the rest of the logs as it burned. Cookie was putting the finishing touches on breakfast over a smaller fire built from his own carefully hoarded supply of dry wood.

The morning meal was leisurely, for there was no possibility of moving the herd until the fog had risen to the height of a scrub cow's horns, and that was going to take several hours. While Ed Porter stalked about, fuming and swearing at this latest perversity of nature, the other men built up their fire and used the forced delay trying to partly dry their bedrolls and clothing.

Despite the dreary weather, Cooter noticed that Peek's usual sunny disposition seemed to have returned after a good night's sleep and an oversized helping of corned beef hash and cornpone. Not even Cookie's ominous mutterings about the fate of big-footed cubs who tracked mud too close to his clean pots and skillets could dampen the young drover's spirits.

He went about his morning tasks with a will, sometimes joining in the rough cow camp humor of his comrades and at other times working alone with a whistled tune on his lips. The older man couldn't see the slightest trace of his partner's ill-tempered exhaustion of the day before.

Cooter could only shake his head in wonder at this flagrant show of youthful resilience. His own body could still feel the effects from yesterday's stampede, and it would have taken him a lot more than one night's sleep to bounce back from all the kid had been through in the last couple of days.

When Ed Porter's bellowed command to "Head 'em up and move 'em out!" came at last, Cooter hoisted himself into his saddle with a grunt and looked up to see Peek already trotting his little Cracker pony out to the waiting herd. Maybe, the veteran cow hunter thought with a grim scowl, he was starting to get a mite long in the tooth after all.

It was three more long but nearly uneventful days before the Rocking JG crew arrived on the banks of the Caloosahatchee River near the tiny settlement of Olga. At that point the river was too deep to ford, which meant the cattle would have to be swum across, guided by the wake of a flat-bottomed barge connected to the far shore with cables.

Life would have been a lot simpler, coming as they had from Brevard County, if they had been able to make the more traditional crossing at Fort Thompson below the falls from

Lake Okeechobee. That natural ford near the river's headwaters had been in use as long as any native Floridian could remember. But a year earlier it had been ruined forever by the clanking, smoke-belching machines of a Yankee land developer named Disston, who had his heart set on draining the state's largest lake dry and turning it into farmland.

There was scarcely a native cow hunter or cowman who didn't curse Disston and wish him ill luck with his crazy venture. But as so often happens, money and high-sounding talk about "progress" counted for more with the politicians in Tallahassee than any needs or concerns of their local constituents.

The sun was well past its high point when Peek and his comrades started the difficult and treacherous job of hazing eight hundred wild-eyed longhorns into the swift, dark current and across to the opposite side. Although the chance of flooding was slight at this time of year, especially in view of Disston's handiwork, no drover would willingly risk the whim of nature. All the late hours and hard work it took to make the crossing before nightfall were nothing compared to the possibility of waking from an early sleep to find a swollen torrent overflowing the banks of what had been a passable stream just hours earlier.

It was a tough, dangerous, bone-wearying job no matter when you started it. Even with the barge's help, getting the balky steers into the water and keeping them moving to the far landing required every bit of skill and fortitude that cow hunters, catch dogs, and horses could muster. Keen-eyed vigilance was needed to stay clear of whirlpools and quicksand, while the splashing, cursing, whip-cracking cow hunters on their hardy little Cracker ponies made endless forays into deeper water to hustle back strays and prevent losses from drowning.

By the time the last of the cantankerous beasts had been prodded up the muddy bank onto solid ground, Peek and his coworkers, both human and animal, were soaked to the skin and almost too tired to move. The sun was below the treetops now, and a chill northern breeze came off the water to add to their misery.

But the long day's labor wasn't quite over yet. A network of rough pens lined the south bank of the Caloosahatchee, built and maintained by the various cow crews for everyone's mutual benefit. They'd make holding a herd for the night a lot easier. But the Rocking JG was the first outfit to come this way since the previous spring, so there were numerous breaks and tumbled rails that had to be repaired before the enclosure was secure.

The men set about these tasks with weary resolve as the last colors faded from the sky. Their only consolation was that from here on out such cow pens were located at regular intervals all the way to Punta Rassa. The reduced need for night guards would give everybody a few more hours of sleep, and the risk of another stampede, though never entirely absent, would be greatly reduced.

By the time all the men were finally gathered at the chuck wagon's fire for a long-postponed supper, it was pitch dark outside the flickering circle of light, and a pale canopy of stars glittered overhead.

"Hello the fire!"

The voice came from a thick cluster of pines and cabbage palms where the river road swung east toward Fort Thompson and Lake Okeechobee. "How's for some coffee? And a mite of comp'ny for the night?"

"Come on in if you're friendly," Ed Porter responded. "Coffee's hot, and they ain't no charge for squattin' on the ground!"

All eyes turned curiously toward the lanky stranger who walked his brindle mule into the firelight and lowered himself from the saddle. He wasn't a young man, but Peek found it hard to guess his actual age, what with the wide-brimmed black hat that shaded his whiskered face and the long, faded frock coat that seemed to have swallowed up his bony body.

There could be little doubt about his occupation, though, from the cut of his clothes as well as the big leather-bound Bible that could be seen weighing down one pocket of the coat as he looped his reins around a tree limb. Cooter filled a cup for him while the man of God approached the fire.

"Thank'ee, brother. I'm obliged." The newcomer took a swallow of the scalding brew and nodded his appreciation. "Best tastin' coffee that's passed these here lips in nigh onto a week." He hunkered down and warmed his hands on the cup while Cooter resumed his place by the fire. "Pert' near the only coffee, as a matter of actual fact."

"They's some supper left," Ed Porter suggested, "if you're of the mind."

"Thanks again. But I caught me a right fine mess of mullet a few hours back. Fried 'em up with some cornpone an' then feasted on loaves an' fishes, just like the good Lord served to the multitude. With vittles like them, and His word here to nourish the spirit,"—he slapped the Bible in his pocket—"I reckon I flat got ever'thing I need."

He finished his coffee and bent to refill the cup. "'Course I might be persuaded to join y'all for breakfast, if they's a tad of hog meat to go with it." He cocked his head to one side and winked slyly. "Them there Jewish folks in the Holy Land didn't rightly know what they was missin'!"

"You're travelin' kind of late, preacher," Cooter ventured after a short silence. "Even for a man like yourself, this ain't real safe country for a lone rider in the dark."

"Sad it is but true, brother," the visitor in the frock coat agreed. "The Devil's bondsmen seem thick as fleas on a hound dog in this age an' place." He tasted his fresh coffee. "But I ain't goin' to live out my life caterin' to such like as them. I've found it suits my nature to ride in the cool of a evenin', when a man can have some time with his thoughts."

He shrugged his thin shoulders and reached to unbutton his coat. "I put my trust in the Lord on such matters. But just in case He happens to be busy someplace when I got need of Him . . ." He pulled the coat aside to reveal a wicked-looking sawed-off shotgun in a hog-leg holster at his hip. ". . . They's always ole Betsy here to kind of take up the slack!"

Peek was impressed, and clearly so was Cooter. "I don't believe I'll worry 'bout you no more, preacher," the older cow hunter remarked wryly. "'Pears to me you're able to fend for yourself."

"I'll do what's needful," the circuit rider answered soberly. "But like the Book here says, it's the meek what'll inherit the earth. A man that hunts trouble generally finds a heap more than he was lookin' for."

Peek found himself nodding at the sense of that. But as he did, his eyelids grew so heavy he could scarcely keep them apart. The day's labors were taking their toll, and it was way past the time he'd ought to be rolled up in his blankets.

He'd have liked to stay and hear more of the newcomer's talk. But sure as the world if he tried, he'd be sound asleep before many minutes had passed. And then he'd have to live with his comrades' joshing about "falling asleep in church."

Some of the others had started drifting off to their beds by this time, and Peek got to his feet to join them. He'd just turned away from the fire when he heard their visitor follow up on his last remark:

". . . You take that shootin' up to Orlando a couple months back. Now, there was a case where a feller'd done a heap better to stopper his pride an' keep his ideas to hisself. But he just had to go on pushin', and that gun-slick Ethan Cabell didn't cut him no slack a-tall!"

7

INSTANTLY WIDE AWAKE, PEEK spun on his heel. "Who . . . Who did you say?"

"Ethan Cabell was the man's name." The whiskered preacher swallowed the last of his coffee and handed the cup to Cooter, who was also watching him narrowly. "Hadn't never set eyes on him before my own self. But some of them folks from up Jacksonville an' Nassau County way 'peared to reckanize him. Seems he's a knowed man in those parts."

"And you say he shot somebody in Orlando?"

"Uh-huh. Kilt that poor young feller deader'n a post. One shot, clean through the brisket an' the kid's gun never even cleared leather." The minister shrugged. "It was a fair killin', far as such things go. Both of 'em was armed, an' the kid come lookin' for it like I said. Reckon he fancied hisself with the six-shooter, only he picked the wrong man to prove it on."

"This Cabell sounds kind of quick on the shoot his ownself," Ed Porter observed from the far side of the fire.

"I hope to kiss a pig he was! The kid started pushin' and runnin' his mouth, all loud an' spiteful like, and Cabell didn't say ary word. He just slid his chair back from that table where he was dealin' faro, and flat opened the ball."

"Faro?" Cooter asked mildly from under his pulled-down hat brim. Peek had come closer and was hunkered down beside the preacher now, listening intently.

"Faro was his game, mostly. I heard he'd deal some after-hours poker down to the ho-tel if the stakes was high enough. But I never seen him anywheres but behind that faro layout." He paused and glanced around at Peek and the other cow hunters who had stayed by the fire.

"I reckon they's a few might find it peculiar for a religious man to be hangin' round saloons an' faro games an' such." He seemed to be reading their minds. "But I take that as a part of my ministry. If you mean to save sinners, you got to go where the sinners are. Anybody don't like it can just take their Bible-thumpin' off some other preacher."

"You're sayin' that Cabell's a professional gambler?" Cooter's tone showed no interest in the minister's choice of congregation.

The whiskered man favored him with a lopsided smile. "'Bout as professional as they come, if you catch holt of my drift. Not that I got so much experience with the pasteboards I could ever prove he was cheatin'. But he surely did 'pear to win uncommon often, 'specially when the bets got up over a dollar or two." The circuit rider paused to yawn and stretch. Then he climbed to his feet.

"Gent'men, I'd dearly love to keep on jawin' with you-all into the wee hours of the mornin'. But I got folks expectin' me in Fort Myers on the morrow, and it 'pears a couple of y'all could do with a tad of shut-eye your ownselves." He winked at Peek. "So with your kind permission, I'll just spread my blankets here in your midst, and mayhap we'll talk further 'bout gamblin' an' gunfightin' on some other occasion."

Peek wanted to protest, but everybody else was moving away from the fire to go fetch his bedroll. He realized that he'd little choice but to wait until morning to ask anything else about Ethan Cabell.

He had small hope of falling asleep now, what with all the questions that were rattling round inside his head, and with his renewed worry about the Westfields and those men who claimed to be their "guides." But he figured he'd lie down and give his tired muscles a rest anyhow.

A second after he put his arms behind his head to start mulling things over, his eyes closed, and when he opened them again it was to bright sunlight.

He'd slept late, and the circuit-riding preacher had already left camp. The only added information he could gather about Ethan Cabell came from what little Cooter had been able to pry out of the man while they shared an early breakfast.

It wasn't much, since both Cabell and the preacher were newcomers to the area. But it seemed clear that the man who had hired on as the Westfields' guide was some kind of a drifting card sharp who used a cold deck whenever he could get away with it. And he was a skilled gunman too, one who wouldn't hesitate to kill. If he had any personal interest in archaeology or Native American history, no one the preacher met had ever heard of it.

Of the other two hard cases that rode with him, there was no information at all. It seemed likely they'd hooked up with Cabell sometime after he left Orlando.

All in all, it was more than enough to make a fellow wonder. And Peek was doing his share.

He didn't rightly know what to do about it, if anything. But he was starting to have some notions, which he kept to himself for the time being. He wasn't sure what Cooter would say about such ideas, and until he'd had time to think them through for himself he wasn't looking for any second opinions.

There was still the hard dawn-to-dusk work of the drive to keep him busy until they reached Punta Rassa. Then it might be time to make a decision.

Not long after sun-up on an already steaming morning three days later, the Rocking JG crew strung out the herd along the broad, sandy main street of Fort Myers, taking the customary and most direct route to the port that lay another twelve miles distant. Peek and Cooter walked their mounts single-file through the narrow space between the town's boardwalks and the noisy, jostling stream of horns and dusky bodies, occasionally popping their whips but for the most part letting the experienced cow dogs handle the task of keeping the cattle in line.

A gaggle of youngsters, distracted from their school bell by the bawling steers and the choking clouds of dust, stood under a nearby awning to cheer and wave their hats as the procession ambled past. Some of the cow hunters smiled and waved back, but Peek was too conscious of his youth and his newfound responsibilities to acknowledge any such public display. He kept his eyes straight ahead, sitting tall and easy in the saddle while doing his best not to show his pleasure at the boys' admiring comments.

Long hours later, with their hats pulled low against the slanting rays of a copper sun, the Rocking JG men hazed their tired charges onto the final treacherous leg of the trail to Punta Rassa—row upon row of rough-hewn logs that formed a corduroy road through six hundred yards of low-lying salt flats and quicksand.

When his sure-footed Cracker horse stepped off onto solid ground at the western end of this makeshift causeway, Peek finally got a glimpse of the ramshackle buildings of old Fort Dulaney and of Jake Summerlin's slightly more appealing Punta Rassa Hotel. Both buildings rose from the sand on pilings within yards of the shimmering turquoise waters of the Gulf of Mexico.

By now even these rough and meager signs of civilization were a sore temptation to the sweating, dusty, trail-weary cow hunters. But they knew that any plans for collecting and disposing of their hard-earned dollar-a-day wages would have to wait until the herd could be sold and loaded aboard ships for Cuba.

When the longhorns were safely inside the port's vacant holding pens, Ed Porter informed his crew that he meant to take care of that task this very night if possible. News of the early drive had preceded its arrival and several Cuban freighters already lay at anchor in the harbor. The trail boss saw no reason to put off his sale of stock for even a day, especially in view of Jake Summerlin's exorbitant prices for feed and other necessities.

While the men wolfed down an early supper and took turns keeping an eye on the herd, Ed sought out the captains and negotiated his deal.

There was some weary grumbling among the cow hunters, for now on top of the day's drive they had a long arduous night to look forward to before any of them could seek a well-earned rest. But such talk was mostly for show. They were used to long hours and lost sleep by this time, and the business of loading the ships would have to be done sooner or later. This way they'd have their pay, and their freedom, just that much sooner.

Peek, for his part, accepted the trail boss's decision with no complaints. It meant that by tomorrow morning he'd be able to turn his thoughts to other matters.

The orange ball of the sun was disappearing behind the level green expanse of Sanibel Island when the first steamer warped up to the pier. A short time before, the tired cow hunters had begun prodding their charges into the narrow board chute that led to the wooden loading ramp beside the port's overseas telegraph station.

To an imaginative stranger the long hours of darkness that followed might have looked and sounded like some rustic scene from Dante's *Inferno*. The flickering glow from lighter knot torches cast eerie highlights and shadows across the ferocious jumble of razor-sharp horns, plunging bodies, and sun-blackened, sweat-drenched faces, amid the ear-splitting din of bawling cattle, barking dogs, pounding hooves, and shouting, swearing, whip-cracking men.

One by one the wild-eyed, violently protesting beasts had to be roped about the horns and fastened to the lines from a block and tackle before being hoisted by brute force over the rail and into the tightly jammed hold of a steamer. Eight hundred times the process was repeated, with only brief intervals of rest while empty freighters replaced full ones at the pier.

Despite appearances, with experienced crews on both ship and shore, it was a better-organized operation than the pandemonium the casual observer might have thought. The loading went smoothly enough. But it was brutally exhausting and time-consuming for all of that.

By the time the last ship was packed to the transom with noisily complaining beefsteaks on the hoof, the sky was gray in the east and the stars had faded from view. Ed Porter treated his weary crew to a farewell breakfast of steak and eggs at the chuck wagon while each man took a turn collecting his pay by firelight.

There wasn't enough of the night left by now to justify even the modest expense of telegrapher George Schultz's barrackslike accommodations. So Peek and Cooter took their bedrolls and spread them on the sand, near where they'd picketed their horses in a grove of cedar a short distance from the buildings. When they'd doused their mosquito bars with water as a defense against the ever-present sand flies, they crawled gratefully into their blankets and were instantly asleep.

Whatever hour they finally awoke would be soon enough to check out the modest but beckoning attractions of Punta Rassa social life.

Miranda cantered her black Morgan gelding within hailing distance of the small stand of oaks they'd chosen for their nooning, and slowed the spirited animal to a trot, then to a walk, before entering the grove's welcome shade. After a brief but careful inspection of her surroundings, she kicked her foot loose from the stirrup of the sidesaddle and dropped lightly to the ground.

There was a small pool at the far edge of the woods, fed by the runoff from one of this region's increasingly numerous artesian wells. Before going near it, she knotted her reins around a convenient branch in order to let her overheated mount recover from its run before leading it to water.

Untying the ribbon that kept her straw sunhat in place,

she used the broad brim to fan perspiration from her forehead and cheeks while she approached the tiny patch of sand that bordered the pool. After taking another cautious glance all around, she knelt and cupped mouthfuls of the clear, cool water to her lips. It was wonderfully refreshing, despite its faint taste of sulfur.

She dabbed water on her face and neck, then drank again. A flat lichen-streaked outcropping of limestone over-looked the pool. It was easily reached from the bank and offered a good view of the woods and the prairie beyond. Here, she sat and folded her arms about her knees, spending several long minutes just reveling in the silence and the soli-tude of this tree-shaded refuge from the south Florida heat.

She'd deliberately cantered ahead of the slow-moving wagon, knowing that her saddle-sore husband wasn't likely to follow, while equally sure of the scolding she'd receive when he finally did join her. He'd be right, of course. There was always a risk to entering such a hidden place alone, despite the fact that they'd seen no sign of Butch or any other trav-elers in the week since the stocky man was banished from their company.

But James had become almost cloying in his attentions following the attack on her—so much so that he could hard-ly be persuaded to leave her side for an instant. And Miranda wanted and needed some time alone with her thoughts.

She'd found herself growing more and more uneasy about the direction their expedition appeared to be taking. She had never entirely trusted Ethan Cabell, and her suspicions had increased since their brief encounter with that young cow hunter. What was his name? Pike? Deke? Tallman? Tillis?

Then had come the brazen assault by Butch. It was true Cabell had intervened quickly and decisively to protect her from his former cohort. But something about the look in his eyes when he drew back the hammer of that pearl-handled revolver still made her shiver slightly, even now in the midday heat.

Lately her misgivings had taken a more ominous turn, based on what she couldn't help but view as her husband's almost total surrender to the unasked-for decisions and "suggestions" of their guides.

To be fair, it was in large part due to Ethan Cabell's sometimes bullying presence that they'd managed to come away from that accident on the prairie with most of their outfit intact. If he hadn't known what was needed and taken charge of the repairs, they almost surely would have had to abandon their wagon and, with it, the expedition. As it was, they'd been able to resume their journey in relative comfort after just three days of backbreaking labor.

But afterward Cabell had taken it on himself—with little or no apparent argument from James—to make a sudden change in their direction of travel. Now, instead of striking west for Fort Ogden as the young cowhand had suggested and they'd originally planned, they had turned sharply southwest—a route that seemed to be leading them away from the Pease River, and from any frontier settlements that might be nearby.

Cabell's excuse—Miranda couldn't say why she chose that word, but to her it seemed appropriate—was that a number of larger, more substantial Indian mounds could be found in this new direction, while there were few of any consequence along the Pease River. This, of course, was at odds with what the cow hunter had told them, and with other reports they'd heard before leaving Tampa.

And then there was the matter of the Spanish coins. . . .

One evening after she'd retired to their tent following a hard day of work on the wagon, she overheard Cabell ask her husband what he knew of Spanish gold, and pirates who buried their loot on the Florida coast.

The question was pointless, given James' almost total lack of interest in or knowledge of recent Caribbean history. Still, he'd long since developed a scientist's healthy skepticism where any such tales of lost mines or hidden treasure were concerned. An archaeologist heard more than his share during his years in the field, and the vast majority of them were just pure wishful fantasy.

He had explained as much to Cabell, who persisted with several more pointed queries before finally dropping the matter when none brought an answer that seemed to satisfy him. Miranda had a feeling that their guide didn't believe James was telling the truth.

The next night she was repacking some personal items in readiness for their journey when Cabell, who might have had a bit more to drink than was wise, asked casually if she'd put the gold coins in a safe place. She had simply stared at him as if she didn't understand. He must have realized his mistake then, for he turned abruptly and retired to his tent for the rest of the evening.

She'd never said a word about those coins to Ethan Cabell or to his associates. In fact, she hadn't had them out of the purse in the bottom of her trunk until the day of the accident, when she'd seen them on the ground and hidden them on her person—where they were at present.

Miranda touched the coins lightly through the fabric of her blouse as she sat by the pool. Then she frowned and considered the facts.

It was possible, she conceded, that she was only imagining problems where none existed. Indeed, when she tried to approach the matter logically, seeking some actual cause for her ominous forebodings, she couldn't put her finger on a single thing. James had accepted their change of route willingly after all; no one had coerced him. And a man who harbored fantasies about buried doubloons might see them in his dreams. Cabell's remark could have been merely the result of an alcohol-induced delusion. . . .

She didn't believe that. Yet taking such vague feelings at face value went against every bit of the scientific training Miranda Westfield had spent much of her young life pursuing.

She put the question aside with an impatient toss of her head, and let her eyes roam from the tree-shaded pool at her feet to the sunlit meadow beyond, as if only now becoming aware of them. It was an oddly peaceful place, this lush green oasis in the untamed Florida wilderness. And like many she'd seen during her present journey, it was a strikingly beautiful one as well—leaving aside the late-September heat and the ever-present insects.

She could easily imagine the kind of reverence early natives must have felt for such a place. And if those feelings were tempered by the ever-present awareness of danger, it was simply an acknowledgment of the tenuous nature of life in these primeval surroundings—so different from the safe, orderly homes and well-policed streets of her native Northeast.

At almost any moment here, whether from savage predators, violent storms, poisonous reptiles, or unprincipled men, the issue of life and death literally hung by a thread. It was something Miranda had become more and more keenly aware of in the wilderness. Perhaps this, and nothing else, was the source of her nagging apprehensions. . . .

She'd almost managed to convince herself of that when the sudden clatter of approaching riders made her start and utter a hastily suppressed cry. The flood of relief she felt when she recognized her husband's khaki campaign hat and his stiff, awkward dismount was as tangible as a warm ocean wave.

As she stood up to go meet him and face his almost comforting words of reproof, she still had no more of a rational explanation for her gloomy premonitions than she did when they parted.

8 🌿

PEEK AND COOTER slept as late as they could, until the insects and the midday heat on the beach at Punta Rassa made further rest impossible. Then they rose, splashed salt water on their faces from the nearby Gulf of Mexico, and set about packing their gear.

When they'd finished this brief task and seen to the needs of their horses, Peek traded in one of the two shiny, new Cuban-Spanish gold pieces he'd gotten in wages for a pocketful of change and a long, luxurious tub bath, followed by a shave and a haircut in the only genuine barber chair this side of Fort Myers. The high price of seventy-five cents seemed well worth it after all those sweaty, unwashed days on the trail. Once he'd freshened his wardrobe with a clean hickory shirt from his war bag, he felt almost civilized again.

Cooter allowed himself to be talked out of the half dollar for a hot bath with soap, but he drew the line at any other tonsorial attentions.

"I reckon my whiskers an' what little hair I still got can take care of theirselves till I make it home to Fort Drum," he said in answer to his young friend's suggestion. "My ole woman does 'bout as good a job in that department as anybody I know. And I'm plumb particular who I 'low next to me with razors an' other sharp objects."

"Besides," he winked at Peek and grinned, "you never can tell what a little private barberin' session with the missus might lead to. Could turn out to be a whole lot better'n anything they sell around here for two bits!"

Peek blushed but could think of no smart comeback to the married man's remark. So he just shrugged and held his peace.

The next item on their agenda was a huge steak dinner with all the fixings. Meals at the Summerlin House weren't fancy, but nobody left the place hungry. And with such worries as storms and the unpredictable moods of bad-tempered scrub cows behind them, they took their time and savored every bite.

"That sure did fill a hollow place," Peek observed finally, topping off his coffee from the pot at his elbow. He sat back in his chair with a contented sigh. "All I need now is to rent me one of these here ho-tel rooms, and stretch out on some nice clean sheets for a long after-dinner nap."

Cooter put down the bone he was gnawing and grunted scornfully. "Pshaw!" he said between gulps of coffee. "That's just the kind of fool notion I'd expect from a young buck what ain't lost his spots yet. Next thing you'll be wantin' to tote a feather bed out yonder on the prairie with you!" He reached up with a hairy paw to pull the napkin from his collar and wipe his face and beard with it.

"Me, I still got two perfectly good blankets, and a whole heap of better things to do with my wages than spend 'em on a li'l ole airless cubbyhole for a couple hours' rest!"

Peek knew there was more to his partner's words than just orneriness. Cooter was a family man, with a wife and a little hardscrabble farm to take care of. His pay from the cattle drive was liable to be the only cash money they'd see for the better part of a year.

He'd no such responsibilities himself, having told his family good-bye and left their homestead in the Florida backwoods the same day he'd heard Ed Porter was hiring cow hunters. All he'd brought with him were his father's dubious blessing and what few possessions he could throw on the back of a horse. And he didn't plan to return until he'd made his mark in the world. Or at least until he had a chance to satisfy that restless longing for new horizons that prodded him onward.

With cash money burning a hole in his pocket for the first time in his life, and the youthful confidence that he could always earn more when it was gone, he saw no particular need to conserve his resources. And since he'd never spent a night in a hotel before, this seemed like a good time to try it. As for Cooter . . .

"Tell you what," he said. "I believe that I'll just go on ahead an' rent me one of those big rooms with two beds in it, so's to have plenty of space to relax in. Once I've done paid the man, you can make up your own mind whether to use that extry bed or let it go beggin'."

Cooter lowered his cup and started to protest, but Peek paid him no heed, turning sideways in his chair and swallowing the last of his coffee with a bland expression on his face. He reckoned a soft mattress and a roof over their heads wouldn't do either one of them any harm, and the couple dollars it cost would be money well spent.

At last the older man sighed and shook his head. "All right," he said, "you go on an' do whatever it is you're of a mind to. 'Pears you're just bound an' determined to squander ever' last penny of your money on foolishness anyhow." He fished a silver dollar from his pocket and plunked it on the table between them. "But in that case this here meal is on me!"

Peek accepted his partner's face-saving tradeoff with an agreeable nod. "I'm pleased you see things my way, Cooter. I got some right lonely travelin' ahead of me come daylight, and I'll be glad of the comp'ny as well as the comforts. Might be the last chance I get at either one for quite some time." He pushed back his chair and started to get up.

"Hold on there, young'un!" The older man's sharp words brought him to a stop halfway to his feet. He looked across the table at the grizzled cow hunter's stern face, hesitated, then eased himself back into his chair.

"You want to explain to ole Cooter just exactly what you meant by that last remark?"

Peek shrugged self-consciously. "Nothin' partic'lar. Just had me a notion to ride up the country a piece an' see what I could see."

"You wouldn't be huntin' anything special, would you?" Cooter's eyes narrowed. "Or anybody?"

Instead of answering, Peek hooked his thumbs in his jeans and stared down at the red-checkered tablecloth in front of him.

"I don't reckon it could be a certain Yankee perfessor you was hopin' to come acrost? Or his good-lookin' wife?"

Peek let out a weary sigh of resignation. He should have known it was no use trying to keep a secret from this wily old fox who'd spent close to every hour of every day with him for over a month. He pressed his lips together and nodded.

Cooter frowned at him in silence for another long moment.

"You give any thought to what you expect's goin' to happen," he said slowly, "when an' if you do catch up to that there outfit?"

"Well . . . not exactly." Peek hesitated. "I mean, I done thought about it a lot, but I still ain't rightly sure what I'd ought to do. It's just that I ain't hardly been able to keep my mind off them folks since we left 'em out yonder on Ninety-Mile Prairie."

"What kind of thoughts you been havin'?" the older man asked bluntly. "Thoughts about the kind of comp'ny them tenderfeet is keepin'? Or thoughts about that there married woman?"

"Aw heck, Cooter!" Peek felt his ears burning. "You know which it is. I mean, all right, I was some took by the lady and I won't deny it. I never met nobody like her, no woman that was so . . ." He paused and shook his head angrily.

"But this here's 'bout Ethan Cabell an' them two owl-hoots that ride with him. You heard what the preacher said back yonder. Cabell ain't even close to bein' what he claims to be. And he's a dangerous man to boot. A killin' man."

Cooter's frown deepened, but he held his peace and let his partner continue.

"Doc Westfield's a mighty fine gent, an' smart as a whip too in his own way. But out in that Florida backcountry the lady an' him are 'bout as helpless as a couple new-borned kittens. I don't believe he'd be much use a-tall if them three was to fetch him trouble. Nor just one of 'em, if it come to that."

Peek shrugged and slumped back in his chair. "Maybe it's a fool's errand from the git-go. Maybe they done called on Judge Ziba King like I told 'em, and he's took 'em under his wing. Maybe Cabell an' them never did have nothin' in mind but some easy money and easy livin' whilst makin' theirselves out to be guides. . . ." He let his voice trail off before adding quietly, "I just got to find out for sure, that's all."

Cooter nodded. "All right. Now, just supposin' you ain't wrong about Cabell an' his *compadres*. Supposin' they do got some kind of mischief planned, and there ain't nobody from the Circle O close enough to help out. Then I'll ask my same question in a different way. What you figure your part'll be in it if you hook up with them folks again up the country?"

"I'll do whatever I can that's needful," Peek said simply. "Or anyhow I'll try."

"You know it could mean shootin' trouble? The way the preacher told it, Ethan Cabell's some kind of hell on wheels with a six-gun, no matter what else he is. An' from what you said, them other two don't sound too far behind him in that department." The older man met his companion's eyes. "You real sure you're up to swappin' lead with three hard-case shootists all by your lonesome? Or do you got some other plan in mind?"

"Hell, Cooter, I don't know!" Peek spoke irritably, for he realized it was the truth. "I'll just have to cross that bridge when I come to it!"

"Anyhow," he went on more reasonably, "who else is there? You know they ain't no law closer'n Key West or Orlando. And ever'body here 'cept me's got family waitin' on 'em to home." He'd thought about all this during the last few days on the trail, and the answer seemed plain enough. "'Pears to me that I got it to do."

The older man didn't answer. He just sat quietly with his elbows on the table and his shoulders hunched forward, still frowning thoughtfully.

After a minute Peek rose to his feet. "Don't you go to frettin' now," he said with more confidence than he felt. "It'll prob'ly turn out to be nothin' but a ol' wild goose chase any-how." A little self-consciously, he shifted his cartridge belt into a more comfortable position.

"An' if it don't . . . Well, I reckon I ain't entirely no slouch with a six-gun my ownself. You've seen me work at it. I get her out from the leather mighty quick, and I don't gen-erally miss what I point her at."

Cooter lifted his eyes from the table to meet Peek's. "Ol' empty bottles an' rusty tin cans," he said gently, "or snakes an' other such varmints. I don't 'call a one of them what ever come up heeled an' went to shootin' back."

There was nothing Peek could say in answer to that, for he knew well enough what his partner meant. The prospect of facing an armed man in the smoke was a different matter entirely.

But none of it changed the fact that two awful fine people might be facing trouble up the country and his gun could be the only thing they'd have to rely on. What he'd told Cooter was the simple truth: It was his job to do. And Peek Tillman never was the kind to fight shy of a job that needed doing.

He turned from his still-seated friend and walked out into the lobby, pausing only long enough to fish two silver dollars from his pocket so as to get the attention of the heavy-lidded clerk behind the counter.

When he'd paid the money and signed his name in the leather-bound register, he turned back to glance at where Cooter had been. He was just in time to see his partner's broad shoulders disappear through the bat-wing doors of the adjacent saloon.

Peek thought about following him but rejected the notion, and made his way instead to the stairs leading to their second-floor room. He was in no mood for the company of strangers at the moment, and his recollection of the morning after his unaccustomed wine tasting with the Westfields was still vivid enough for alcohol to hold little temptation. He figured he might as well take full advantage of the money he'd just shelled out, and catch up on some much-needed rest.

Not that he expected to sleep. His talk with Cooter had brought into the open a whole army of self-doubts that had been skulking around the edges of his brain ever since he decided to ride after the Westfields.

In spite of his confident words, he wasn't sure how much help he would be against the likes of Ethan Cabell and his men if it came to a showdown. And if it did, he hoped he'd have the grit to follow through once all the chips were on the table.

He found his room and entered, then turned the key in the lock behind him. A gentle offshore breeze was stirring the thin curtains on either side of the open window, and a faint lapping of waves could be heard from the shallow waters of the Gulf a short distance away. Most of the hotel was empty at this hour, and no other sounds reached his ears.

The room had a soothing feel about it after all his rough days and nights on the trail.

When he'd unbuckled his cartridge belt and hung it over the post of the bed nearest the window, he sat in a chair to pull off his boots. Without troubling to undress further, he stretched out at full length on the thin cotton coverlet, gazing moodily up at the rough pine ceiling with his hands behind his neck.

Cooter was right about one thing. For him to meet three

seasoned gunmen in a face-to-face shootout made no sense at all. The trouble of it was, he didn't have the slightest glimmering of a plan for how else to approach the situation. It was, he admitted glumly, a problem completely outside his experience.

Like most boys growing up on the frontier, Peek was no stranger to rough-and-tumble fights with fists, feet, elbows, and whatever else was at hand, including cow whips and various farm implements. His introduction to such affairs began when he was scarcely out of the cradle. By the time he turned twelve he'd whipped every boy within walking distance of his house at least once. Several had been twenty pounds heavier and a full head taller at the time.

In those cases he'd learned the surest tactic was just to wade in swinging, land the first punch, then follow it up to a conclusion. Planning wasn't much a part of anybody's thinking, and the fellow who hesitated generally paid a price for his caution.

He knew there were some who took the same approach to a shooting scrape, and he'd seen his share in this lawless Florida country. But when it came to killing a man or being killed, Peek was inclined to believe a tad more reflection was in order.

It wasn't a matter of fear, though no one could be certain how he'd react when the lead started flying. It just looked like plain common sense to him. No thinking man ever risks his own life lightly, or lightly takes that of another.

But there would always be some who viewed violence

and killing as the simplest and fastest means to an end—whether that end be wealth, reputation, or power over those without the will or ability to resist. For such men violence was a policy to be used over and over for as long as it yielded success. The only thing that would make them abandon such a policy was the more immediate threat of violence to themselves.

This was the reason lawmen carried guns, even in the most "civilized" parts of the nation. And it was why on the frontier, where formal law was scarce and all law-abiding citizens shared the responsibility of enforcing the law, the law-abiding citizens carried guns.

Peek Tillman had grown to manhood in a country where the dangers were many and the chances for outside help were few. Wild beasts, poisonous reptiles, and human predators all had to be dealt with by whoever was on the spot at the time. Since no one but a fool carried a weapon without knowing how to use it, he practiced with the six-gun whenever he had time and could afford the cartridges, actively honing his skills in the hope he would never need them.

But here was the possibility of such a need, and it was staring him in the face.

True, Ethan Cabell had offered no threat to him personally. And because a man fought his own battles on the frontier, there were some who could say this applied to James Westfield as well. But Westfield was a tenderfoot, hopelessly outmatched by Cabell and the others in any kind of a physical contest.

And of course there was Miranda. . . .

No, it was like he'd told Cooter. If the Westfields needed help, it was up to Peek to offer it. And he'd noticed his partner didn't state any objection to that part of his argument.

He sure did wish the older man could ride with him though. For all his peace-loving ways, Cooter had seen and survived about everything this country could throw at a man, from rustlers to range wars, to floods, droughts, and hurricanes. He'd be a powerful comfort to have at your back with trouble on the horizon.

Only Cooter had cares of his own, and it had been too long already since he'd been home to tend to them. This was Peek's job, come hell or high water—or the six-guns of Ethan Cabell.

At last his eyelids grew heavy and, in spite of himself, he slept.

9

THE SLANTING RAYS of the late afternoon sun felt hot on Miranda's cheeks as she knelt to unpack the dinner dishes from their crate by the linen-covered camp table. She removed the last one from its nest of wood shavings and finished arranging the place settings, then stepped back to take advantage of the tarpaulin's shade and a slight breeze off the open prairie, opposite the small stand of laurel oak and cedar where their tents were pitched.

As she brushed back a stray wisp of hair, the suggestion of a frown creased her sun-darkened forehead.

It had all seemed very gay and elegant in the beginning, to dine each night from blue china dishes, with clean white linens and cut glass stemware—as if that somehow set them above and apart from the harsh realities of the Florida wilderness.

Lately, she'd found herself wondering why they went to so much trouble.

The wilderness, for its part, made no concession to these pale trappings of "civilization." With or without them, its primal nature was unchanged. The savagery and beauty of this land, with its unyielding laws of survival, endured as they had for countless generations. To Miranda it was starting to appear more sensible to live with such elemental forces instead of against them, as had the ancient peoples she and James studied.

She allowed herself a wry smile as she went to the cook fire to check on their dinner. If she were truly honest, she would admit that at least part of that feeling was brought on by weariness, and by her resentment toward Ethan Cabell and Quint for what seemed to be a growing disdain for the day-to-day chores of the camp.

When the three men had first joined them as guides, they'd gone out of their way to be helpful, even volunteering for such unmanly duties as setting the table and cleaning the dishes. Now it was a trial to ask even the most simple tasks of them. Unloading the wagon, putting up the tents, and repacking for travel were no longer begun without James and herself pitching in to do most of the work. And what little the others did was done sloppily, with more than a little grumbling.

Nor had it escaped her notice that their once-ample supply of wine and spirits had become seriously depleted.

In camp the two men usually stayed in their tent, except when one or the other rode off on some unexplained "reconnaissance" that frequently lasted till mealtime. Both still enjoyed hearty appetites, Miranda observed sourly, but now they kept to themselves when eating, and never took part in after-dinner conversation. It seemed Ethan Cabell had lost interest completely in discussions of archaeology, and his manner had grown increasingly sullen.

She returned the lid to the pot of beans she'd been stirring and hung the ladle back on the iron tripod before lifting her gaze past the empty tents to the grassy clearing where their mules were picketed. No one was in sight now, and that itself made her uneasy. Quint was away on one of his mysterious rides, but until a few minutes ago her husband and Cabell had been talking together at the edge of the trees.

They'd evidently moved farther off now. So she couldn't overhear? It might be just her lively imagination at work. But the fact remained that she wanted desperately to know what the two of them talked about.

The recent attitude of their guides both annoyed and disturbed her. But it was the change in James that caused the greatest concern. For all his cultured and scholarly upbringing, until now he'd always been confident and decisive. In fact, it was his calm self-assurance that first attracted her to him, when she was still a sophomore at Vassar and he a nationally known lecturer in anthropology.

Yet now, in the face of Cabell's increasingly high-handed and callous behavior, this man she loved and admired seemed incapable of action. More than once she'd seen his face grow grim and he'd appear on the verge of speaking out, only to swallow his words and retreat behind a mask of tight-lipped indifference.

In her heart Miranda was sure this wasn't due to cowardice, nor to James' belief that Cabell posed any personal danger to him. But if it wasn't that . . . then what?

After another furtive glance toward the spot where she'd last seen her husband, she sat at the table and clasped her hands together, trying desperately to shut out the sudden thought that she feared held the answer.

The sun was below the horizon when Peek blinked awake, groggy from sleep and a little disoriented by his unfamiliar surroundings. The sparsely furnished hotel room seemed dreary and lonely in the gathering dusk, and he reckoned he'd had enough time with his thoughts. He felt a powerful need right now for some bright lights and company.

Swinging his feet to the floor, he rose, belted on his six-shooter, and sat down again to pull on his boots. After splashing cold water on his face at the wash stand and running his fingers through his hair in place of a comb, he took his hat, closed the door behind him, and made his way down to the hotel saloon.

The big room was noisy and crowded when he entered. Since it was early in the season the only cow hunters present were a half dozen familiar faces from the Rocking JG. But there were a number of Cuban sailors off the ships in the harbor, and these had been joined by a boisterous mob of fishermen from Sanibel, Boca Grande, Marco, and elsewhere, all of who seemed to have chosen this particular night to converge on Punta Rassa.

Cooter stood at a corner of the bar, talking to a tall, copper-skinned man in a wide-brimmed black hat, to which the distinctive black-and-white wing feather of an osprey was attached.

"Hey, Peek!" the older man called when he spied his friend in the doorway. "We was just talkin' about you. Belly on up to the bar here an' have yourself a beer!" He turned to get the bartender's attention while Peek started threading his way through the crowd to join them.

It was a delicate task among the constantly shifting throng of jostling, boozing, sweaty bodies. At one point he zigged when he should have zagged and stumbled against the muscular back of a huge sailor with tattoos on both arms and gold rings in his ears. "Watch your step, *chiquito.* There are men in this port, and we require space to do our drinking."

"Sorry, *amigo.*" Peek deliberately ignored the challenge in the big man's words and turned again toward the bar. In the process he trod on the toes of a small hawk-nosed sailor who'd edged suspiciously close during the encounter.

As he opened his mouth for a second apology he felt the little man's fingers enter his pocket. Instantly, Peek's work-hardened fist shot down, clamping like a vise around the thief's knuckles and holding them inside his pocket so they couldn't be withdrawn.

"You got you just two seconds to let go them coins, *amigo.*" The cow hunter's words were a low-voiced purr as he tightened his grip. "Or I'm goin' to bust ever' bone in your slippery little hand."

"*¡Ay, Diablo . . . !*"

"One second." Peek increased his crushing hold and the smaller man whimpered with pain. Then, with a sharp intake of breath, he let the coins drop and was allowed to withdraw his arm.

"*Pendejo*," the pickpocket glared at Peek as he stepped back to rub circulation into his fingers, "*hijo de cabrón.*"

Peek knew enough Spanish to understand the insults, and he couldn't resist a wry impulse to turn it back on the speaker.

"I'm mighty pleased to make your acquaintance, *Señor Cabrón*," he drawled, touching the brim of his hat in mock politeness. "Peek Tillman's my name."

Before the red-faced thief could respond, Peek turned quickly and strode to the bar. The incident seemed to have gone unnoticed by anyone else in the crowd. Their attention was being drawn to the far end of the room, where a little gray-bearded man in greasy overalls was spinning some colorful but unlikely yarn about pirates and Spanish doubloons and beautiful dark-eyed women captives.

Peek was tempted to move in that direction himself out of curiosity. But Cooter was impatiently waving him forward.

He elbowed his way next to them and nodded a greeting to Cooter's companion, who responded with a curt tilt of the head. Even apart from his size—the copper-skinned man was a good two inches taller than Peek and much broader in the shoulders—this appeared to be one mighty tough *hombre*. His long raven hair hung straight past his collar, only partly concealing a jagged scar that extended across one high cheek-bone. As he stood next to the bar with his arms folded, powerful muscles seemed to ripple under the loose-fitting calico of his shirt. He carried no firearm, but the huge bowie knife in a deerhide scabbard that was thrust into the belt outside his shirt looked both well used and businesslike.

Cooter dropped two coins on the bar and turned toward them with a bottle of beer in each hand. "Peek, say howdy to my old friend Chekita Joe, Cheeky Joe for short. His folks been makin' out in this Florida country since before ole Ponce de Leon was a pup."

"Any friend of Cooter's," the younger cow hunter said seriously, "is a man worth knowin'." They shook hands while Peek put his partner's words together with the other's appearance. "Seminole?" he ventured, in a tone that held respect as well as curiosity. The Indian wars had ended before Peek was born and encounters with the surviving natives were rare nowadays, but they were usually cordial.

"Calusa," the man with the osprey feather corrected him. His features betrayed no emotion, but his dark eyes flickered with savage pride. "Full-blood or near it from my mother's family." The muscular shoulders lifted in the suggestion of a shrug. "Spanish, African, a touch of what-have-you for the rest."

"Cheeky Joe don't drink," Cooter explained as he handed a bottle to Peek and kept the other for himself. "He just comes here for the talk an' news of the settlements. And he don't do that so terrible often. It was just pure-dee luck that he showed up today." Something about the way his partner said that made Peek glance at him curiously.

Cooter saw the look but ignored it, resting his back against the bar to take a long pull from his beer. After a minute he set the bottle down and wiped his mouth with his hand. His eyes went from Peek to Cheeky Joe, and then back again.

"Y'see," he said slowly, pushing his hat away from his forehead, "how it appears to me is this. You got it all fixed in your young mind to go traipsin' off up the country huntin' bad men, and likely gettin' your tail in a crack in the process. Me, I'd admire to tag along an' see you don't go bitin' off anything bigger'n you can chew. But I got to be gettin' home to the missus, and I can't spare the time for no extry sight-seein' trips. . . ."

Peek had an idea he knew what was coming. But he kept quiet for the time being, swallowing his annoyance with a long pull of beer.

". . . That there bein' the case," the older cow hunter went on with a jerk of his head at his Indian friend, "I reckon it's mighty lucky ole Cheeky Joe turned up when he did. He was just tellin' me he ain't got no special plans for the next couple weeks. So he'd be willin' to ride along, 'case you needed some help."

Peek glanced at the Calusa's inscrutable face. Then he took a deep breath and turned to his partner.

"Now look-a here, Cooter," he said evenly. "It ain't that I'm not grateful for all your mammy-like frettin' over my personal welfare. But with eighteen summers behind me, the last eight or so doin' a growed man's work in this here man's country, I was startin' to get the notion I was almost full-growed my ownself." He paused to take a swallow of beer.

"So I reckon I can do my own askin' for help when I want it. An' if I didn't ask, it's 'cause I figured I can look out for myself, without no nursemaid to make sure I eat reg'lar and stay dry from the rain."

There was a brief awkward silence when he finished; and it occurred to him, belatedly, that he might have used a little more tactful language in declaring his independence.

"I don't mean no disrespect towards you, Cheeky Joe," he added quickly, turning to the big man at his elbow. "I can tell you're a man to ride the river with, and I'm grateful for the offer. But I wasn't plannin' on no comp'ny on this here expedition, and I reckon I'll allow things to just stay like they are."

The Calusa nodded. "You want to go alone, it's your business. No bad feelin's." He touched the brim of his hat to the cow hunters and started to turn away. Then he glanced back over his shoulder at Peek. "You change your mind, I'll be here till mornin'. Camped out by the horses."

"One of these days," Cooter said quietly after they'd watched the door close behind Cheeky Joe's huge form, "that stubborn streak is goin' to cost you a heap more'n you want to lose." He drained his beer and set the empty bottle on the bar. "That there feller's went up the creek and over the mountain 'fore you was in long pants. He's the best they is at follerin' a trail, be it animal or human or you name it. An' if it was me had some tom-fool notion about bracin' three hard-case gun artists somewheres up the country, there ain't a soul in this world I'd sooner have at my back."

Peek just shrugged and nursed the last of his beer in silence. He knew he'd spoken hastily, mostly from anger at Cooter's meddling and treating him like some wet-behind-the-ears greenhorn. But he had to admit that if it came to a showdown with Cabell and his henchmen, he might be sorry he didn't take Cheeky Joe's offer.

He'd be danged if he'd go back on his word now, though. He'd spent a lot of time working himself up to tackling this business alone, and he meant to see it through. Besides, a man shouldn't get in the habit of always expecting help when he'd some unpleasant chore to do.

After a minute he turned his eyes to the crowd of men clustered at the opposite end of the bar.

"Say," he said, deliberately pushing his gloomy thoughts aside and indicating the bearded storyteller with a nod of his head. "Who's that feller yonder? He sure does 'pear to have a uncommon talent for drawin' a crowd."

"Him?" Cooter shrugged. "That's just old John Gomez. He's got more tall tales inside of him than that there Sir Walter Scott feller. Mostly 'bout sailin' ships an' pirates an' buried gold an' such. Swears ever' word of it's gospel. Says he used to sail with some buccaneer named Gasparilla a real long time back."

"No kiddin'?" Peek eyed the bearded man with fresh

interest. "You reckon it's true?"

"T'aint likely. I calc'late he'd have to be upward of a hundred year old if he done all he says he done. And he don't look a day over sixty to me. I got a notion 'long as anybody keeps buyin' him them rum drinks he's so partial to, he'll tell 'em 'most anything they want to hear."

"Well, he sounds like a interestin' feller just the same. Let's listen a mite an' see what he's got to say."

Cooter started to protest, but Peek had caught the bartender's eye and ordered two more beers. The older cow hunter accepted his with a shrug of resignation and joined his friend at the edge of the crowd.

10🦅

"EVER' ONE OF these islands herebouts got its name from Jose Gaspar an' his crew," the self-styled former sea rover was explaining. "Captiva, that's where they kept all them beautiful gal captives they took off the Spanish ships. Useppa, what used to be called Joseffa's Island, is where Gaspar built his favorite wife a house. And then o' course there's Gasparilla Island itself. . . ." He paused, swaying a little on his feet while he drained his latest glass of grog.

"An' you know these so-called Injun mounds you'll find ever'where up an' down this coast?" Old John dried his beard with a swipe of his shirtsleeve and handed the glass across the bar. "Well, maybe a couple of 'em was made by Injuns . . ." Somebody tossed a quarter to the bartender and he turned to replenish the drink. "But most was the work of Gasparilla and his men."

Gomez winked a watery eye. "I guess I ought to know, 'cause it was me that helped 'em do it!" He paused and lowered his voice almost to a whisper. "Now what you suppose is inside all them mounds?"

Peek had an idea that everybody else in the room had heard the story and knew the answer as well as Gomez. But no one offered a reply. And in spite of his skepticism, he found himself leaning forward with the rest in order to hear better.

"Gold!" the gray-bearded man said dramatically. "Spanish doubloons, pieces of eight! And rubies, diamonds, em'ralds . . . ever' kind of precious jewel you can think of! All of it stole off them Spanish galleons!" He winked again, slyly. "An' snatched from the white necks of them beautiful dark-eyed *señoritas* we took along into the bargain!"

When Peek straightened up and glanced at Cooter, his partner seemed to be studying the rafters over their heads. Both could recognize a tall tale when they heard it. They'd been known to spin a few of their own when the occasion was ripe for it.

Still, Peek enjoyed the old fraud's stories and he took his time finishing his beer. Each yarn grew less likely than the last, and more outlandish with every fresh swallow of grog. Finally, after Gomez had told about meeting Napoleon some ninety years earlier, and of fighting alongside General Zachary Taylor in the Seminole wars—at the tender age, by his account, of sixty-five—his audience in the saloon started drifting away. The old man was deep in his cups by then, and he was beginning to repeat himself.

Cooter put his empty bottle down and pushed away from the bar. "Come on, young'un," he said. "Let's grab a mite of fresh air to get the smoke out of our craws. Then we'll have a look at that highfalutin room you paid for. You said you was wantin' to be up in the saddle come daylight, so we'd ought to try an' get a part of your money's worth out'n that accommodation anyhow."

As they were crossing the sawdust-covered floor to the exit that opened onto the verandah and the outside stairway at the front of the hotel, Peek had a sudden feeling that everyone's eyes were on them. A second before following his partner outside, he glanced back over his shoulder.

The Cuban sailors seemed to have mysteriously disappeared. But there were enough furtive glances from the remaining crowd of fishermen to confirm his suspicion that they were all waiting for something. And just a tad too eagerly for Peek's taste.

As his eyes scanned the lamp-lit room for the faces of their own Rocking JG crew, he realized that each cow hunter was now surrounded by two or three big dungareed bodies, effectively blocking them from the exit.

The hairs rose at the base of his neck and he turned sharply to call out into the night: "Hold up a minute, Cooter! I got me a real bad feel—"

But it was already too late.

A heavy shoulder propelled him out the door and down the short flight of wooden steps to the ground. As he rolled over in the sand, clutching a badly bruised knee, he heard Cooter's sharp yelp of pain and surprise from the darkness a dozen yards away.

Before Peek could get to his feet, a boot heel in the small

of his back threw him face down again in the sand. He had a fleeting glimpse of the little hawk-nosed pickpocket as his pistol was jerked from its holster and tossed away underneath the building.

A noisy drunken mob had started pouring out onto the verandah to witness the expected blood-letting, while Peek crouched in the rectangle of light from the saloon's open door and peered warily about him into the shadows. Angry cries in Spanish seemed to issue from every direction:

"¡Malditos!"

"¡Sinvergüenzas!"

"¡Vaqueros mariquitas!"

"¡Gitanos hijos de puta!"

"¡Vamos! ¡Mátenlos como perros!"

Peek understood enough of what was said to sense the fierce and unreasoning rage that was directed against him and his partner. And he knew it must have taken some imaginative lies from the pickpocket and his tattooed accomplice to incite more than a dozen men to carry out such an attack, while at the same time keeping the American fishermen from any efforts to help their outnumbered countrymen.

It made no difference what kind of lies they were. The drunken sailors were well past listening to words, even if the words had been spoken in their own tongue. They'd armed themselves with a wicked assortment of oars, marlinespikes, boat hooks, and belaying pins. And they showed every intention of using these until the two unlucky cow hunters were either dead or crippled for life.

From the corner of his eye Peek caught a glimpse of a large body hurtling toward him out of the dark. He tucked in his head and straightened his legs, throwing the attacker over his shoulder to hit the ground with an earth-shaking thud.

The hard-swung toe of his boot brought a yelp of agony from a second man as it connected below the knee-cap, and he managed to rake a third with his spurs on the backswing. Turning, he followed this with a solid left and a right to the jaw, then wrestled an oar from his latest assailant and began laying about him in all directions.

Angry shouts and crashes from inside the saloon announced that the outnumbered Rocking JG crew had now taken the brawl to the fishermen in an attempt to come to the aid of their fellow cow hunters. The knowledge gave Peek renewed strength, and he bared his teeth in a ferocious grin as his enemies closed in around him. He meant to make them pay a price before this set-to was over, no matter what the outcome might be.

He drove one sailor to his knees with a vicious round-house swing of the oar, smashing it to splinters across the man's muscular neck and shoulder blades. Its jagged end ripped flesh from a second man's face as Peek recovered and brought the weapon up for another blow. But then the mob rushed in all at once, and the makeshift club was torn from his hands.

They all tried desperately to pin his flying fists and elbows behind him. But Peek still managed to pulp a sailor's nose and knock another sprawling before he was wrestled to the ground. The pain of a dozen cuts and bruises served only to feed his rage as he lashed out like a cornered wildcat, clawing blindly at the sea boots that pummeled his body while with churning feet and spurred heels he fought to keep the enclosing forest of legs at bay.

Suddenly brilliant daggers of fire exploded before his eyes and he felt his body go weak. The heavy butt of a marlinespike had opened a deep gash in his forehead and he was stunned and blinded with blood. More from instinct than from any conscious thought, he curled himself into a fetal position and raised his arms to cover his head, still trying as best he could to ward off the torrent of blows.

A glancing kick to the chin rocked his head back, and his eyes snapped shut. An instant later he was tumbling down a bottomless sinkhole into darkness.

❖ ❖ ❖

How long he was unconscious he had no way of guessing. When he finally groped his way back to awareness he felt sick to his stomach, and his breath came in agonized gasps. But mercifully, the punishment to his tortured body seemed to have stopped.

For what felt like many long minutes he lay without moving, shivering a little in the cool air off the Gulf while having to breathe slowly and shallowly to ease the pain of bruised or broken ribs. Above the roaring in his ears he thought he heard men's voices. But at the moment they sounded faint and far away.

When the red fog in his head began to clear, he pawed blood from his eyes, gritted his teeth, and lifted his body into a wary crouch. If those men from the ships had a mind to finish what they'd started, at least he meant to look them in the eye while they did it.

But a fresh wave of nausea came over him, and he dropped to his knees and elbows, retching silently with his face inches above the churned-up sand. After a long time he managed to sit back on his heels and rest, trembling miserably and drenched with sweat.

Gradually he became aware of muted voices from the direction of the saloon. A quick glance revealed that the door was partly closed now, with only an occasional flicker of movement beyond its thin yellow rectangle. What had happened to the brawling mob of fishermen?

Still groggy and confused from the blows to his head, he peered cautiously around him. There seemed to be a number of shapes lying here and there on the sand. But none of them were moving that he could tell.

Gritting his teeth against the pain in his ribs, he climbed unsteadily to his feet. Almost in the same instant a bright crescent moon rose above the treetops, spreading its pale silver light over the immediate surroundings. When his eyes took in the scene, Peek found himself gaping in disbelief.

Close to a dozen Cuban sailors lay sprawled on the ground, each showing the effects of the brutal kind of treatment they'd meant for him and his partner. A few were beginning to stir now and moan softly, but most remained still, either dead or unconscious.

For a long minute the young cow hunter could only look stupidly about him, unable to make any sense of the spectacle. He'd given a good account of himself under the circumstances, but nothing that would explain the devastation he saw here. Nor was Cooter likely to have done much better, outnumbered and surprised as they both were from the beginning. The others of the Rocking JG crew? They'd faced heavy odds themselves inside the saloon.

"You finished with your li'l nap now?"

The sudden quiet voice at his back made Peek turn sharply, nearly causing him to lose his balance and fall in the process. He clutched at his midsection to still the shooting pain in his ribs while his attention was drawn to two dark shapes on the ground a little distance off. After a second he recognized the big kneeling form of Cooter's friend Chekita Joe.

The man's bowie knife glinted evilly in the moonlight as its razor-sharp tip probed with excruciating gentleness the left inner nostril of a muscular sailor stretched out by his side. Peek saw the faint reflection of gold earrings and realized it was the same tattooed ruffian who'd been with the pickpocket earlier in the saloon.

It was to this man Cheeky Joe was speaking, so softly that Peek could barely make out the words:

"Soon as they're able, you help those others get back on their ships. Then you stay there till you sail. I ever find you messin' with my friends again, I'll take that pretty tattooed hide off you, real slow, and make me a shirt." He drew the knife back a scant quarter of an inch. "*¿Comprende?*"

"*Sí.*" The sailor took a gulp of air and nodded feebly. "*Sí sí, comprendo.*"

Out of the corner of his eye Peek saw that Cooter was now standing beside him. He looked at his partner and breathed a sigh of relief. There was blood on the older man's balding head, his shirt was in tatters, and one eye was swollen nearly shut. But he was grinning broadly and appeared to have suffered no serious injury.

With a single catlike motion, Chekita Joe unfolded his huge body and rose to stand gazing down at the man at his feet. Peek caught a sudden fleeting glimpse of another dark figure creeping from under the porch of the Summerlin House. The barrel of a pistol caught the moon's rays as it lifted, and the cow hunter opened his mouth to call out a warning.

But even before he could find his voice their companion's arm flashed up from his side, releasing the bowie knife in a deft underhand throw. There was a soft and sickening *thud* followed by a low moan from the would-be assassin. Then the pistol-wielding figure collapsed and was still.

Cooter approached the body warily and knelt to recover the weapons. Peek followed a little more hesitantly. He'd seen a lot during his young life on the frontier, injury and death included. But a man with a bowie knife sunk to the hilt in his stomach was a grim and sobering vision.

The older cow hunter took up the pistol, glanced at it briefly, and held it out to Peek with a wry look on his face. It was Peek's own Colt, which he'd had stripped from him at the start of the fight.

Embarrassed at being so easily disarmed, Peek silently checked the loads and dropped it in his holster. Then he bent to examine the dead man's face in the moonlight. He turned quickly away when Cooter seized the knife to pull it from the body.

"Well," he said hoarsely, choking back the bile that rose in his throat, "I don't reckon he'll be pickin' no more pockets any time soon."

"Nor shootin' folks from ambush," Cheeky Joe said calmly as he approached to take the weapon from Cooter. "He made his play and he come up short."

With the bloody knife once more in hand, the big man darted a wary glance at the sailor he'd left on the ground. But it looked like the other had no more fight left in him. He was on his knees now, crossing himself and gazing at the body of his former partner. After a minute he uttered a low-voiced curse in his native tongue before rising to go see to his more fortunate comrades.

Cheeky Joe watched him leave, then reached up to pull some Spanish moss from a nearby tree. He seated himself cross-legged with his back to the trunk and began methodically cleaning his blade and rehoning it on his boot sole, while sparing only an occasional glance for the gradually recovering seamen.

While Cooter disappeared into the shadows in search of his hat, Peek eyed the man before him with growing disbelief.

It seemed Chekita Joe had no plans to volunteer anything more about the fight, and Peek's curiosity was almost more than he could stand.

"What the dickens happened out here?" he blurted finally, his voice sounding loud in the night's restored stillness. "I can recall the first part pretty good, and I reckon I just seen the last. But in between there I must of missed a li'l somethin'."

The other shrugged without interrupting his task. "Not much to tell. You an' Cooter was havin' some troubles and the odds didn't seem right. So I took a hand an' settled things."

"Settled th—" The words died on Peek's lips as he stared about him. The battered and bloody seamen were limping toward their boats now, supporting one another and grumbling softly like a pack of beaten curs.

"Well," he said bluntly, "I guess you sure 'nough done that. Only how in the . . ."

"Hey," the seated man interrupted, calling to a handful of less seriously hurt sailors who were passing nearby. "Don't forget to take that with you." He pointed to the dead pickpocket with the tip of his knife. "He ain't mine, and I don't plan to hold no funerals."

The sailors glared at him, but they kept a rein on their tongues and bent to remove the body.

Peek felt his knees growing weak as the aftereffects of the fight set in and his injuries started taking their toll. Yet his burning need to know what happened wouldn't let him drop the matter:

"What about that big crowd of fishermen?" he asked. "I was afeared they'd be takin' a hand in things next."

Cheeky Joe shrugged again. "Reckon your friends gentled 'em some. Then they kind of lost interest when they looked at these here." He tested the knife's sharpness on the hair of his arm, grunted, and resumed his honing. "Most of 'em back on the water now, headed for home."

There was an angry throbbing at the side of Peek's skull, and despite all his questions about how just one man could wreak so much damage, he no longer seemed able to find the words to ask them. His legs started to give out and he was close to falling when Cooter arrived and took hold of his arm.

"Steady up, young'un." The older man handed Peek his hat, which he'd recovered along with his own, and turned him gently toward the steps to the hotel verandah. "Let's us get inside there an' see can we patch ourselves up a mite."

Before Peek could take more than a few shambling steps he was halted by Cheeky Joe's soft voice at his back:

"You still got in mind to be ridin' tomorrow?"

The young cow hunter took a moment to place his hat on his head and draw himself up to his full height before turning around.

"Way back when I was thirteen an' a half," he said deliberately, "I got kicked by a mule and had two ribs busted together with a broke arm. I caught up that sorry critter an' rode it eighteen miles to the house without ever gettin' down." He favored the other with a lop-sided grin. "So I don't expect none of these here li'l hurts will keep me from travelin'!"

The big man's face remained impassive while he pulled a hair from his dark mane, sliced it neatly in two, and dropped the bowie knife back in its scabbard. "Still plannin' to go it alone?" he asked mildly.

Peek hesitated, then his grin became broader. He winced as the loose skin peeled away from the cut on his forehead.

"Well," he said, "I reckon if some big ol' mean Injun had a notion to ride that way too, I wouldn't be such a almighty fool as to make a issue of it."

Cheeky Joe crossed his arms and settled his back more comfortably against the tree trunk.

"All right," he said, reaching up to draw his hat brim over his eyes. "I'll be here come daylight."

11

DESPITE PEEK'S BOLD words of the night before and all his youthful resolve to leave Punta Rassa at first light, the copper-colored sun was well up in the sky by the time he'd gulped down his second cup of coffee and ventured out with Cooter onto the Summerlin House verandah.

With a knowledge and skill gleaned from years on the frontier, the older man had bound up his partner's sore ribs—which had fortunately turned out to be only bruised and not broken—and tended to his other cuts and hurts as well as any doctor would. But Cooter also knew that sleep was the most powerful medicine. So after explaining things to an understanding Chekita Joe, he'd deliberately put off waking his young friend until an hour before noon.

When Peek finally did roll awkwardly out of the soft hotel bed to dress and struggle into his boots, the aches and stiffness in every part of his body left him small temptation to complain about the delay.

Cheeky Joe had his Cracker pony saddled and ready to travel when he finally emerged, squinting, into the bright midday sun. It stood three-legged at the rail next to a short-coupled gray horse of the breed known to the natives as a marshtackie.

The big man rose lazily from the shade of a tree when he saw the cow hunters appear. He nodded a silent greeting, then strode forward to tighten the cinches on the waiting animals.

Peek negotiated the wooden steps carefully, carrying his saddlebags and bedroll under one arm. When he'd rounded the end of the hitch rail he took a deep breath and swung those objects into place on his pony's back. The stabbing agony in his side that accompanied his sudden movement made him gasp and bite his tongue to hold back the yelp of pain that tried to leap from his throat.

Neither of his companions seemed to notice, and he let out a long slow sigh before raising a hand to wipe tears from his eyes while pretending to fiddle with the strings of his bedroll. He took his time securing the gear to the saddle, pausing afterward to lean heavily against his horse for several long moments.

Finally he turned to his partner. "You take care, Cooter." He held out a hand and the older man gripped it firmly. "I reckon I'll be seein' you come next fall's cow hunt, if not before."

"You take it careful your ownself, young'un." The older man laid a gentle hand on Peek's shoulder. "And you pay real close attention to whatever Cheeky Joe here tells you. He ain't much on idle talk, so when he does say somethin' it'll be a thing worth heedin'."

Peek nodded and climbed stiffly into the leather. Cheeky Joe was already mounted, and together they swung their ponies' heads east toward the road to Fort Myers.

Just before they lost sight of the port behind a thick stand of cedar, the younger man turned in his saddle and looked back at the familiar form of Cooter, squinting after them with his thumbs hooked in his suspenders and his slouch hat pushed back off his forehead. Peek was going to miss the ornery old cuss, with his unvarnished ways and all his sharp-tongued kindnesses. He raised one hand in a purposely casual farewell, then swallowed hard and forced his eyes to the front again, drawing his own hat brim lower against the hot Florida sun.

He did his best to endure the early torture of the corduroy road in tight-lipped silence. The cut on his forehead throbbed painfully and its bandage was soaked with sweat under his now too-tight hatband. But that was nothing compared to the searing daggers of fire that stabbed his ribs with every rocking step of his sure-footed mount on the rough-hewn causeway.

He had no intention of letting his new companion know the extent of his misery, nor of halting to rest until they'd put two or three miles behind them. Only a little farther now, he kept saying to himself between tightly clenched teeth. When they reached solid ground the ride would be easier. His eyes were narrowed to slits against the glare of sand and water as he watched the trees grow closer. . . .

But pride and grit could take him only so far. No sooner

had they stepped off onto the soft white earth of the mainland than Peek felt his stomach churn, and the sour taste of coffee rose in his throat. Unable to prevent what he knew was coming, he drew up and knotted his fingers in the Cracker pony's mane. Then he leaned far out beside the animal's neck and was violently and painfully ill for several long seconds.

Cheeky Joe halted a short distance off and waited patiently with his eyes on the trail ahead, while his companion recovered and sat up in the saddle.

After he'd unlimbered his canteen to rinse out his mouth, Peek sat still for a minute or two, taking in slow deep breaths of the fresh salt air. Surprisingly, he felt better after his brief bout of nausea. He swallowed some of the lukewarm water from his canteen and hung it back on the saddle. Then he clucked to his horse and rejoined his guide.

The loose sand road did help ease the journey once his Cracker pony settled into its native "coon rack" gait—a comfortable single-foot stride not unlike the Spanish *paso fino*. But Peek offered little objection when Cheeky Joe—without ever appearing to take the slightest notice of his discomfort—drew up to rest their mounts after only another half an hour.

"No use lettin' the animals get wore to a frazzle," the big man said when they'd dismounted to take advantage of the shade from a stand of cabbage palms a hundred yards from the river. "Got a long ways to go. Li'l break now an' then won't make us much difference."

Peek was tempted to stretch out on the soft warm sand and close his eyes. But he was afraid his ribs would stiffen up, and make the rest of the day's ride just that much harder. Instead, he hunkered down and rested his back against the rough bole of a palm, gazing idly out from under his hat brim at a dragonfly that darted and hovered a few feet away.

He already felt a little more spry than when they'd left Punta Rassa. Not that he wasn't still sore all over and tired to the bone. But being out and doing in the fresh air and sunshine always did seem to help a body get over his hurts quicker than laying up feeling sorry for himself. Peek hadn't known much else in life but hard physical work and the rough knocks and bruises that frequently went with it. He figured if he could manage to keep up with Cheeky Joe for the rest of the afternoon, another good night's sleep might fix him up almost as good as new.

He dozed then in spite of himself. The next thing he knew the other man was striding past him to fetch their horses, grunting a terse, "Okay. Let's ride," back over his shoulder.

They crossed the Caloosahatchee southwest of Fort Myers, willingly paying a boatman's modest price to save themselves more than a day's travel upstream to the nearest ford and back again. The narrow strip of beach where Cheeky Joe had them put ashore was almost invisible among the dense thickets of mangrove and saltbush—a low-growing wall of green that stretched along the water's edge for as far as the eye could see.

There were no signs of human settlement close by, and

only the barest suggestion of a trail winding north through the shadowed jumble of twisted limbs and spiderlike prop roots of the red mangrove. Yet no sooner were they mounted again than Cheeky Joe struck out along this hidden path without a second's hesitation, deftly guiding his marshtackie through its tortuous bends and switchbacks at a shambling, distance-eating walk.

Peek's nimble-footed Cracker pony followed readily enough, but the cow hunter shook his head in wonder at the unerring way his companion navigated the dense confusion of woodland in the absence of any obvious landmarks. Such hidden forest travel seemed as familiar to him as riding the military roads was for a settler. Which, of course, was probably the case.

The late autumn heat and humidity of the Florida interior were galling and oppressive to a seaman used to the fresh salt breezes of the Gulf; and the unaccustomed jolting of the hard McClelland saddle did nothing to improve Juan Castro's surly disposition. Every few minutes the big tattooed sailor would rise up in the stirrups and shift his massive bulk, hoping for some relief for his painfully tender backside. But none of it helped. After a time he drew rein, cursing bitterly while he mopped his florid face with an outsized bandanna.

"¡Malditos caballos!" he growled as his shipmate Miguel came abreast. "If ever was a creature of Satan put on the earth for man's mortification, it was the horse!"

Miguel was privately inclined to agree, but he was too well aware of his companion's sudden rages to call unneeded attention to himself at such a moment. He merely shrugged.

"How far you think we've ridden since crossing the river?" the big man persisted, shaking out the sodden bandanna and reknotting it around his bull-like neck.

Miguel hesitated, then shrugged again. "Three kilometers maybe," he ventured mildly. "Possibly four."

"*¡Mierda!*" By now the *yanqui* and the *indio* would be a good two hours ahead of them. And because they knew the country and were accustomed to travel by horseback, they would increase their lead with every minute of daylight.

It had cost Castro and Miguel a nettlesome delay while they convinced the boatman to show them where he'd put the *norteamericanos* ashore. He'd been stubborn and close-mouthed at first. But at the end he'd almost begged for the opportunity to talk. That's the way it usually turned out when Juan Castro asked the questions.

After they'd landed on the north side of the river with their stolen horses, they had pushed the man's boat adrift with his shattered body inside. Perhaps others would discover him before he breathed his last under the Florida sun, and perhaps they would not. Either way he would do no more talking in the near future.

Castro had never been looked upon as a clever man by anyone, least of all himself. That reputation had belonged to

Pico, his former partner in theft. Now Pico was dead. So much for cleverness.

Castro's own methods tended to be more direct than devious; and for this he was superbly well-equipped. Single-minded and ruthless, with the native cunning of a predatory beast, he combined in his huge frame the irresistible power of a bull and the deadly quickness of a stalking panther.

Yet above all he was persistent. Once he had a clear object in mind—such as the price in blood to be paid for the death of a partner, with a little extra for his own humiliation by that *indio* outside the Summerlin House—Juan Castro was as relentless as a feeding barracuda.

The men they pursued might outdistance them for now, possibly for as much as several days or even weeks. But like any quarry, they must sooner or later come to ground. And when they did, he would be there—no matter how long or how far it took him.

It might be at some lonely camp or nooning in the wilderness, or in the dark vacant street of some frontier set-tlement, or—best of all—in the home of friends or family where they believed themselves safe. . . .

Whatever the place, only one thing was certain. It would be at a time when the *gringos* least expected it. And Castro would give them no more warning than was needed to reveal who struck them down. That much he owed them as a mat-ter of revenge. He owed them nothing at all by way of a chance to defend themselves.

❖   ❖   ❖

The day was well along and the shadows of the forest that walled in Peek and Cheeky Joe on every side were growing deeper. Yet at this time of year it wouldn't be completely dark for several hours yet. And although they had continued to make regular stops to rest the horses and themselves, nothing had been said of camping for the night.

That suited Peek, for he seemed to have gotten his second wind as the sun slipped toward the horizon. And every mile they put behind them now, he knew, would bring them that much closer to the Westfields.

After a time the forest opened up and they were able to ride abreast for longer periods. They took these at a leisurely pace, using the opportunity to continue their discussion—begun during earlier stops—of the archaeologist's expedition, Ethan Cabell, and the problems that might lie ahead.

It was Peek who did most of the talking, something he'd already come to expect during his brief association with his taciturn saddle partner. The big man listened carefully but seldom interrupted while Peek filled in the gaps in Cooter's earlier sketchy account, describing his visits to the Westfields' camp, his impressions of Cabell and his followers, and concluding with what they'd heard from the circuit-riding preacher a few days afterward.

Yet each terse remark or question from Cheeky Joe focused on something that Peek hadn't yet considered. Or it brought out details that made the situation clearer as they slowly began to piece together the framework of a plan.

Finding the Westfields was their first task, of course. And it looked like the best approach for the time being was to head straight for Fort Ogden, some thirty miles away to the north-northeast. With luck they might come across cow hunters from the Circle O or some other outfit who had news of the expedition.

If the archaeologist had followed Peek's advice and paid a call on Judge Ziba King, it could be that they'd have no need to look further. Peek had every reason to expect the influential cowman would be delighted to welcome two such interesting visitors, and would place them under his personal protection. In that case Ethan Cabell's plans—whatever they were—would likely come to nothing.

If, on the other hand, the Westfields—or Cabell—had decided to bypass Fort Ogden and had turned southwest instead, Peek and Cheeky Joe would have a good chance of cutting the heavily loaded wagon's trail in the course of their journey. Such a rig would leave deep ruts in the soft prairie grass that not even Florida's torrential rains could wash out quickly. What's more, the tenderfoot outfit's unusual appearance would surely be remembered and cause comment among any locals who happened to cross its path.

Other directions of travel were possible but less likely. To the north of Fort Ogden were lots of scattered settlements and cabins—not the best sort of country for an outlaw who wanted privacy for his schemes, nor a place with many large and substantial Indian sites to tempt the archaeologist.

It could also be that they'd never left Ninety-Mile Prairie. That was the possibility Peek found most worrisome. But as Cheeky Joe pointed out, there was nothing Cabell or his companions could have done after the cow hunter's visits that they couldn't do beforehand, and with less risk to themselves. So it looked like the man who claimed to be their guide had a particular destination in mind. Anyway, Peek hoped so.

If worse came to worst they'd just have to backtrack to where he'd last seen Westfield's camp and pick up the trail from there. It would mean miles of extra riding and a frustrating delay, but it shouldn't be hard to do otherwise. And even then they ought to catch up with the slow-moving caravan after only a few days.

When they found them . . . Well, that was something neither Peek nor Cheeky Joe seemed ready to speak of at the moment. It was like Peek had told Cooter: They'd just have to cross that bridge when they came to it.

The sun was down but the sky was still light when they finally stopped for supper at a hidden spring a little way off the trail. Ringed about on all sides by a thick growth of elm, dahoon holly, and other plants, the spot was all but invisible from a few yards away.

Peek took charge of the horses while Cheeky Joe began sweeping dead leaves from the sandy soil and collecting dry wood for a fire. He glanced up as his young companion was leading the animals to a nearby patch of maidencane and said quietly, "Don't unsaddle. We'll move on after we eat."

Peek glanced at him curiously, then shrugged and did as he was told. By the time he'd loosened the cinches and run a tether to let the ponies crop grass and pull Spanish moss from the low-hanging limbs, a blaze no bigger than the crown of his hat was crackling softly, sending up pale fingers of smoke to dissipate among the branches overhead. Before long the welcome smell of coffee filled the clearing from a small blackened pot thrust in among the coals.

Hardly a stranger to making do in the out-of-doors, Peek still couldn't help but marvel at the speed and efficiency with which his new companion worked. His movements seemed unhurried, even careless, as he went about putting together a simple meal of bacon, fried bread, and warmed-over sweet potatoes. But there were no wasted motions, and in a matter of minutes they were sitting down to eat.

"Hope you don't mind me cookin'," he said as they hunkered down with the tiny fire between them. "Don't make any special claim for it. Just used to doin' my own fixing."

"You can keep right on doin' it far as I'm concerned." Peek grinned at him between mouthfuls. "You ever taste my cookin' and you'll prob'ly insist on it. Cooter says with just a tad more practice I might get the knack of boilin' water." He paused to take a swallow of coffee and wipe his mouth with the back of his hand. "From where I sit, you fix a fine mess of vittles. Although hungry as I am tonight, I reckon I could eat a whole boiled saddle, cinch rings an' all!"

"Up to you," the other responded soberly, not meeting his eyes. "No extra trouble." He picked up his own cup from a log by the fire. "But I wouldn't want anybody thinkin' I was tryin' to be his nursemaid."

12 ⚘

PEEK SWALLOWED AND felt himself getting red around the ears.

"All right," he said after taking a second to drain his cup and toss the grounds into the fire. "I guess I'd got that comin'. One of these days I'll learn to use my noggin, 'fore I open my mouth up so wide I can stick both feet inside. It's just that I was some put out at Cooter right then for tryin' to do my thinkin' for me, an' . . ."

"And you've got your pride," Cheeky Joe concluded with a nod of his head. He took a stick and began spreading apart the few coals from the fire so they'd extinguish more quickly. "Pride's good to have. Fellow with no regard for himself can't expect much from others." He took up the coffee pot and frying pan, and rose to his feet.

"But you're right about the other too." He turned to go wash the utensils at the spring. "I helped bury some real proud men who couldn't put common sense with it."

They rode for another mile and a half, then unsaddled the horses and made their camp among a stand of hardwoods with a thick carpet of fallen leaves all around. The September night was warm, and though it was dark by the time they finally spread their bedrolls on the soft ground, Cheeky Joe made no move to light a fire.

When Peek had pulled off his boots and stretched out under the whispering canopy of branches, he asked why they hadn't just stayed at the place where they'd eaten supper.

"Habit," Cheeky Joe answered simply. Then, after a minute: "Not a good idea to sleep where you been leavin' your scent around. Don't know who might come along in the night—followin' maybe, or just lookin' for sound sleepers."

Peek reckoned that made sense, although it looked to him like they had a heap more to worry about from what was in front of them than anything behind. But as he lay on his back waiting for sleep to come, he began to see that nothing his companion ever did in the wilderness was done without purpose.

Not only was their current resting place well hidden from casual passers-by, but the layer of dead leaves made it almost impossible for anyone to come near without revealing his presence. Nor was it an accident that their horses were tethered a few feet away. The frontier-bred animals would give warning of intruders even if some late-night rain or wind came up to mask the other sounds.

Much of Peek's young life had been spent in the Florida backcountry. But until now it had been a life made up of mostly peaceful pursuits. There were dangers, of course, from bad men as well as wild beasts. But these were the exception instead of the rule, and the last hostile Indian raids took place before he was born. There had been no reason to dwell on those habits of wariness that could protect a man from attack by a resourceful human enemy.

It was clear he had a lot to learn about such things—and he'd best learn it quickly if he meant to cope with men like Ethan Cabell and his friends. And this was a decision he'd already made. For if law-abiding citizens like him didn't take a stand against the Ethan Cabells of the world, who would?

They rose at first light. After a brief reconnaissance of their surroundings, Cheeky Joe set about fixing a quick breakfast of pan bread, bacon, and coffee while Peek stowed their gear and saddled the horses. When these chores were done, the cow hunter squatted near the fire to clean his six-shooter and wipe the dew from the cartridges with a piece of cloth from his saddlebag.

His companion watched in silence as he rose from the ground and dropped the empty weapon into its holster, then spun and practiced a half dozen fast draws before reseating himself and starting to shove cartridges into the cylinder.

"You ever do that facin' a man?" the Calusa asked quietly. "One that was heeled and able to shoot back?"

"No." Peek knew what was behind the question, but still he couldn't help feeling a little annoyed by it. He'd been all over this with Cooter.

"And I'd just soon not have to," he added seriously. "But like our movin' on before sleepin' last night, it don't cost much for a feller to be ready if trouble comes huntin' him."

"That's so." Cheeky Joe nodded agreeably and reached for the coffee pot to fill both their cups. "You mind a bit of advice? 'Case it finds you?"

Peek shrugged while his eyes flicked to the bowie knife in his associate's otherwise empty belt. So far there'd been no suggestion that the big man even owned a sidearm, much less that he was skilled in its use. But who could tell?

"If it comes to a shootin'," Peek said frankly, "I reckon I could use all the advice an' help I can get."

"Most could," Cheeky Joe replied dryly, "and luck to boot. But it's not how fast a man pulls iron that keeps him alive when the lead starts flyin'. It's how straight he shoots. You'll feel bad if your first shot kicks dust at your enemy's feet. But you'll feel worse if you don't get another."

He paused to swallow coffee and Peek reached for his own cup. "Could mean you'll have to take some lead. . . ."

Peek looked across the fire with his cup halfway to his lips. This talk wasn't doing much to build his confidence.

". . . But no matter what, you take your time and make the first one count. Aim right over the belt buckle where the body's widest. Then follow up with as many as it takes. Don't ever stop shootin' till the other man's down."

Peek nodded to show he understood. It wasn't the first time he'd heard something of the kind, and he had no doubt it was good advice. But he figured it would take every ounce of nerve a man could muster to remember it while being shot at. And he wished he was sure he'd have that much nerve when push came to shove.

He'd little appetite for breakfast now, and was anxious to be back in the saddle. His sore ribs still troubled him, but not so badly as the day before. Of the other hurts he'd gotten during the fight at the Summerlin House, he was scarcely even aware.

They made good progress during the cool hours of the morning. By the time they drew rein for an early nooning among cabbage palm and laurel oak, Peek guessed they'd covered ten or twelve miles. The country around them had grown more open as they rode, with occasional stands of trees like the present one, separated by coarse meadows and low-growing palmetto thickets.

The site Cheeky Joe had chosen for a halt was on a gentle rise of ground that afforded visibility in all directions. They seemed to be at the westernmost edge of the long prairie now: a broad sea of green sweeping off to the horizon, interrupted here and there by widely separated islands of darker hues that marked the location of woodlands and hammocks.

Before dismounting, Cheeky Joe walked his marshtackie to the edge of the trees and studied the expanse for several long minutes. Then he made a circuit of their stopping place, taking his time and pausing occasionally to peer off toward the distant clumps of forest. When he got back to where Peek stood taking parcels of leftover bread and meat out of his saddlebag, he dropped to the ground and squatted on his heels with a thoughtful expression on his face.

He accepted food from Peek and chewed for a time in silence.

"They's a kind of a trace," he said finally, "out yonder in the grass a bit. We'll have a look when we get done here. Might be the track of a wagon. More likely just somethin' different in how the land lies."

As they rode from the cover of the trees to study the prairie's surface, Cheeky Joe's gaze was wary under his wide hat brim. Peek's own eyes were on the ground, but he still had to look twice to see the faint marks in the sod that had drawn his companion's attention.

When they came near, it was obvious this was no trail left by a heavy mule-drawn wagon.

"One horse, one rider," the big man grunted after dismounting for a closer look. "Maybe two, three hours ago. Grass hasn't had a chance to straighten up good."

He followed the tracks on foot for a dozen yards, letting his marshtackie's reins trail on the ground. "Big, long-stridin' animal, maybe seventeen hands . . ." Pausing at a small clump of saw palmetto, he knelt to examine the fronds. When he rose he held several dark hairs between his fingers. "Bay color, on the legs anyhow."

"Butch," Peek said suddenly. "That Butch feller was ridin' a big bay horse the first time I seen him."

"Could be." Cheeky Joe turned and squinted off toward the northwest. "He's alone now. Headed for somewhere on the coast, looks like." He glanced back at Peek. "No sign of a wagon passin' this way, nor other riders. We need to watch close from now on, though. Where one of 'em is, there's liable to be . . ."

All of a sudden he fell silent, gazing off at some trees a mile or so south of them.

"What is it?" Peek asked, following Cheeky Joe's eyes.

"Don't know. Nothin', maybe." He returned to where his pony waited and gathered the reins. Mounting, he walked the marshtackie close to where Peek sat his own horse and spoke softly without turning his head:

"You 'call that thicker stand of trees 'bout a quarter mile north of where we ate?"

"Uh-huh." Peek nodded.

"Ride with me real easy back over that rise, and when we're out of sight from the prairie lope your horse for those trees. Get among 'em and stay put. I'll be along after while." He prodded his pony forward and Peek had to rein around to catch up.

"Nothin' to fret about," Cheeky Joe explained under his breath when they were stirrup to stirrup again. "Just take a li'l rest while I do some scoutin'."

"Scoutin' for what?" Peek's voice matched his companion's as they walked the horses past their nooning place.

"Not sure. Just a feelin'."

"A feelin'?"

"Somebody back there." The big man shrugged. "Maybe a couple wanderin' cow hunters. Maybe not."

In another minute they dipped down behind some trees and Cheeky Joe swung his marshtackie's head southwest to disappear into the forest. Still puzzled but with little choice except to trust his companion's judgment, Peek reined his own mount north and lifted it into a canter.

He spent an uneasy hour cooling his heels in the wooded thicket, trying to rest but unable to sit still for more than a few minutes. His Cracker pony seemed content with the enforced intermission. There was good grass nearby, and tender clumps of Spanish moss on the low-growing branches.

He'd just returned to his horse after another restless circuit of his surroundings when Cheeky Joe appeared leading his marshtackie. The big man took the canteen from his saddle and hunkered down on his heels while Peek approached to join him.

"Could be trouble," he said in answer to the younger man's questioning look. "Couple of those seamen we had dealin's with in Punta Rassa." He pushed his hat back from his forehead, uncorked the canteen, and raised it to his lips. "Figure they're prob'ly lookin' for us."

After drinking sparingly, he rose to hang the canteen on his saddle again. Then Peek watched while he removed an ancient but well-cared-for Army Colt and cartridge belt from his blanket roll, checked the loads and action, and belted it on outside his colorful shirt.

"Look to be pilgrims," Cheeky Joe said as he gathered the reins and stepped into the leather. "But it don't pay to take anybody that's huntin' you light. Mount up an' we'll see how they like a li'l trek in the woods!"

He made a careful survey of their surroundings while Peek went to fetch his pony. Then he turned the marshtackie's head west and led off at a brisk trot. Before long they came to a small freshwater creek that lost itself in a dense wilderness of reed-choked sloughs and vine-shrouded hammocks.

It was the ideal place to discourage pursuers, and Cheeky Joe plunged into the thick of it with stony-faced relish, leading them on a twisting, tortuous, exhausting journey through stretches of the most hellish terrain a man could find anywhere.

The afternoon heat had turned the leafy fastness into a steaming cauldron. In minutes both horses and riders were drenched with sweat. Peek could already feel his homespun shirt and trousers growing heavy and starting to chafe as he dodged whiplike branches and moss-laden limbs, emerging into the open for brief periods only to curse the galling clouds of gnats and no-see-ums that darted about his eyes.

At times they rode through thickets so overhung with strangler fig and mulberry that passage even for a man on foot seemed at first glance impossible. In other places they waded stirrup-deep through dark stagnant pools and marshes from which all trace of their passing would be lost to sight in minutes. Occasionally they were forced to dismount and lead their ponies, but not as often as Peek would have guessed. Over and over again they reversed themselves, backtracked for a short distance, then turned sharply off in some new and unexpected direction.

As hard as this was on himself and his companion, Peek knew it would be worse for anybody on their backtrail—especially if the pursuers weren't used to such country. Trying to track the two of them through this hellish maze of green wasn't a job that he'd want if he could avoid it.

Most of the time they traveled in silence, with only the creak of their saddles and the persistent chattering of insects and birds to tell of their passing. Cheeky Joe was even less inclined to talk than usual, but his eyes roamed constantly under his broad hat brim, from the sandy ground below to the moss- and vine-draped limbs overhead, to those rare expanses of marsh or prairie that could be glimpsed from a distance.

He turned often to study their backtrail, a habit any woodsman learns whether he expects pursuit or not. A path in wild country can look completely different from the opposite direction, as many tenderfeet have found to their sorrow when they tried to return to some place they'd just been.

It seemed to Peek that they were slowly working their way north and east, occasionally coming in sight of the open prairie, but always from the leaf-shaded depths of some bordering woodland. From these locations they could study the grassy plain at leisure, without betraying their presence to any who might be watching.

It was in such a hidden glade that they drew rein at last for a much-needed rest, after more than three hours of weary plodding through sweltering forest and marsh. The late afternoon sun was behind the trees now, so Peek had no way of guessing how much progress they'd made toward Fort Ogden, if any. At best he doubted if it was over a mile or two as the crow flies, which was mighty little to show for all the trouble and sweat it had cost them.

But if the detour served its purpose, he supposed it was worth it. They'd have enough problems once they located the Westfields, without the added worry of more enemies behind them.

Even after all this it shouldn't be more than a day's ride farther to Judge King's ranch headquarters, and Peek felt a nagging urge to press on tonight in the hope of meeting up with the archaeologist and his wife as quickly as possible. For reasons he couldn't explain, he had a gnawing sense of foreboding that grew stronger with each passing hour.

Yet continuing on now was clearly out of the question. Their horses were badly used up and would need time to recover from the day's draining heat and humidity. Not to mention the fact that they'd little hope of cutting the supply wagon's trail after dark. Cheeky Joe meant to travel only a mile or two farther, and then call a halt to save their mounts for the long ride tomorrow. Peek knew it was the sensible thing to do, but he still couldn't help chafing at the enforced delay.

When he'd unfastened the cinch and pulled the saddle from his pony's back, he spread the sodden blanket over low-growing limbs to catch whatever breeze might reach it from the nearby prairie. Then he wiped sweat from the animal's coat with handfuls of Spanish moss. Finally he took a long drink from his canteen while gazing fretfully about the limited confines of their shaded resting place.

Cheeky Joe, it seemed, didn't share his companion's anxious forebodings. When he'd made a brief inspection of their
surroundings and tended to his horse, the big man had pulled
together a makeshift cushion of leaves under the spreading
branches of a live oak and was now stretched out comfortably
with his face covered by his broad feathered hat. He was, to
all appearances, sound asleep.

13

MIGUEL SLUMPED IN his saddle and wiped sweat from his eyes with a shirtsleeve. He looked on tensely as Juan Castro aimed a vicious swipe of his fist at his own mount's neck after it shied from a sawgrass-bordered marsh they'd carelessly blundered into. The wily buckskin snorted and twisted its head to avoid the blow, coming within a hair's breadth of throwing its off-balance rider to the ground.

"We could all do with a rest, *amigo*," the smaller man interposed quickly but gently, having no wish to see his enraged companion kill the hapless beast out of hand. If one of them was to be set afoot in this seething wilderness, Miguel had a very good idea who it would be.

He got down from the saddle and took a metal flask from his blanket roll, lifting it up like a priestly oblation while stepping forward to suggest in a calming voice: "*Toma algo, compadre. Un poquito de aguardiente* to settle the nerves."

With a sullen grunt, Castro seized the offering in his huge fist and drew the cork with his teeth. Spitting this away into the bushes, he raised the flask to his lips and drank for long moments without pausing for breath. At last he belched agreeably and tossed the almost empty container back over his shoulder.

"*Gracias, amigo*. It is little enough in this *maldito infierno*, but it is something."

Miguel grinned with relief while he scrambled to rescue the flask and drain its few remaining drops to calm his own badly frayed nerves. Then he ventured tentatively, "Maybe we walk a bit now and save the horses, you think?"

Castro's reply was another surly grunt. Yet he was forced to admit the wisdom of the proposal, and after a minute he lowered himself stiffly to the ground and stood rubbing his sore backside, taking advantage of the respite to more thoroughly study their surroundings.

"Where do you think we are?" he growled fiercely.

Miguel bit his tongue rather than voice the too-obvious answer that they were hopelessly lost. "Somewhere between the Gulf, I think, and that open *sabana* we saw earlier." When his heavy-set companion glowered at him he knew his reply wasn't satisfactory. But what else could he say?

"Perhaps," he suggested hesitantly, putting words to a doubt that had been nagging at him for more than an hour, "the *indio* knows he is being followed? And is purposely leading us in circles to discourage us? . . ." He broke off, then added quickly: "It is only a thought."

Castro frowned and was silent for several seconds. "You may be right," he acknowledged grudgingly. "I myself had the feeling we have already passed this place at least once." He was quiet for another moment, then exploded angrily: "But they will not succeed! We will make our way out of this *jungla infernal*, and we will pick up their trail afresh!"

He glanced up at the sky between overhanging branches. "The sun is in the west now, *verdad?*"

"*Sí.*"

"So that way lies the *Golfo de México*. And in the other direction is the prairie."

"*Sí.*"

"Which way would they most likely travel if they did not believe themselves followed?"

Miguel considered the question. "The prairie," he said finally, "or so it seems to me. If they wished to reach some place on the coast, they could more easily get there by boat."

"Aha! Then it is east we must travel to find them!"

Pausing only long enough for another hasty glance at the sky, the big tattooed sailor knotted a hand in his horse's reins and began shouldering his way through the dense undergrowth that ringed them round to eastward. He no longer had any thought of paths or trails, but charged straight ahead like a maddened bull, with only the sun at his back to guide him.

Miguel struggled gamely to keep up, his progress made only slightly easier by the broad wake of crushed and trampled plant growth that marked his companion's passing.

At times they were forced to detour around some pond or boggy slough, but afterward they resumed their eastward march using the shadows of trees to point the way. On rarer occasions the forest opened up enough to allow them to ride for short distances, before they once more had to dismount and proceed on foot.

Late in the day it clouded up and started to rain. Juan Castro cursed bitterly and hunched his massive shoulders, but he kept slogging ahead relentlessly. Miguel sighed and held his peace till the brief shower was over. By then it was growing dark, and he wondered if he dared to suggest a halt for the night.

A few minutes later his burly associate grunted triumphantly, then waved him forward and pointed past the shadowed trunks of trees that encircled them. As Miguel trudged wearily closer leading his horse, he could see open sky in the distance and—at last—the green expanse of the prairie, stretching away to a blue-gray horizon.

"You see!" Castro clapped his smaller companion painfully on the shoulder. "You follow Juan Castro, and he leads you out of the wilderness!"

Out of one wilderness into another, Miguel thought wryly. But even so he was pleased. From now on the traveling was sure to be easier.

Neither had much energy for conversation as they knelt at the edge of the forest, looking out across the open plain and breathing deeply of the humid night air. Like their horses, they were soaked to the skin with rain and sweat. All of them were close to exhaustion.

Where they were exactly, they couldn't venture a guess. Nor did it seem to make much difference in the long run. If the two *norteamericanos* had come back east as they supposed, then their trail would be found sooner or later. Sooner, if the *gringos* were so foolish as to show themselves in the open. For from this place vast tracts of treeless prairie could be easily observed.

Perhaps tomorrow, or the day after, would be the time for a reckoning. At present the two sailors could barely muster the strength to unsaddle their horses and tether them out of sight among the trees before they collapsed on the soft ground for a long and welcome sleep.

The air in the clearing Ethan Cabell had chosen for a camp, surrounded by pine-palmetto flatwoods near a wide mangrove-bordered arm of the Gulf, was dank and heavy from the late afternoon rain. What small breeze had accompanied it was not from the sea, but from the swamp-dotted prairies and hammocks of the peninsula, bringing with it clouds of mosquitoes so dense that they turned the white tents black with their numbers.

There was no hope of any such leisurely outdoor dining as they'd enjoyed earlier. Instead, they were forced to scurry about frantically, gathering what partly cooked food they could before being driven into the relative security of their tightly buttoned shelters. No lanterns were lit, lest they serve as magnets for the ravenous insects and contribute still further to the sweltering heat of the canvas interiors.

James Westfield seemed thoughtful and withdrawn while he and Miranda shared their makeshift supper and hurriedly retired to adjacent cots. Woolen blankets and thick mosquito bars were a final defense against the persistent intruders that found their way past the buttoned flaps. But as an unpleasant consequence, they made the heat even more oppressive.

Miranda was tired from the day's journey and the work of setting up camp, but the hour was early and she had no desire for sleep. She would have welcomed some words of comfort—or just small talk—from James at the moment, but none were forthcoming.

She lay on her side with her eyes closed, her head resting a few inches from her husband's but separated from it by heavy netting, and tried without success to close her ears to the strident angry whine of millions of bloodthirsty insects. It seemed the entire universe outside those flimsy canvas walls was vibrating in time with their never-ending drone. The raw intensity of it was eerie and even a little frightening in the tent's black interior. It was like nothing the young New Yorker had ever before experienced.

Finally, after what seemed hours, the reassuring sound of her husband's voice came from the darkness beside her:

"Well," he said calmly, as if commenting on the weather, "at least I don't think anyone will be listening at our tent flaps tonight."

Miranda opened her eyes and turned her head toward him, though she could see nothing in the all-pervading gloom. "What did you say, James?" She wasn't entirely sure she'd heard him correctly.

"I said," he responded in a mild but deliberate voice, "that I'm reasonably confident neither Ethan Cabell nor his associate will brave that plague of insects to eavesdrop on our conversation tonight. And even if they did, I doubt they'd hear much with this infernal buzzing to mask our speech."

It took Miranda several seconds to digest her husband's words. Then she asked softly, "You have reason to believe they would do such a thing?"

"The best of all reasons, I'm afraid. I've caught them in the act."

There was another brief silence while Miranda awaited his explanation with the patience of long habit. It was one of James' more maddening traits, this pregnant pause before he revealed something important. One of the small prices, she reminded herself, of falling in love with a professional lecturer.

"Two nights ago," he went on finally, "you'll recall that I left my notebook outside on the table. I was afraid the heavy dew would damage it, so I interrupted our conversation to go and retrieve it. My abrupt exit surprised Quint as he knelt by our tent. The next morning he offered some lame excuse about adjusting the ropes, but his true purpose had been clear from the expression on his face."

"But . . ." Miranda choked back the sudden flush of anger she felt rise inside of her. "But why in the world would either man be interested in our private discussions? To a stranger they must seem terribly mundane. I mean, it's not as if we have any dark, lurid secrets we're hiding!" Despite the truth of her words, she felt violated and outraged. How dare they intrude on her rare personal moments with James? How *dare* they!

"You know that," her husband replied gently, sensing her mood even with the darkness between them. "And I know it. But I'm afraid our Mister Cabell is not easily convinced." He paused again, characteristically, but this time Miranda was too angry to notice.

"Somehow," the archaeologist continued with a hint of irony in his voice, "our guide has conceived the idea that our purpose in Florida is other than scientific. He is under the impression—as preposterous as it sounds—that we have come here in search of buried pirate treasure!"

Miranda opened her mouth—to laugh, to cry out, to mock the sheer absurdity of the idea—she wasn't sure what. But then she closed it again and made herself be silent. She realized now that James had been waiting for such a moment, for some chance occurrence that would let them speak privately.

She knew the man she'd married, and if he couldn't predict when the opportunity would come, or how long it would last, he would have planned what to say with meticulous care. For her to squander precious moments in an emotional outburst would not only be wasteful, it might be dangerous.

James' somber tone as he went on fully justified her assessment:

"I've no idea how this notion was arrived at, or why anyone would think such treasure, if it existed, could be found in pre-Columbian middens. What matters to us is that Mister Cabell believes it, and he has revealed himself to be a man of few scruples. He's been employing thinly veiled threats to extract information from me ever since we resumed our travels after repairing the wagon. At first I tried not to worry you about it, in the hope that a solution might present itself. But now . . ."

When her husband paused this time, Miranda could almost picture his helpless shrug.

"I've tried everything I know to reason with him, but he simply does not listen. It seems he had a glimpse of the gold coins we received in Tampa, and they have further whetted his greed—though one would think the difference between ancient doubloons and modern *reales* would be patently obvious, even to a layman!"

He fell silent again, and Miranda reached under the folds of mosquito netting to take hold of his hand. "So," she said, putting unfelt confidence into her voice, "what do we do?"

"We?" The word seemed to hang in the darkness while he squeezed her fingers briefly, then released them. "I haven't spent so much time thinking about 'we' during these last few days, as I have about you."

"Me?"

"I'm afraid it's finally become clear to Mister Cabell that his threats against me will produce no useful information about hidden pirate gold, though not for the reason he suspects. Lately he has begun replacing those threats with more pointed remarks about you!"

With a start, Miranda felt something cold and metallic pressed into the hand that had earlier clasped her husband's.

"When that occurred I knew my most urgent goal must be your escape, from Cabell and his friends to some place of safety. With luck I'll go with you. But at all events . . ."

Miranda suddenly realized what she held under the mosquito netting.

". . . Keep that pistol about your person from this moment forward. It will offer some measure of protection whether I'm with you or not."

James waited while she took the weapon and slipped it under her pillow. She wasted no words in pointless protest, for her husband had thought this all out beforehand, and his thinking made sense. Both knew she was no stranger to firearms, although most of her experience until now had been with rifle and shotgun.

"This estuary beside us," the archaeologist continued when their fingers had joined again under the mosquito netting, "opens into a long bay that enters the Gulf of Mexico past a series of barrier islands to the south. Directly west, if I've read my map correctly, is an uninhabited peninsula of thickets and swamps. To the north, although I'm not sure how far, is the entrance to the Pease River. . . ."

Miranda shut her eyes and concentrated on forming a mental picture of the land and water features as James described them. She understood his reason for doing so, but deliberately put that from her mind while he completed his summary of the area's geography. Such knowledge might be needed by either or both of them in order to plan and carry out a successful flight.

"There are fishermen living here and there along the coast and among the islands," he said finally, "and farther south is the town of Fort Myers. But I believe the nearest settlements where we might seek refuge, and the most favorable means of reaching them, will be along the Pease River. If we can obtain a boat—to which I've some reason to think Mister Cabell has access—we might make it to Fort Ogden in two or three days, perhaps less."

He fell silent, and Miranda knew he expected a response from her.

"I'll be ready whenever you say the word." Her fingers tightened around his. "We'll each be watching for our chance now, and it will give us twice the opportunity to make a getaway . . ." After a bare fraction of a second she added firmly, ". . . together."

"Yes," James Westfield agreed. "Together, if at all possible."

14

PEEK AND CHEEKY JOE were up at first light, shaking the heavy dew from their blankets and saddling their horses for the day ahead. Their hidden campsite in a dense thicket of dahoon holly and wax myrtle was dripping and clammy. It had been an uncomfortable night from the start, what with the late afternoon rain that drenched the ground, and the army of mosquitoes that followed. A sporadic breeze off the nearby prairie had done little to relieve the night's muggy heat or to provide relief from the plague of hungry insects.

To make matters worse, they'd had no fire to make coffee or fix a hot meal since the previous morning, with the promise of a cold breakfast today into the bargain.

"Too many folks about," Cheeky Joe had explained curtly when they'd stepped down from their saddles in the gathering darkness. "And none that 'pear friendly."

Peek had offered no argument, for he was beginning to see the wisdom of his companion's constant vigilance. With the probability of enemies both behind and before them, it would be foolish to risk such an obvious advertisement of their location. Even a small, well-hidden fire could be smelled for some distance on the humid air.

Once their beds were rolled and tied behind their saddles, Cheeky Joe left his marshtackie tethered beside Peek's Cracker horse and walked to the edge of the leafy enclosure. The big man was wearing moccasins now; his boots had been knotted together with rawhide strips and slung across his horse's neck.

"Wait here," he told Peek quietly. "Maybe we lost those two yesterday. Maybe not. Want to have a look around." Peek reluctantly shrugged his acceptance while the other man slipped, ghostlike, into the forest.

He'd a lot rather be up in the middle of his pony making tracks for Fort Ogden right now. But he also saw the need to keep a wary eye out for their pursuers. With a half sigh he resigned himself to cooling his heels a little longer, and went to fish a piece of jerked beef from his saddlebag in an effort to quiet the rumbling in his stomach.

The minutes dragged by, and before long Peek found himself drawn to the outer edge of the thicket, where a small stand of laurel oaks and half-grown cedars offered a vantage point overlooking the prairie.

For some minutes he stood with his thumbs hooked in his belt, drinking in the view and the fresh scents of growing things on the early morning air. The golden ball of the sun was just now peeking over the horizon, still not high enough to warm the breeze that stirred the grass at his feet. A trace of mist clung about the distant hammocks and woodlands, lending a kind of reverence to the far-reaching scene.

Even with all that had happened in the past couple of days, Peek couldn't help but reflect what a fine thing it was to be alive on a morning like this.

After a bit he grew restless again. For lack of any more productive way to occupy the time, he took a seat in the shadow of a small cedar and began to study the grassy expanse before him, trying to pick out anything unusual in appearance, such as the trail Cheeky Joe had found on the day before.

He went about the task methodically, dividing the scene into pie-shaped wedges bounded by plants and other convenient landmarks, then breaking these up into smaller tracts of a few dozen square yards apiece. It was a way of searching wild country that he'd learned in childhood—useful, among other things, for hunting nervous scrub cattle out of wooded terrain.

He took his time, scanning each piece of ground with care before moving on, gradually shifting his search from right to left and from close by to farther away.

It wasn't until he'd finished with his immediate surroundings and was beginning a more distant sweep that his eyes picked out a slight reflection from a clump of grass some hundred feet off. He couldn't tell what was causing the reflection, but he knew it wasn't anything put there by nature. Only men made objects of glass or metal that shone when they caught the sun's rays.

He fixed the location in his mind and continued his search, but there was nothing of interest except for some faint disturbance in the sod a little beyond where the shining object rested. For all he knew, it might be nothing but some natural fold of ground.

Peek clasped his arms about his knees and frowned in thought. He knew if he ventured out in the open to make a closer inspection, there was a chance, however slight, that he'd be seen by one of those men who were following them yesterday. At the least, that would render their long, sweaty detour for nothing. And if they were the sort of men who went in for dry-gulching . . .

He didn't know that, of course. He didn't really know anything about their intentions. He'd only Cheeky Joe's habitually suspicious instincts to go by.

It was also possible that he'd be seen by Ethan Cabell or one of his henchmen, although they could just as easily be miles away at present. Cabell might think it a coincidence if he saw Peek in the neighborhood. But it could raise suspicions—something that would better be postponed until the Westfields had been found.

Balanced against these uncertain possibilities was the equally troubling thought that if he didn't check out that man-made object, he could miss some vital clue to the archaeologist's whereabouts. Yet he had no way of knowing it was a clue unless he took the chance of approaching it.

Uncertain what to do, he rose and walked back to where their horses were tethered in hopes that Cheeky Joe had returned in the meantime. But there was still no sign of him.

Peek thought about it some more while he shifted the animals to fresh grass and took a long slow drink from his canteen. Then he made his decision.

Returning to his earlier shaded vantage point, he knelt and spent long minutes watching each stand of trees or other possible hiding place within his field of vision. When he'd seen nothing that suggested the presence of others, he moved forward in a half crouch until he was a dozen yards into the open. Then he turned and knelt again to study the woods behind him. He took care to do it thoroughly, letting his eyes move slowly from one distant edge of the tree line to the other.

Still seeing nothing that concerned him, he took a deep breath, rose, and strode quickly to the place where he'd noticed the reflection. It took only seconds to locate the object that caused it, half-buried among the tall prairie grass.

It was a bottle of an unusual shape that Peek recognized instantly, even before his fingers reached out to grasp it. The only time in his life he'd seen such a bottle, with its squat dark body and its deeply indented base, was in James and Miranda Westfield's camp the night Doc Westfield had offered him a glass of brandy.

So the Westfields had been here! Or . . . Peek's eyes narrowed as he turned to look about him. There was nothing nearby to suggest the passage of a wagon, heavily loaded or otherwise, only a thin ripple in the grass leading in a roughly straight line from northeast to southwest. A closer examination revealed the hoof marks of a solitary horse and rider.

Peek made no claim to equal his companion's skill at tracking. But he wasn't exactly a tenderfoot either. And the story these marks told was plain enough. They'd been made sometime the previous day, for they were partly washed out by the afternoon rain. And they were clearly not left by the same horse and rider Cheeky Joe had found sign of earlier.

Like the other, this was a big, long-gaited animal. But the rider was heavier than Butch, who was no more than five feet seven inches tall for all his muscular bulk. The hooves of this man's mount had cut deeply into the moist prairie sod, and he rode at a purposeful canter, like he'd someplace to go with no wasting around about it.

It was then that Peek recalled Ethan Cabell's fondness for Doc Westfield's brandy.

He squinted against the glare of the newly risen sun, following with his eyes the pale line in the grass toward its beginnings on the distant horizon. Cabell—for Peek was now certain whose trail he'd discovered—seemed to be heading in the same general direction as Butch, although he'd traveled at a later hour. That the two were planning to meet somewhere near the Gulf was a reasonable assumption. But it didn't explain why they'd started from such widely separate locations. Nor did it offer any clue to where James and Miranda Westfield were at the moment, along with their supply wagon.

Had the couple been waylaid, perhaps murdered, somewhere on the prairie? And had the three men who did it split up to hamper pursuit? If so, why did they ride toward a common meeting place now, instead of just leaving the country separately? It didn't make sense. Yet Peek forced himself to consider the possibility.

He swallowed a lump in his throat, remembering Miranda Westfield's lively dark eyes and her warm smile. . . . Then he put the image from his mind. He could not—would not—think of her dead while there was any chance she still lived.

He blinked his eyes a few times—at least partly because of the sun's glare—and turned to make a mental note of the place where Cabell's tracks entered the woods a quarter of a mile off. They'd be easy to follow, for the ground here was soft and the big man had made no attempt to hide his passing.

The question was, should they? Or should they backtrack him onto the prairie instead? Could Westfield and his wife still be out there somewhere, alive and in need of help?

That, Peek decided, was a matter to discuss with Cheeky Joe. He'd made enough decisions on his own for one morning.

After taking the time to let his eyes roam in a circle, checking once more for unwanted observers, he strode quickly from the open to the hidden thicket where their horses waited.

The morning air felt dank and heavy when Miranda unbuttoned the flaps and stepped out from their tent to greet the new day. Low tendrils of fog lurked among the pines and palmetto brakes, clinging stubbornly to rough trunks and exposed roots as if trying to escape the slight offshore breeze that stirred the mangrove tops to westward.

Enclosed as they were here by dense woods on every side, it would be several hours until the burning Florida sun put in an appearance. Yet the sky overhead was a clear azure blue; and already she could feel a faint moisture on her neck and upper lip, promising another stifling hot day.

She tried to make no noise that would wake her gently snoring husband, while pulling the flaps apart and tying them to let what breeze there was reach the shelter's dim interior. Neither had slept well after their secretive conversation, and it was a blessing that James had at last fallen into a deep slumber in the hours before dawn. He would need all the rest he could get for the trials that lay ahead.

For her part, Miranda had little hope of any more sound sleeps, until she'd seen the last of Ethan Cabell and his companions once and for all.

She walked a little way from the tents and stood with her hands clasped behind her, breathing deeply in the cool moist air. It was very quiet at this hour. The night birds and insects had long ago fallen silent, while the day creatures, it seemed, had not yet started their rounds. Mercifully, only a few stragglers were left from the army of mosquitoes that plagued them earlier.

Turning her head to glance back at the camp, she felt a faint tinge of guilt when her eyes fell on the cold cook fire.

On any other day at this hour she'd have already stirred the coals and begun making breakfast. But the guilt was short-lived. She'd not the slightest intention of waking her husband prematurely. And if necessary, their "guides" would just have to delay their morning meal.

Or fix it themselves. Miranda had more important things to think about today than catering to Quint's and Ethan Cabell's appetites.

In any event, there was nothing to suggest that the two were up and about as yet. Their tent was still tightly buttoned, and no sounds issued from it.

Not even that of snoring, she realized curiously. And Quint, at least, was a decidedly noisy sleeper.

Well, they'd wake soon enough, no doubt. And in what little time she had to herself, Miranda needed to think.

To plan, actually—although at the moment her mind couldn't seem to conjure up even the barest hint of a strategy.

The object, of course, was escape. She and James must somehow manage to leave this camp, and to elude Cabell and his companion long enough to reach a place of safety. But how? And where would they go? Clearly, it would be no easy task for two novices in the Florida wilderness.

James had given thought to both questions, and she agreed with him that the Ziba King ranch seemed the most likely refuge, based on what the cow hunter had told them. Fort Myers was a more distant possibility, though she knew nothing about the place. The only other town on this coast that she'd even heard of was Tampa, and as nearly as she could guess it was more than a hundred miles away.

How would they travel if they did make good their escape? Horseback seemed the obvious choice. But James wasn't a very skillful rider, even with the added experience of the past several weeks. And Cabell and Quint were both superbly mounted, which made the prospect risky at best. Yet perhaps, if they could slip away during the night and gain a few hours' head start . . .

Making their way on foot through these trackless swamps and hammocks was entirely out of the question. Even if they could find their way to that open prairie again, it would just make them more visible and vulnerable to capture.

James' notion of fleeing by boat offered one definite advantage: a boat left no tracks for a pursuer to follow. But Miranda hadn't seen any boats so far; nor any indication that Ethan Cabell might have one. And to her logical mind there was no use making plans based on hopeful conjecture. When and if a boat became available, they might consider schemes for taking advantage of it. Until then . . .

She frowned and bit her lower lip in frustration. There were too many variables, too many things beyond James' and her control. Yet they had to do *something*. And the longer they delayed the fewer options there might be.

A sound from beyond the mangroves suddenly caught her attention, and she looked in that direction. Nothing could be made out past the dense hedge of greenery. But a second or two later the noise was repeated: a rhythmic sloshing and splashing from the unseen estuary. It was louder now than the first time she'd heard it, and was evidently coming closer.

Some large beast? An alligator? Her thoughts of Ethan Cabell were momentarily thrust aside in the face of this immediate and unknown threat. Miranda turned and quickly started retracing her steps toward the camp and her sleeping husband. As she did, her hand dropped to the pocket of her dress where the awkward bulk of James' revolver pummeled her thigh in rhythm with her steps.

A few feet from the tent's entrance she stopped to glance over her shoulder. And found herself riveted to the spot by the new sound of hard-ridden horses.

An instant later Ethan Cabell and Quint burst from the trees, skirting the canvas enclosure to draw rein on each side of her. Cabell swung his big gelding sideways, blocking her most direct route of escape, while Quint slid to the ground and pushed roughly past into the tent where her husband was.

She spun on her heel and started to protest but was halted by the sounds of a scuffle inside the tent. A brutal blow could be heard, then another, and then a stocking-footed James Westfield was pushed rudely through the opening to sprawl at his wife's feet.

Miranda dropped to her knees beside him, cradling his head in her hands. She could find no serious damage apart from a split lip and one blackened and badly swollen eye. But she shifted her body instinctively to shield him as Quint reappeared and stood over them. Then she turned her furious gaze on the still-mounted Ethan Cabell.

"We're done foolin' around," the man in black said calmly, ignoring Miranda to address the archaeologist. "You've had your chances to make this easy on you an' the lady. But you just couldn't get it into your head that the two of us meant business."

There was a crunching noise from the mangroves a dozen yards away, and Miranda glanced over her shoulder to see three newcomers elbow their way through the slender-branched thicket.

The face of the leader was turned away as he spoke to one of the hard-eyed strangers who followed; but Miranda recognized the thick neck and muscular shoulders instantly. Icy fingers gripped her spine as Butch stepped into the open and strode insolently toward her. When their eyes met she saw the stocky little man's swollen lips curl into a triumphant grin.

The other two new arrivals stood a little behind and on either side of him. One had a pistol and a bowie knife shoved down in his waistband; the second carried a wicked-looking machete.

"Now then," Cabell went on, sidestepping his horse and drawing his pearl-handled revolver, "we're all of us goin' to take a little boat ride out to those islands in the harbor. They's a whole bunch of mounds yonder, made by that pirate Gasparilla. But I got a idea most were just put there for show. We'd prob'ly spend a month of Sundays diggin' all over ever'where, and still not find any treasure to speak of." He tilted his pistol barrel toward the couple on the ground.

"That's where you-all come in. We know you found gold, 'cause I saw it in your belongin's. I don't reckon you'd be stayin' in this country," he finished smugly, "'less you knew where there's more."

Still keeping his pistol leveled at the Westfields, Cabell kicked a foot loose from the stirrup and dropped from the saddle. He stepped around his horse to face them.

"Now, you can save ever'body here includin' yourselves a heap of time an' trouble, if you'll just let us in on the right place to dig."

James Westfield gripped Miranda's arm and they rose from the ground together. "This is all utter nonsense!" he protested angrily. "Those mounds were made hundreds of years before your so-called Gasparilla was born—assuming he existed in the first place!"

"That there's your story." Cabell's manner was cool. "And I reckon you can tell it however you'd like to." He came closer and laid his pistol next to the archaeologist's nose. "Only if you ain't come up with somethin' different by the time we reach those islands, I'm goin' to let my li'l pardner here . . ." He indicated the still-grinning Butch with a jerk of his head ". . . have his chance with your woman."

Miranda shuddered and took an involuntary step back, clinging tightly to her husband's arm with her left hand while her right slipped to the pocket in her skirt. She was conscious of the revolver's weight just under her fingertips, but to draw it while Cabell's own weapon pointed at her husband would have meant James' certain death.

"And if that ain't enough to help you make up your mind," the man in the broadcloth suit went on coldly, "we'll just let ol' Quint have a go at what's left. And then all the rest of who's here, turn an' turn about!"

15 🌿

CHEEKY JOE WAS waiting when Peek arrived at the horses, kneeling motionless and almost unseen among the thick bushes where the animals were tethered. He did not look pleased as he rose to face the young cow hunter.

"Saw you movin' in the open," he said, his voice barely over a whisper.

"Yeah, an' . . ."

"Not good. Others watchin'." Before Peek could explain about finding Cabell's trail, the other turned and started untying the reins. "We ride now, talk later."

Peek hesitated, then decided his news couldn't wait. If they lit out now in some fresh direction, there was no telling when, or if, they'd cut sign of Cabell or the Westfields' party again. Keeping his voice low to match his companion's, he quickly described his discovery while they led their horses from the thicket and stepped into the leather.

Cheeky Joe listened without comment, his eyes on the forest around them, until Peek paused for breath. "Where'd you say he went into the woods?" the big man asked shortly.

Peek pointed south, where the tops of three royal palms could be seen rising above the other trees nearby. "Just past them big ol' palms."

Cheeky Joe nodded and wordlessly swung his marshtackie southwest, leading off at a fast walk. A few minutes later, without halting their progress, they picked out Cabell's hoof prints in the soft earth and changed direction to follow them. When they'd covered perhaps half a mile he slowed the pace long enough to let Peek come alongside.

"Takin' a chance doin' this," he said softly. "Those two from the ships are back there, loaded for bear. Want to keep a sharp lookout, before an' behind. . . ." Then, after a couple seconds of silence: "You figured where these tracks are goin'?"

Peek shook his head grimly. "I ain't even for certain this is the way we'd ought to be trailin' 'em." He explained about seeing the tracks come from the northeast, and his fear that the Westfields might still be in that direction. He tried, without much success, to keep the annoyance from his voice: "But you was in such a all-fired hurry to be ridin' . . ."

The big man grunted mildly. "Could be right," he admitted. "But if they're out yonder an' nothin's happened to 'em yet, they've two less men to trouble 'em now. An' if somethin' did happen . . ."

Peek pressed his lips together and nodded. Nobody needed to paint him a picture. In that case, the Yankee couple was probably beyond helping.

"Anyway," his companion went on, "where they are's a guess. Where your Mister Cabell is, is at the end of these tracks. Might do better askin' him where to find your friends." He urged the marshtackie forward with his knees and Peek fell in behind.

The horses' hooves made almost no sound on the sandy earth as they followed the trail southwest through hardwood hammocks and palmetto flats, changing direction only occasionally to skirt reed-choked sloughs or stagnant ponds. They rode warily, for now there could be enemies on every side. It would never do to come up blindly on a gunman of Ethan Cabell's skill, especially if he was engaged in something suspicious. Their only hope was to locate him first, before he knew he was being followed.

Nor could they forget the men at their backs. Cheeky Joe was sure the Cuban sailors were hunting them, and they'd made no friends among that crew.

Peek saw his companion keeping an eye on his pony's ears, and he made it a point to do the same. The animals' keener senses were apt to detect another horse or human some time before their riders did. But his own senses had grown sharper too, honed by the presence of imminent danger. His eyes and ears reached out into the country around them like sensitive feelers, alert for even the slightest of warnings.

He rode loose in the saddle, with only the toes of his boots thrust into the stirrups. The leather thong over the hammer of his pistol was off now, and his left hand rested lightly on his thigh, just inches from the butt of his tied-down revolver.

He guessed they had gone two or three miles when Cheeky Joe drew rein in a small clump of hardwoods to give the horses a breather. In all that time they'd seen and heard nothing to indicate the presence of others in the vicinity.

"Charlotte Harbor's less'n a mile off," the big man said quietly when Peek came alongside. "He's not goin' much further, 'less he's got fins or a boat."

Peek didn't reply. So far he hadn't been able to make head or tail of Ethan Cabell's movements, nor of his intentions. His having a boat was as likely as anything else.

Cheeky Joe was silent for a minute or two, listening and sniffing the slight offshore breeze. Then he leaned toward his companion and whispered in his ear:

"Keep a sharp eye behind. Got a feelin' 'bout those sailors. We're not careful, we'll be caught between two kinds of trouble!"

They started off again, in single file and more slowly than before, with Cheeky Joe in the lead and Peek turned sideways in his saddle to keep watch over his shoulder.

Miranda could see two flat-bottomed rowboats pulled up among the mangrove roots as she and James were ushered roughly through the tentlike canopy of leaves that overhung the inlet's sandy bank. While the men who'd arrived with Butch went to untie the bow lines, Ethan Cabell pointed with his pistol to the nearer craft.

"You go on an' climb in the back of that one," he told her brusquely. "Quint an' Billy'll keep you comp'ny for the *time bein'*. . ." He stressed the words deliberately, then turned a cold eye on his stocky companion, who had taken a step to follow her. "Butch an' me'll ride in the other boat with your mister."

Butch swung his head around to meet Cabell's eyes but saw nothing there that he liked. Scowling savagely, he plodded off in the direction of the farther boat.

For several long seconds Miranda stood without moving, racking her brain for any plausible excuse to delay or avoid following Cabell's instructions. Once she was aboard the skiff and seated in its stern, with two strong men between her and the shore, she'd not only be cut off from escape, but from her husband as well.

Yet what else could she do? The muzzle of Cabell's revolver hovered inches from her bosom, and she had little doubt that he'd use the weapon if she forced his hand. There was no longer even the slightest pretense of gentlemanly consideration in their former guide's manner.

She glanced beyond him at James, standing a dozen feet away with Quint's pistol in his ribs. He seemed to be watching her closely, and when their eyes met she saw his chin drop in a barely perceptible nod. With no workable plan of her own, she had little choice but to trust her husband's judgment.

Tilting her head slightly in reply, she gathered her skirts and stepped over the gunwale, making her way awkwardly past the thwarts to the stern of the gently rocking boat. As she turned around to seat herself, she had the presence of mind to slip a hand inside the pocket of her dress, letting her fingers close around the butt of James' revolver.

Butch and the second boatman seated themselves in the other skiff, some thirty feet away and partly hidden from view by the tangled branches of mangrove. The man called Billy came forward and tossed the bow rope into her boat. Then he lifted one foot aboard while Quint advanced to join him. Ethan Cabell lowered his pistol and started to turn away.

And in that instant James Westfield moved.

It was a scene that would be etched in Miranda's memory for the rest of her life. Roughly elbowing Quint aside, the archaeologist lowered a thin shoulder and struck Billy a terrific body blow that knocked him out of the skiff and face down into the shallows beside it. Then, without pausing or losing momentum, he seized the boat with both hands and started manhandling it away from shore.

"The oars!" he shouted wildly as his eyes met Miranda's. "Take up the oars and pull yourself away!"

For one bare instant Miranda hesitated, torn between keeping a grip on the revolver in her pocket and doing what she was told. Then there was a stab of flame from the barrel of Quint's pistol and she saw her husband stagger.

"For God's sake, Miranda!" James' voice rang hoarsely over the fading echoes of the shot. He was knee-deep in the water now, leaning red-faced into his task while an ugly dark stain spread out over his shirtfront. "Get yourself away from here! Never mind me! I . . ."

For the first time in her young life, Miranda Westfield felt the urge to kill. Half-blinded with fury and disbelief, she jerked the revolver from her pocket and swung the barrel toward Quint. Their shots racketed in unison as the man on shore fired a second time into her husband. She saw the outlaw turn suddenly and claw with his free hand at a bloodied ear. Then, howling a curse of pain and rage, he spun and leveled his pistol at Miranda.

"Stop it, you idiot!" Ethan Cabell was beside his associate in two headlong strides. He viciously struck Quint's weapon down with a bone-jarring swipe of his own, and the bullet plowed a harmless furrow in the sand. "We got to have one of them alive to show us where the gold's at!"

Miranda let go of her revolver and stumbled blindly forward, heedless of the bruises to her knees and ankles from the wooden thwarts and floorboards. She leaned over to clutch at her husband's sleeves while he continued to push weakly against the slowly moving boat. The water was up to his chest now, and tinted pink with his blood.

"No, no . . ." he gasped, shaking off her futile attempt to drag him onboard. "Too late . . . for me. . . . Use the oars . . . and save yourself! Hide from them among the mangroves!"

Her fingers lost their grip as the boat's backward motion separated them. She could see her husband stumble and lose his balance. Then, screaming his name at the top of her lungs, Miranda watched helplessly while James Westfield's khaki campaign hat sank beneath the bloody water. It did not reappear.

Sobbing uncontrollably and blinded by tears, she fumbled clumsily at the oars lying beside her in the skiff's bottom. Somehow she managed to wrestle them into the locks and position herself on the center thwart. Then, scarcely able to think but grimly determined not to let James' sacrifice go in vain, she sculled the bow around and started pulling with all her strength for open water.

As she lowered the oars and lifted them, putting all her youthful energy into each desperate stroke, Miranda kept her jaws tightly clenched to choke back the screams. She wanted to scream, over and over again, to vent her loss and rage and hurt in one furious orgy of animal keening. But she bitterly refused to give those murderers onshore the satisfaction of hearing it.

Instead, she bent her lithe shoulders to the work at hand with hardly a sound, forcing all thoughts of vengeance and release to the farthest depths of her psyche.

At least for the time being.

The flat reports of pistol shots echoed harshly through the still morning air. Peek drew rein abruptly and glanced at Cheeky Joe, who had brought his own mount to a halt and had risen in the stirrups to listen. The shots came from the west, perhaps a mile or less away. But it was never easy to judge distance where small arms were concerned.

"Four of 'em," the larger man said in a low voice, after

several seconds had passed and the forest was quiet again. "Two real close together, like more'n one was shootin'." He looked at Peek. "You reckon they're shootin' at each other?"

The cow hunter shook his head. He'd like to believe that but didn't think it likely. He walked his pony next to his companion's. "I don't know 'bout you, Cheeky Joe, but I got a f—"

He saw the other's sharply upraised hand and broke off in mid-sentence. From far away, borne on a westerly breeze that gently stirred the treetops, came the long drawn-out echo of a woman's scream.

Miranda! Peek had no doubt whose voice it was, nor that its sound meant the lady was in desperate trouble. He tightened his grip on the reins and bent to put spurs to his pony.

In that instant a thundering volley of shots rang out from the shadowed forest behind them. One bullet whipped over Cheeky Joe's head, barely missing him as he suddenly lowered himself into the saddle. From the corner of his eye Peek saw the big man kick free of the stirrups and drop to the ground.

Peek's left hand was darting for his six-gun even as he swung his pony to face their hidden attackers. He felt the weapon come up, fast and smooth as in practice, and then it was bucking in his fist.

But he never saw the effect of his bullets. For sometime in the midst of that reflex act of firing, a brilliant crimson star exploded in his head. He felt himself falling. . . .

And after that was blackness.

Miranda halted to catch her breath behind one of the low mangrove islets that dotted the watery expanse beyond the estuary where she'd left her attackers. Already she could feel her shoulders and upper arms starting to cramp from the unaccustomed exertion.

As an active young girl growing up on the Hudson River, she'd had more than a little experience with boats, from birch-bark canoes to gaff-rigged sailing vessels. But that seemed a long time ago now. And this flat-bottomed skiff made of cypress was heavier and more awkward than any she recalled from her youth.

Nosing the stubby bow in among the dense tangle of prop roots to hold it in place, she shipped the oars and massaged her aching biceps for several long minutes while she took stock of her situation.

She'd neither the strength nor the stamina to outdistance Cabell and his henchmen once they appeared from the inlet behind her—something she expected at any moment. Not only were they all more muscular than she, but their numbers would allow them to take turns with the rowing. Her only hope lay in finding a hiding place where she could stay until nightfall. After it was dark she could try to evade pursuit and start making her way toward the Pease River.

The tiny islet where she rested was too small for that purpose. As soon as anyone passed behind it she'd be in plain view. What she needed was a larger island, or some spot along the shore, with a narrow bay or estuary concealed by dense foliage. She knew there would be such places, and suspected they were common. But finding one in her present circumstances was another matter entirely.

The pressing issue was time: time to search for a refuge without being seen in the process. And that meant doing her best to avoid open water.

There were, fortunately, quite a few mangrove islets like this one strewn about the bay. If she could keep one or more of them between herself and her pursuers . . .

But she had to move quickly now, to gain enough distance to afford a choice of routes. And because she couldn't use the islets for concealment without knowing where her enemies were, she must first spare a few precious moments to learn what was behind her.

There was no more time for rest. Using the prop roots as handholds, she backed the bow free and drew the skiff sideways until she could see the distant inlet through the jumble of leaves. Forcing herself to patience lest she miss something in her haste to move on, she studied the bay and its overgrown coastline with care. To her surprised relief, there was still no sign of Cabell's second boat.

Perhaps that had something to do with the distant shots she'd heard while making her escape. Surely Cabell and his companions would have wondered, as she did, at the sounds of so much violence in this unsettled wilderness—especially coming almost on the heels of their own exchange of gunfire.

Miranda had had more urgent concerns at the time, and it wasn't until now that she thought about that other shooting. Nor had she the leisure for much speculation even now. If it offered some delay or difficulty to those criminals behind her, all well and good. Otherwise . . .

She unshipped the oars and lowered one into the water, using it to swing the awkward craft about before taking a fresh grip on the handles with palms that were chafed and blistered from her earlier exertions. Then she inhaled deeply and bent her aching shoulders to the task of pulling as quickly as possible for another low islet a quarter of a mile away.

The sun was over the treetops now. And there seemed to be storm clouds gathering to the westward.

16 🌾

COLD. PEEK WAS shivering with cold. Or was it from the dull steady pounding at the back of his skull? One or the other must have awakened him.

That or the rain. For now he could hear the sounds of heavy drops rustling through the leaves overhead to spatter on the earth nearby. His face was cold and damp. Tiny streams of water trickled past his ears and ran off from his chin.

After several long minutes he forced his eyes apart. It took a few seconds more to bring his surroundings into focus.

He was lying on the earth under the sheltering limbs of a large magnolia, protected from the worst of the rain by its broad, glossy leaves. Somebody—Cheeky Joe almost surely—had taken the trouble to spread his poncho over him, and had put his bedroll under his head as a pillow. He could feel the comforting weight of his six-shooter pressing against his thigh under the poncho.

Slowly and carefully, he raised a hand to his throbbing skull. There was a crude bandage there, holding what felt like some kind of poultice of leaves over the most painful spot. His hat lay upside down a few inches away, where it must have fallen when he shivered himself awake.

He reached out and brought it close, using it to cover the bandage and part of his forehead. Then for a time he simply lay there without moving, trying to gather his thoughts along with his strength. His tongue was dry and his throat ached with thirst; but it seemed like too much effort even to roll onto his side, let alone try to locate his canteen. Instead he opened his mouth and let the sparse but soothing drops of rain trickle inside. After a bit he slept again.

When his eyes opened next, the sky overhead had turned a deep royal purple and one or two stars had begun to twinkle. The tops of the trees were streaked with gold from the last rays of the sun. It wasn't raining now, and the damp Florida woods seemed eerily still.

Memory came to him slowly, in ragged bits and images. He could recall hearing distant shots, and his horse turning toward the sound. Then something had happened . . . something that left him on the ground with this throbbing ache and a head filled with cobwebs. He closed his eyes and took several slow breaths. Well, maybe it hadn't all happened right at this spot. . . .

Finally he gritted his teeth and pushed himself up on one elbow, stifling a groan as he did it. Even that small movement left him feeling lightheaded and sick to his stomach. After several seconds his hand went gingerly to the bandage under his hat brim. The pain wasn't as bad as it had been earlier, though it was still doing its dangdest to get his attention. Something in that poultice did seem to help. . . .

Cheeky Joe. It must have been he who'd tended his wound and left him here in the shelter of the magnolia.

After . . . ?

Gradually, like bubbles filtering up from a deep underwater spring, more memories returned: a violent explosion of shots, his hand dropping for his pistol, and then blinding, searing agony—as if somebody had laid a red-hot poker across his scalp.

He closed his eyes while his fingers tenderly explored the shape of his wound through the layers of bandage. No doubt about it: He'd been creased by a bullet, and he was almighty lucky into the bargain. The act of swinging his pony to face their attackers had probably saved his life.

Their attackers—

Peek's eyes jerked open and he fumbled for the pistol at his side, ignoring the shooting pain as he turned his head to peer about him into the gathering gloom. There was no one in the range of his vision. Nor were there any sounds but the ever-present crickets and frogs, chanting their strident refrain into the moisture-laden air.

Where had they all gone? Where was Cheeky Joe? And what of the men who'd dogged their trail to ambush them?

He kept a firm grip on his six-gun while he threw off the poncho and got clumsily to his knees. In the process his eyes fell on his canteen a few feet away, and he was sharply reminded of his unslaked thirst.

With his ears tuned to the surrounding woods for even the faintest suggestion of unwanted visitors, he dragged the canteen to him and removed the cork with his free hand.

With a grateful sigh, he raised the container to his lips and drank long and deep. Following a brief pause to catch his breath and listen again, he drank some more and replaced the cork. The water had been chilled by the rain and the lengthening shadows, and its coolness seemed to have an almost magic effect. His mind was growing sharper, and he felt as if a little strength was returning as well.

After another, more careful study of the small clearing beside him and the vine-shrouded forest beyond, he clenched his teeth and climbed unsteadily to his feet. His knees felt like they were made of India rubber. But that, he told himself stubbornly, would pass after he'd stirred around a bit. A powerful urge to know what had happened in the hours since he lost consciousness, along with a nagging but less clearly defined sense of foreboding, made it impossible for him to stay put in any case.

He had a notion his associate had gone after their ambushers, and for all he knew the Calusa was miles away by this time. Cheeky Joe could also lie hurt or dying in some hidden thicket in the wilderness. Tomorrow when it was light, Peek could look for his trail. For now, it seemed each of them was entirely on his own.

He found his Cracker horse picketed among the trees a dozen yards away. And with no idea what dangers might be lurking in the vicinity, nor where his companion was at present, it seemed the best idea was to saddle up and be ready for any possibility.

Even that familiar task needed longer than usual, with many pauses to rest and catch his breath. It wasn't until he'd tied his bedroll and poncho behind his saddle that his disjointed mind conjured up one last chilling image from the jigsaw puzzle of events that happened before his injury.

The sudden recollection of Miranda's far-off scream sent a shiver up his spine in the gathering darkness. To make matters worse, it was followed by the helpless realization that many hours had passed since he'd heard those keening echoes. He closed his eyes and tried not to think about what could have happened in the meantime.

Then he bent to tighten his cinch with a deliberate jerk, and spent another minute checking the loads and action of his Colt revolver.

"Well, old son," he said between his teeth as he shoved a sixth cartridge into the weapon's empty chamber, "you ain't exactly covered yourself with glory so far on this here expedition. An' it could be you're too late to help the lady now. . . ."

With a sudden rush of anger he broke off to spin the cylinder and drop the pistol into its holster. Then he gripped the reins and stepped up into the leather.

"But by the Lord Harry they's goin' to be some folks called to accountin' for it if I ain't! An' that's my personal promise to you, Miz Miranda."

A sort of icy calm came over him as he turned the

Cracker pony's head toward the faint remaining glow in the western sky—a hard-edged readiness for battle unlike anything he'd ever experienced. All the fears and doubts he'd fretted over before seemed far off now, as if they'd belonged to some other young man he'd only met in passing.

He let his pony move forward at a slow walk, riding light in the saddle with just the toes of his boots in the stirrups. The trees around him were cloaked in darkness under their softly whispering canopy of leaves, and Peek's senses were even more keenly attuned to his surroundings than they'd been that morning with Cheeky Joe.

It was no longer likely that any rapid advance would be of help to Miranda and her husband; and charging in like an angry bull to face gunmen such as those before him was an invitation to disaster. The Gulf Coast wasn't more than a mile off at this point, so it shouldn't take long to locate them if they were still in the neighborhood. And in that case a silent, cautious approach offered the best chance of surviving long enough to plan his next move.

What that move would be Peek had no idea. All that seemed certain was he'd have only himself to carry it off. Everything that happened from now on was his responsibility alone.

He'd been smelling the smoke from the campfire for several minutes before he was able to make out its ruddy glow among the trees. By the time he drew rein a hundred yards away, the low and indistinct rumble of men's voices could be heard easily in the still night air.

He lowered himself from the saddle and tethered his Cracker pony among some cedars at one edge of a small clearing. Then he knelt and quietly unbuckled the spurs from his boots. After stowing these in a saddlebag, he turned and began inching his way toward the fire in a wary half-crouch.

He took his time, making sure to lift each foot with care and put it down gently so as to keep the rustling of leaves to a minimum while avoiding any dry twigs that might betray his presence. When possible he kept the thick boles of trees or clumps of palmetto between himself and the fire's flickering light.

This was no time for recklessness or haste, and Peek wasn't a stranger to stealthy woodland movement. He'd been stalking deer and wild turkeys since before he turned five—although, he reminded himself grimly, his quarry tonight was infinitely more dangerous.

It took him the better part of an hour to cover the distance to the outskirts of the camp. When he was finally crouched in the shadows of a dense stand of palmetto some twenty feet off, he was able to make out most of the words the men spoke. Some of their voices were those he remembered:

". . . time Billy gets back here with that other boat it'll be comin' on noon." That would be Butch. And the stocky little man didn't sound happy. "Even with two boats we'll play hell tryin' to find her. They must be a million li'l nooks an' crannies out yonder where she can hole up, what with all them islands an' the mangroves an' what-not."

"We'll find her," Ethan Cabell's voice replied coldly. "It may take a while, maybe two, three days. But sooner or later that tenderfoot woman's just naturally goin' to slip up and show herself." Peek hunched lower as a stick of fat pine flared up when it was added to the fire.

"Might not be altogether a accident, either," the gambler went on. "There wasn't no food or water in that skiff she lit out with. A night or two in the woods without 'em could change her thinkin' considerable." He allowed himself a dry chuckle. "Even Butch here might start to look appealin' to her, with a full canteen in his fist."

"Huh! I wouldn't put no serious wages on that!" The third voice had to be Quint, who appeared to be seated some distance from the others. "Nor on her lettin' herself be took whilst there's any breath left in her. That woman's got steel inside of her, with a fair helpin' of wildcat besides! Maybe she ain't got no water or food, but she's got that six-shooter of her husband's. An' I'm here to tell you she ain't shy about usin' it!"

Gradually, from their conversation, Peek began to piece together what had happened. Earlier in the day Miranda Westfield had managed to take a boat from these men and make her escape. Now they wanted her back. And they must want her powerful bad, judging from all the trouble they were willing to go to. Why they'd do it—and risk almost certain lynching if anybody caught them at it—was something the cow hunter still couldn't fathom.

And where was Doc Westfield? Was he here in the camp? Or had he made his own escape separately? That seemed unlikely, knowing how the Doc felt about his wife. But it was clear from the conversation that he wasn't with her at present.

From what Quint said, she had a pistol belonging to her husband and she knew how to use it. That was some comfort anyhow. And when you came right down to it, why Cabell and them wanted the lady didn't make much difference. The fact that they did was reason enough to stop them.

The voices around the fire grew quieter after Quint's remark, and a little more sullen it seemed to Peek. He could still make out a word here and there, and apparently a bottle was being passed around. But apart from a sometimes passionate curse directed at the ever-present mosquitoes, followed by less frequent slaps, there was nothing of interest he could manage to decipher.

At last he figured it was time to move. One of his legs was starting to cramp under his weight, and the mosquitoes in the palmettos where he crouched were a constant source of torment. Unable to swat them for fear of making his presence known, he'd been forced to content himself with silently crushing one now and again with a finger while it feasted on his neck or hand.

He rose slowly in place, keeping his balance with difficulty and trusting to the darkness and the effects of liquor to protect him from discovery for the few seconds it took to get circulation back in his leg. Then he started backing away from the camp, moving as carefully and silently as before.

He had the beginnings of a plan now. But before he could put it into motion, he needed to return to where he'd left his Cracker pony.

Butch had spoken of using two boats in the search for Miranda, one of which wouldn't arrive until late tomorrow morning. That meant there was one boat here now, and if Peek could find and make off with it under cover of darkness, Cabell and his men would be left high and dry—at least until the second boat arrived.

It went against the grain to set his dependable little mount loose in the Florida backcountry. But he had no idea when—or if—he'd return to this place. And the wilderness-bred pony was capable of fending for itself if left free to do so. Horses were sociable animals, so with a little luck it would seek out others of its kind before long. And with a tad more luck, some honest rancher might hold it until Peek had a chance to come looking.

The shaggy-maned creature acted as if it understood when he spoke quietly in its ear, only lifting its head and standing motionless while its master took what he needed from the saddlebags. That was little enough: a small bundle of cornpone and jerked beef Peek had kept for emergencies, some fishing line and hooks in a carved wooden box, and several hands full of spare .44 cartridges. When he'd shoved these into his pockets, he slung his canteen over his shoulder and undid the tether rope, coiling it and fastening it along with the reins to the front of his saddle.

"So long, pardner," he whispered, running his fingers through the horse's thick mane. "I hope we'll meet up again when this is all over. . . ." He felt a lump come to his throat and turned away quickly to start retracing his steps toward the outlaws' camp.

After he'd gone perhaps a dozen yards he glanced back over his shoulder. The Cracker pony was nibbling peacefully at the dew-wet grass of the clearing, showing no inclination for the moment to seek out greener pastures.

The fire had burned itself down to coals by the time Peek finally got another glimpse of it from a stand of trees some fifty feet away. He'd angled slightly to the right on his return, in the direction of the unseen coast that he knew was close by. The round trip had taken him well over an hour, moving as cautiously and patiently as before.

When he could make out the tent's ghostly rectangle against the pitch black of the forest behind it, he stopped and went down on one knee, listening intently for any sound of voices or other activity that might come from that direction.

There was nothing. It appeared Cabell and the others had turned in for the night.

Even so, Peek waited where he was for a good ten minutes to be sure. There was still plenty of time until daylight, and what he meant to do was avoid calling attention to himself while he found that boat and made his getaway onto the trackless waters of the Gulf.

At last he rose and started circling to his right, staying

as far from the camp as possible while still keeping it in view. Before long his nose caught the scent of brackish water, and he could sense its coolness through the dark hedge of plants at his elbow. Somewhere nearby there ought to be some kind of a path that would lead him to the boat.

Suddenly his boot sank up to the ankle in loosely packed sand. Now what in the world—?

17 ✹

WITHOUT MOVING HIS feet, Peek crouched in the darkness and let his fingers explore the soft ground in a cautious half-circle. There were no leaves or grass near his boot, nothing but what seemed to be a low oblong mound of freshly turned soil. A few inches away the earth felt solid and natural.

The cow hunter's jaw clenched and he felt the hairs on his neck rise as he located the roughly straight line that separated the two textures. He slowly withdrew his foot and backed away on hands and knees. Then he traced the line of separation for its full extent: pretty near six feet, give or take.

There could be little doubt that he'd stumbled on a grave: recently dug and hastily filled in by the feel of it. He caught himself shivering a bit in the dank night air. The sudden awareness of death is always a shock to the living; and here in this gloomy place a few scant yards from the men who were most likely responsible, it was a grimly upsetting surprise.

But Peek had no time to spend dwelling on it, or even

to speculate about whose grave it was—though he'd a melancholy suspicion that he knew. It made no difference to his plans for the present. Miranda Westfield's safety was the most pressing concern.

He rose quickly and stepped gingerly past the disturbed earth. A few yards beyond it was the path he'd been seeking. With his right arm he gently parted the thin curtain of branches, taking care to make as little sound as possible. Then, on cat's feet, he made his way to the shore of the inlet.

Silver ripples shimmered under a late-rising moon as he approached the water, which he learned to his surprise was no more than thirty yards wide at this spot. He looked hurriedly around and was relieved to see the dark silhouette of a boat pulled up on the sand, its anchor rope looped carelessly over some red mangrove prop roots. A closer inspection confirmed that the oars were still in the craft, and everything seemed ready for a speedy departure.

But he'd been expecting to find open water when he reached the mangrove-bordered coast—if not the Gulf itself, then at least the wide expanse of Charlotte Harbor. Making good his escape only to be trapped in some dead-end channel had no part in Peek's plans to help Miranda—nor did increasing his risk of discovery by having to backtrack repeatedly while hunting an outlet.

Frowning in thought, he took a few guarded steps to the edge of the shallows. His boots made soft sucking noises as he lifted them and changed position to gaze left and right along the overgrown banks of the waterway. He couldn't see far enough to be sure, but the inlet seemed to grow wider on his left. And judging from the position of the moon, that made sense—for the direction was roughly west, which should take him toward the Gulf.

That looked like his best bet, at any rate. And once he was out on the water he'd be able to see farther.

Having made his decision, he turned and strode quickly back to the skiff. He'd undone the rope and was bending to pick up the heavy lump of scrap iron that served as an anchor when he heard a faint noise behind him.

It was no more than a whisper of coarse fabric against branches, but to Peek's sharpened senses it might as well have been a warning shout. Somebody was moving along the path between the outlaws' camp and the water!

Instantly he froze where he was, hunched awkwardly above the anchor with both arms extended. Maybe the new arrival wouldn't come close enough to notice his still form among the shadows. It was a desperate hope, but the only one that would give him even a slight chance of avoiding detection.

Nor was it meant to be. The rustling continued until the new arrival was less than a dozen feet away. Then it stopped. There was an agonizing moment of silence, followed by a sharp intake of breath.

Peek didn't wait for any warning shout. His fingers gripped the rusted hunk of iron and he spun on his heel, flinging the heavy missile at the sounds with every bit of force his work-hardened muscles could summon. Without knowing the result, he lowered his shoulders and followed it in.

A brief and startled cry was cut short by a sickening thud, and the cow hunter's charge knocked the man sprawling to the ground. Turning swiftly to recover his balance, Peek finished the job of silencing him with a brutal kick to the head from his booted foot.

It was no one he'd ever seen before, which meant Cabell must have recruited extra help. How many? Peek wondered. How many men did it take to hunt one lone woman out of the Florida wilderness? And how many would he have to face before Miranda could finally be shut of them?

As many as it took, he told himself grimly while bending to retrieve the blood-spattered anchor and its jumble of rope. At least this one wouldn't cause much trouble for a while—if he lived.

He knew the time for stealth was past, for although the confrontation had been short, its sounds would carry in these quiet hours of the night. Dumping the anchor and rope into the skiff's bow with no more worries about silence, he gripped the gunwales with both hands and inhaled deeply. Then he gave the flat-bottomed craft a mighty shove with all his strength behind it, propelling it over the sand and into the water in one constant movement.

Peek uttered a low-voiced curse as his foot plunged into a hole a few feet from shore, soaking his boots and his trousers up to the thigh. But he didn't let the mishap slow his clambering aboard, and in seconds he'd unshipped the oars and begun swinging the craft's blunt bow toward the western leg of the inlet.

He was pulling hard for what he prayed was open water by the time he heard angry voices and had a glimpse of dark forms milling about the landing place behind him. A minute afterward there were the flash and bark of a pistol, followed by the flat smack of a bullet striking water a few yards away. Before whoever it was could manage a second shot, Peek had rounded a small headland and was lost to view behind dark thickets of mangrove.

Miranda raised herself on one elbow from the rough cypress strakes of her captured boat, where she'd finally collapsed into an exhausted sleep. Her clothing still wasn't entirely dry from the previous afternoon's rain, and she shivered a little in the faint breeze off the bay while her ears reached out into the moonlit night.

More distant gunshots? She had a vague impression that was what had awakened her. But all she heard now was the gentle lapping of water against the skiff's hull, together with the muted whine of hunting mosquitoes.

It could have been her imagination. Or more likely some half-recalled image from her latest nightmare: the one in which James' arms kept reaching out for her, but an instant before their fingers touched . . .

Her breath caught in an unvoiced sob, and she pulled

herself up to a sitting position. The horror of that nightmare was that it had been no dream. Yet whenever she closed her eyes she was forced to relive it—with such frightful vividness that each time it took all of her willpower to keep from venting her feelings with ear-rending shrieks.

But she couldn't do that. Not in this place, where any sound above a whisper might be heard across the still waters by those cold-blooded savages who'd murdered her husband. And if there was to be any positive outcome at all from yesterday's disaster, it must lie in avoiding their clutches until she could see justice done.

She gazed up at the moon and pulled a matted wisp of hair from her eyes with cracked and blistered fingers. She'd slept longer than she'd meant to, once she'd finally been able to sleep at all. The night seemed well along now. There was no telling how much precious darkness she'd lost that could have been used to increase the distance between herself and those men who—she was positive—would be hunting her again at first light.

But it couldn't be helped; and it did no good to fret over lost opportunities. She'd needed the rest badly. When she'd finally located this hidden estuary among the dense clumps of mangrove on the bay's western shore, she could scarcely have rowed another stroke if Ethan Cabell or Butch had been ten feet behind her.

Even now the thought of gripping those rough-hewn oars with her lacerated hands, and of more long hours of rowing with muscles already sore and knotted, made her close her eyes and utter a weary sigh.

Yet it had to be done. And the sooner she started, the sooner she might hope to arrive at some friendly settlement or other refuge where her pursuers dared not follow.

She bent forward on her knees and reached out to dip her hands in the cool salt water. The first sharp pain brought tears to her eyes, but the brine seemed to have a mildly cura-tive effect—or so she tried to convince herself. Afterward she made a few halfhearted attempts to wipe the sleep and grime from her face with the sodden sleeves of her blouse.

If only she had something to drink! She'd been too occupied with finding a place to hide for such thoughts dur-ing the brief afternoon shower; and now it had been almost twenty-four hours since she'd tasted food or water. Yet it was thirst that caused her the greatest distress. Her lips had become dry and cracked, and she was starting to have trouble swallowing. How ironic, she thought, that with water in every direction its need could pose such an urgent threat to survival!

At last she rose to her feet, balancing with care in the gently rocking craft while she turned to study her moonlit surroundings. She could make out the faintly shimmering expanse of the bay some thirty yards behind her. Everything else at a distance was gray and indistinct.

Her present refuge was walled in by a close-growing mass of roots and branches that rose almost to eye level as she strained on tip-toe to peer beyond it. When she was seated on the thwart she and the shallow-draft vessel were invisible from a dozen feet away, even in daylight.

The tangled mangrove roots had collected dirt and other flotsam over the years, giving a deceptively false appearance of solid ground. But when she'd tested it earlier with her hands and a cautious toe, she'd discovered the footing was dangerously unstable. Nowhere nearby was there any place that might support her weight. And even if there had been, the plants grew so densely together that making progress among them seemed all but impossible.

She knew from earlier observations that the maze of mangroves extended for at least a quarter of a mile to the west of where she was now, interrupted only occasionally by reed-choked marshes. Dry land, if there was any, must lie somewhere beyond that. And since the estuary she'd found came to a dead end at this point, the chances of discovering a passage to shore without countless hours of searching were so remote as not be worth considering.

Her husband's ideas on the subject had been right as usual. The only practical route was on the open waters of the bay, making her way north to the entrance of the Pease River. The risk of discovery would be greater, but balanced against that was the possibility of coming on some closer settlement—or at least a source of fresh water!

No sooner was the choice clear in her mind than Miranda set about translating it to action. She bent to take up one of the oars, then stood and began poling her unwieldy craft back to the mouth of the winding estuary.

Here the moon's light revealed itself in all its brilliance, turning the expanse of water to liquid silver under the starry dome of the sky. The wooded banks, by contrast, loomed dark and forbidding in the distance.

Suddenly and uncomfortably aware of the increased visibility, together with the night's all-pervading quiet, Miranda drew the boat up in the nearest shadows and spent several minutes muffling the oarlocks as well as she could with strips torn from her petticoats.

Then, steeling herself to ignore her hurts and exhaustion, she wrestled the oars into place and started pulling for the north end of the bay, trying to keep as much distance as possible between herself and the eastern shore, where her enemies were camped.

She had to pause more frequently than she liked to catch her breath and give her aching muscles a few seconds of rest. Yet even so she made progress. The moon proved a blessing as well as a danger, for it allowed her to hold a steady course without having to rely on the deceptive contours of the mangrove-shrouded coastline.

After perhaps an hour she began to encounter a slight but noticeable current, and knew its source was probably the outflow from a river. Suddenly she froze in midstroke, recalling something that had escaped her troubled thoughts until that very instant.

James' account of their surroundings a couple of nights earlier had mentioned *two* major rivers, both of which flowed into this bay from the north. Belatedly, Miranda realized that the one she wished to enter, the Pease River, was the more easterly of the two!

With a weary sigh, she raised one of the oars from the water and used the other to swing the skiff around so she could see her direction of travel. Then, sculling gently to hold her position against the current, she considered the situation.

By moonlight the shore in every direction appeared as a thick solid line. There was no way she could guess its configuration from a distance, no way to distinguish between island or headland, river or inlet, until she was just a few yards away.

It was painfully obvious that if she kept on as she was, the most likely result was that she'd become hopelessly lost. At worst, daylight might find her trapped by some cul-de-sac, with no means of escape from her pursuers.

Traveling at night as she must, it appeared her best hope of entering that easternmost river was by following the east bank of the bay. And that meant crossing to the opposite side—an almost impossible distance in her present state of exhaustion.

But if not now, with the moon already low and daylight approaching, it would have to be tomorrow, after another long day of hiding among the mangroves.

It was her overwhelming thirst that decided her. Another day and night without water were totally unthinkable. She would still need luck to find some spring or fresh stream on that far coast, but at least she'd be nearer her destination. And whatever dangers and hardships the long crossing involved would be less than those of delay.

Calling upon what she felt sure were her last reserves of

strength, Miranda gritted her teeth and swung the skiff's bow to the east. The oar blades bit deep into the water as she struck out gamely for the distant shore.

Peek eased his own stolen craft in among the shadows of some saltbush and quietly shipped the oars. Then he spent several long minutes resting and catching his breath while his eyes roamed the moonlit expanse of Charlotte Harbor from one end to the other.

He'd left the inlet where the outlaws' camp was located almost a mile behind, and had no worries about pursuit. The problem at the moment was what to do next.

There was no sign of any boats on the water—at least none that Peek could make out from his current vantage point. Nor had he expected there would be any. Miranda Westfield was a smart woman, and he'd a notion that if she didn't want to be found, not even the Devil himself could make an easy job of it.

And that was just the trouble. How could he manage to track the lady down before Cabell and his men did? Especially when she didn't know he'd come hunting her. She had no reason to expect help or friendship from any man hereabouts, and was as liable to avoid him as anybody else.

One thing was mighty clear: He wasn't going to have much luck finding her by moonlight. His best chance would be tomorrow morning, while Cabell was still cooling his heels waiting for that other boat. If Peek started at first light, he might have five or six hours before they got on the water. And if he could guess which direction she'd gone during her flight today, and about how far, he could try to be that much closer to her when he did start looking. . . .

Had she traveled north? Or south? Or straight across the bay to the mangrove islands on the other side? He frowned as he pondered the question, turning the possibilities over in his mind.

The fact was, he couldn't know for certain; he'd just have to pick a direction and hope for the best. But since the lady was smart, he might as well assume she'd done the smart thing—which was to make her way north toward the closest and most populated settlements.

How far had she gone? That was even harder to guess. It seemed better to err on the conservative side, though. So he'd only go another mile or two now, and hole up till first light. Then he'd start rowing north and see what he could see.

Any way you looked at it, Peek knew his chances of finding Miranda ahead of the bad men were slim. But since this was the only plan he had, he reckoned he'd have to make it work.

18 🌿

TIME AND DISTANCE ceased to have meaning as Miranda bent and drew back the oars again and again, repetition without end: a straining of the back, a hoarse gulp of air, then a hunch forward to do it once more.

Her entire world was a rippling expanse of silver, its only sounds the monotonous gurgle and plash of the blades as they lifted and fell, the gentle creak of muffled oarlocks, and, through it all, the dull but never-ending pain in her hands, arms, shoulders, and back.

Charlotte Harbor was more than five miles wide at this point. But Miranda had no thought of that. Her progress was measured one stroke at a time. Each agonizing pull was a victory. Every gasping stretch to return the blades to the water was another.

When the handles grew slippery with blood from her ragged palms, she bit her lower lip and simply gripped them more tightly.

Again and again she was certain she could go no farther. Again and again she told herself between rasping breaths:

"Just one more pull; only one more! And then you can give it up!"

Somehow she found the will to keep going.

And then, miraculously, just when the stars were blinking out in the lightening sky, she found herself among the comforting shadows of a wooded coastline.

With one last desperate pull, she thrust the skiff into the tangle of mangrove roots and shipped the oars so they wouldn't float away. Then, not troubling to sit erect or straighten her shoulders, she rested her arms on her knees and let her head drop forward, staying like that for many long minutes until her chest stopped heaving and her ragged breaths became more regular.

She was perspiring from her exertion, and the salty drops on her lips seemed to mock the aching rawness of her throat. Her thirst was a tangible thing now.

If only it would rain! Just a little predawn shower, enough to cool her fevered brow and let her catch a few precious drops in her mouth. She opened her eyes and gazed hopefully up through the branches. But there wasn't a cloud in the sky.

Then, abruptly, the realization struck her: That dull expanse had taken on a pinkish tint even in the short time she'd rested here; it seemed to be growing brighter as she watched. In less than an hour it would be full daylight!

She sat up hurriedly to take stock of her surroundings. She had to get herself and the skiff out of sight, and she had to do it soon. Ethan Cabell and his men could even now be setting out to resume their pursuit.

She had neither the time nor the strength for a prolonged search for a hiding place; she'd have to make do with whatever was close by. Which seemed awfully little to a first probing glance. She could see nothing like the estuary she'd found the day before.

Yet there were occasional narrow openings among the mangroves where a boat might be less noticeable from the open waters of the bay. Pulling herself painfully along by the prop roots, she managed to reach the nearest of these openings, and nosed the skiff inside.

It was imperfect cover at best, for the passage ended after just a few yards and the blunt stern of her craft would still be visible to someone on the water directly opposite. But maybe, with the help of some odds an ends she'd found onboard earlier . . .

She used a rusty scaling knife to hack branches from the onshore side of some mangroves, then combined these with a scrap of discarded fishnet to make a rough screen of camouflage over the exposed end of the skiff. It was crudely done, for the knife was dull and even that small chore took an added toll on her hands. She doubted her handiwork would deceive anyone who was closer than fifty feet. But it was the best she could do in the circumstances, and she'd simply hope for the best.

After removing her husband's pistol from the pocket of her skirt and placing it on the center thwart in easy reach, Miranda climbed into the bow and prepared to curl up for a much-needed rest. She could hardly keep her eyes open as she shifted her aching limbs around in a vain effort to find a more comfortable position on the hard wooden strakes.

One bare instant before she lowered her head, she happened to glance at the rough varnished wood alongside the pistol. A heavy coating of dew had collected there, and was forming on the weapon's steel barrel as well. It glittered bewitchingly in the soft morning light, and in that instant Miranda recognized it for what it was.

Nor was she one to be fastidious when survival was at issue. Rising up on her elbows, she touched a dry and swollen tongue to the thin film of moisture and reveled in its coolness. It had a faint, salty flavor, and a trace of what may have formerly been some creature of the sea. Yet she couldn't remember ever tasting anything so delicious.

There wasn't nearly enough, of course. Only a few scant teaspoonfuls in all. But when she'd licked what was on the seat and the metal parts of the revolver, she felt remarkably refreshed.

And for the first time since James' murder, she had a firm conviction that she'd make it through this ordeal. And that she would live to see his killers punished.

The sun hadn't yet burned the night's coolness from her hiding place when Miranda grew aware of the rhythmic slosh and creak of oars out on the bay. Blearily, her eyes slit open;

and with stiff and clumsy fingers she fumbled for the pistol on the thwart above her head.

She dared not sit up or stir about, for fear of calling attention to her already precariously exposed position. She scarcely dared to breathe.

Her ears strained for any clues to the craft's direction of travel or its occupants, but these were pitifully scarce. There were no voices, only the relentless cadence of the oars, approaching, approaching . . . Her index finger found the revolver's trigger and she gripped the weapon tightly with both hands.

But then—thank Heaven!—the noises passed her by. Breathlessly, she listened while they receded gradually into the distance as the oarsman continued northward up the bay.

Very slowly and by degrees, Miranda let the tension drain from her body. At long last she placed the pistol back on the thwart.

For the present she'd escaped discovery. Another small victory, but still a victory. Whatever dangers lay ahead would be dealt with as they came. Her chapped lips curved into a wry smile.

"Sufficient unto the day," she quoted softly to herself, "is the evil thereof!"

Exhaustion, both physical and emotional, took its toll then, and tears of fatigue blurred her vision. She slumped back into the bow of the skiff, falling almost instantly into a deep but troubled sleep.

How long she slept she'd no way of knowing. But as she

began to climb slowly back to awareness with her eyes still tightly shut, she had a vague sensation of another presence close by. When she was conscious enough of the skiff's hard bottom to stir and mutter a soft complaint, the feeling that someone was watching her became almost tangible.

For an instant, stark panic took over. Her eyes snapped open and her hand darted for James' pistol. But the weapon wasn't where she'd left it!

"It's all right, ma'am. You won't need no gun for me." The male voice was gently soothing as she lifted her wary gaze toward it. She blinked with surprise, then let out an involuntary gasp as she recognized the slim young man seated in the stern of her boat.

"I took it up so's you wouldn't have no chance to hurt yourself accidental whilst you was sleepin'." Peek slid the revolver from his waistband and held it out to her butt first. "You can have it back now, if it'll make you feel more comfortable."

Overcome by shock and disbelief, Miranda could only stare at the cow hunter for several long seconds. Finally she reached out and took the weapon from him with a barely audible "Thank you."

"I'm awful sorry if I give you a fright just now," her new companion said seriously. "I 'magine you've already had enough scares an' fearsome surprises to do you for a lifetime." He reached down and took up a large canteen, which he uncorked and placed on the thwart between them. "But you was sleepin' so peaceful, and I knew you prob'ly needed it, that I just couldn't bring myself to rouse you."

"How . . . How long was I asleep?" Without waiting for an answer, Miranda raised the canteen to her lips and took several long breathless swallows.

"Don't rightly know when you started, but it's a little before noon now. . . . Here, have a care with that! They's plenty. You don't got to swallow it all to onct!"

Miranda lowered the canteen and took a breath, wiping her lips with the back of a dainty but blood-stained hand. "I know. Small sips. Restore it to the system gradually. But that's a lot easier said when you're not the one who's thirsty!" She allowed herself another tiny swallow, then returned the canteen to Peek.

He replaced the cork and reached in his shirt pocket. "Figure you prob'ly missed some meals too, whilst you was hidin' from them bad men." He handed her a small oilcloth-wrapped package. "They ain't a lot there," he said apologetically. "Just a li'l cornpone an' jerky. But it'll help till somethin' better comes along."

His eyes went to her hands while she was unwrapping the oilcloth, and he grimaced in sympathy. "That's about as mis'able a case of tore-up skin as I seen in a coon's age!" He bent for a closer look, then shook his head. "Sure wisht I'd some bacon grease to put on 'em. They must pain you awful fierce."

"If you'd known," The young woman forced a game smile to her lips. "I'm sure you'd have brought some with you. You seem to have come prepared for every eventuality." She glanced down at her hands as she opened the package. "But it's not as bad as it looks. I've been dipping them in salt water from time to time, and that seems to help."

"I reckon," Peek conceded, "if you're able to stand it. But they's some plants an' roots that'd take the fire out, if I had a chance to go lookin'. . . ."

"You're very kind," she said quietly, swallowing a bite of cornpone. "And I'm awfully glad you found me. I've been so frightened and alone, ever since . . ." She fell silent and turned quickly away. For a moment Peek wondered if she had something in her eye. But then she raised her head and looked at him curiously.

"What are you doing here? Weren't you taking your cattle to some place far to the south? A port of some kind?"

"Yes'm. An' we done that. But all the while I couldn't help thinkin' about you and the Doc an' that Cabell feller. And no matter which way I looked at it, I just couldn't shake the notion that he was up to no good. Cabell, I mean. . . ." He paused, and noticed that Miranda had finished the cornpone but was eyeing the jerky suspiciously.

"That there's dried beef, ma'am. It's tougher'n ole shoe leather, but a tad more flavorful. And all the chewin' you got to do so's you can swallow it fools your stomach into thinkin' you done et somethin'."

Miranda shrugged and put a piece in her mouth. "Well, when in Rome . . ."

"Huh?"

"Actually, this is very good," she observed, chewing vigorously and ignoring his question. "You were saying . . . ?"

"Well . . . when we'd got done with the drive I just fig-ured . . ." He felt himself starting to blush. "I mean . . ." Miranda said nothing, watching him in silence while she gnawed on the jerky.

"Anyways," Peek concluded with a self-conscious shrug, "I come up the country huntin' you-all. Thought maybe I could help if you was in some kind of trouble." He saw the young woman swallow and passed her the canteen, which she accepted gratefully.

"But we run into some troubles of our own back down the trail, and I was fearful I wouldn't make it in time. . . ." He saw an odd look come into her eyes, and he let his voice trail off.

Miranda felt a momentary flush of anger—not at this young man, who'd already done more than anyone could have expected—but at the random cruelty of fate. If he hadn't been delayed, if he'd arrived at their camp just a few hours earlier, perhaps . . .

She closed her eyes and inhaled deeply. Such thoughts were worthless, and she perfectly well knew it. What had happened had happened. Letting herself get caught up in a twisted maze of "what ifs" and "might have beens" could only lead to madness. The past was in the past, and what mattered now was the future.

"I'm very grateful to you for coming," she said, "Mister . . ." Then she paused, suddenly embarrassed. "I'm ashamed to say I've forgotten your name!"

"It's Tillman, ma'am. Peek Tillman. No partic'lar reason you'd ought to remember it. We just knowed each other for a couple hours, an' that was some weeks ago now."

"All the same, I'll not forget it again. If you hadn't found me when you did, Mister Tillman . . ."

"Peek, ma'am. Nobody ever mistered me before, not in my entire life. I ain't rightly sure how to answer to it."

"Peek," she repeated firmly. "And you must call me Miranda. 'Ma'am' makes me sound like some old maiden schoolteacher!"

"You sure ain't that!" he said with feeling. Then to hide the blush he felt coloring his cheeks, he changed the subject: "I reckon you know Ethan Cabell and them ain't give up their hunt for you. I took their only boat from 'em durin' the night. But they'd already sent for another."

"At least you've managed to delay them for a while. It seems your arrival came just in time" She broke off, and he saw her shoulders slump. She buried her face in her hands before concluding in a near-whisper: "for me."

The cow hunter listened somberly while she described James Westfield's murder and the events leading up to it. She was trying hard to keep a rein on her feelings, and she told the story with no wasted words. When she'd finished, Peek nodded grimly.

"I'd had the feelin' since I laid eyes on that bunch that they was evil to the core." He was silent a moment, then he shook his head. "But who'd of thought all the mischief they done would be 'cause of some drunk ole man's storytellin'?"

Then it was his turn to explain about Old John Gomez and his fictional tales of hidden pirate treasure. Miranda's jaws clenched together when she finally came to understand what was behind Cabell's actions and her husband's senseless murder.

It took a supreme effort of will to keep a grip on her sanity at that moment, let alone any semblance of outward composure. The sheer insanity of it! The vile, depraved, misbegotten stupidity of these savage little men with their all-consuming greed! Inside, she seethed with an animal rage that wanted to vent itself in guttural shrieks and the tearing of her hair.

If the cow hunter noticed, his features betrayed nothing. He'd kept his eyes averted during most of his narration. When he was finished he turned to her and said seriously, "I'm terrible sorry about your husband, ma'am . . . Miz . . . Miranda. He was a mighty fine gent. And a genuine hero too, there at the last. I just wish I'd of been closer so's I could of helped out. Or tried, anyhow."

"You're here now." Miranda took a deep breath and even managed a faint smile through the blurring of tears. "And no one ever asked or expected you to become involved in our problems."

"No'm, that ain't just exactly so. I done asked an' expected it of myself, onct I'd realized the kind of a low-life Ethan Cabell was." He squinted briefly up at the sun, which was almost directly overhead now. "See, down here in Florida we got us a custom. Whenever we see a snake go slitherin' up into a neighbor's henhouse, we don't wait to be told he don't want it there. We just roust the critter out an' mash its sorry head in. Then we hang its carcass over the nearest fence post for ever'body to look at!"

He paused and glanced over his shoulder. "Now if you'll pardon me sayin' it, we already done tarried here a heap longer'n we'd ought to. We best be seekin' out a better place to hole up in. Them killers'll have 'em that other boat by this time. An' 'fore you know it they'll be out rootin' round these mangroves wantin' to stretch both our hides!"

Miranda wiped her eyes with the sleeve of her blouse and raised herself up onto the center thwart of the skiff. She looked past Peek at the boat he'd taken from the outlaws. It was only partly hidden among the branches and prop roots, and wasn't likely to escape even a casual glance from anywhere on the water opposite them.

"I seen a li'l crick 'bout a half mile up the coast," he said as he turned to transfer his canteen and the oars from Miranda's craft to his. "Figure our best bet's to sink this here boat so them others can't find an' have the use of it, then light out for there in the one I brung. Couldn't rightly tell how much of a crick it was from where I was lookin', but 'least it 'peared big enough to get us round a bend an' out of sight from open water."

Wasting no more time on conversation, he stood and helped Miranda into the second boat, then followed and knelt in the bow to take hold of the other craft's side with his powerful hands. It needed several strenuous minutes of rocking and pushing before the vessel started to fill with water; but then it sank to its gunwales and was nearly invisible among the clustered roots of the mangroves.

"Can't hardly make a hole in them ol' cypress boards without shootin' or takin' a ax to 'em," he explained as he seated himself on the center thwart of the remaining boat and unshipped the oars. "'Sides, it don't seem right to wreck a good boat like that when there ain't no need for it. Somebody might come acrost her later on, and once they empty her out she'll be 'most good as new."

19 ☀

WITH PEEK'S MUSCULAR arms and shoulders
to propel them, it seemed no time at all before they came in
view of the inlet the cow hunter had noticed. Miranda was
fully awake now, and she scanned the sun-flecked expanse
behind them anxiously, shading her eyes with a hand against
the harsh midday glare.

They'd almost reached the entrance to the estuary when
Peek, with all his attention on nosing the blunt bow of their
craft toward it, heard his companion's sharp intake of breath.

"What is it?" His voice dropped almost to a whisper, in
spite of his conviction that no one could possibly be closer
than a mile away. "You see somethin'?"

Miranda hesitated while her eyes narrowed to slits to
study the hazy division between water and sky. "Another
boat," she said finally. "I'm sure of it, though they're still a
long way off!"

Peek hadn't allowed the exchange of words to interrupt
his rowing, and they were already entering the shadows of the
dense hedge of green that bordered the bay. After another

minute he put all his strength into one mighty pull, then lifted the oars as they glided noiselessly between the mangroves on either side of the inlet.

"That was a right near thing," he sighed, taking in two or three deep breaths before lowering the oars to row them upstream past a bend in the waterway. "You reckon they seen us?" Neither he nor Miranda had much doubt as to who was in the distant boat.

"I don't think so." The young woman's brow furrowed as she considered the possibility. "They were very far away, and with all the trees and plants behind us. . . ." She lifted her slim shoulders. "But of course they weren't near enough to make out any reactions."

Peek guided the boat around another bend and shipped the oars to give his arms a rest. "I reckon we'll know it soon enough if they did. We ain't goin' much of anyplace else till after it gets dark." He turned his body sideways to study the inlet ahead of them. "She 'pears to narrow down considerable up yonder a ways. I got a notion the only way out is how we come in."

Yet even as he said this he wondered. Among Cooter's favorite tidbits of wisdom when it came to choosing campsites or other places of lodging—including hotel rooms—was that even a rabbit doesn't trust itself to only one hole. With men like Ethan Cabell and his friends behind them, Peek figured it made sense to consider every possibility.

He lowered the oars into the water and rowed a little farther, to where a canopy of slender branches overhung the estuary. At this point he saw another narrow channel that led to a dead end some thirty feet off. Neither passage appeared to offer any outlet, but at least the second one was less noticeable from a distance. He glanced at Miranda, who seemed content to leave the decisions up to him for the time being, and swung the boat into it.

After looping the anchor rope around some convenient prop roots, he shipped the oars and rose stiffly to his feet. For several long minutes he stood motionless, contemplating what little he could see of the landscape around them. Then he stepped carefully up on the thwart in order to gain a better view. Miranda watched curiously but asked no questions—for which Peek was mightily grateful. He hesitated to admit even to himself the crazy notion he was mulling over in his mind.

Yet it did appear the pines and palm trees of the mainland were closer to this place than to most other points along the coast—possibly no more than a hundred yards off. And beyond the nearest thicket of mangroves was a broad reed-filled marsh with what appeared to be higher ground at its far end. The water ought to be shallow enough for wading, barring occasional deep holes, for even the open bay hereabouts was just a few feet deep for some distance offshore.

So it *might* be possible, if worse came to worst . . .

He shook himself out of his reverie and glanced at Miranda. The young woman was curled up in the stern of the boat now, once more fast asleep. She was clearly exhausted from her recent ordeal. And unlike her earlier slumber, this time her peaceful expression and regular breathing seemed to suggest complete confidence in Peek's ability to protect her and to do whatever planning—and worrying—needed to be done.

He wondered what she'd think if she knew of the wild scheme he'd just been considering: a hundred yards of wading through mangroves and sawgrass, with the ever-present dangers of quicksand, hidden drop-offs, and savage predators below the surface—including saltwater-dwelling alligators! A body would have to be almighty desperate to try something like that.

But it did offer another way out. . . .

Well, he told himself, stepping gently down from the thwart and resuming his seat, it wouldn't help things to fret about it. More than likely they'd just need to sit tight here until dark, when they could make their way back out into the open bay and resume their journey north.

Still . . . He reached to undo the anchor line and quietly took up an oar. There was no harm in seeing how far he could work the skiff in among that thicket of mangroves in front of them—which just happened to be another dozen yards closer to the distant mainland.

At all events, they'd be a little better hidden there.

Miguel's toe caught under a palmetto root, and he fell to his knees in the soft sand. He glanced up at his companion's broad back a few feet ahead and gasped hoarsely: "¡Momentito, amigo! Only a second to catch the breath, ¡Dios mio!"

Juan Castro halted, then turned and slowly retraced his steps to stand with both fists on his hips, glowering down at his fallen comrade. One of the fists was crudely bandaged with the bandanna he'd worn earlier about his neck. He was breathing heavily himself, but it seemed to Miguel that no amount of trekking through this ungodly wilderness ever managed to slow his partner's bull-like progress.

Both men's faces were marked with a livid tracery of cuts and scratches—galling reminders of their wild night's ramble among briar-filled brakes and whiplike tree limbs. It was more than twenty-four hours since they'd had any real chance to rest, much less to sleep.

They'd given in to a kind of panic, Miguel admitted reluctantly—and only to himself—once their original ambush of the *norteamericanos* had failed. Who would have thought the younger one could draw and fire so quickly? And so accurately? With nothing to aim at but the flashes from their two guns, he had succeeded in striking Juan Castro in the hand, wrecking his pistol and removing two fingers in the process.

Miguel's own desperate shooting had knocked the *gringo* from his saddle; but the *indio* survived. And that one was a devil incarnate! They'd been fortunate to evade the savage's first counterattack with breath still in their bodies. And in their mad dash to escape they'd had to abandon their horses.

Ever since, Cheeky Joe had given them no rest. Each time they thought they'd left him behind or gained a tiny bit of breathing space, there would be a jarring shot from some unseen direction—or worse, the spine-chilling cry of some bird that was no bird, often so close that it seemed at their elbows. They'd been reduced to lashing out at shadows. And each time they did, they found only the jungle!

All of those encounters had been too close for comfort, but so far none had drawn blood. Which led Miguel to the disturbing conclusion that the *indio* was toying with them, like a cat with a mouse.

"*¡Vámonos*, little one!" the larger man growled after only a second or two had passed. "*¡No hay que parar!* We must keep going until we find a place to seize more horses. And weapons!"

Miguel still had his own pistol, shoved down behind in the waistband of his trousers. But he saw no need to call this fact to his brutal partner's attention. Juan Castro might want the remaining firearm for himself. And Miguel had no plans to yield up his surest means of protection.

"All right, *amigo*. Just another few moments, while I . . ."

But Castro had already turned away, and he began striding into the woods before the smaller man could climb to his feet. Miguel glared after him and muttered a silent curse under his breath. Then he rose and started to follow.

What happened next was so sudden that it froze him in his tracks.

The big tattooed sailor had just ducked his head to pass

under one of the low-hanging branches of a huge and ancient live oak, when another large figure dropped noiselessly from the upper limbs and smashed him to the ground. Miguel instantly recognized the bright-colored shirt of the *indio*, and his hand went for his pistol. Yet he hesitated, unable to fire without the risk of hitting his *compadre*.

Even as the smaller man stared in open-mouthed fascination at the two enormous bodies grappling furiously in the dirt, it began to appear that his muscular associate was being swiftly subdued. The *indio* had avoided Castro's fists and arms with the quickness of greased lightning. Now he was bearing down relentlessly with a scissors hold that had Castro bent almost double.

Should Miguel rush to his aid? Yes, certainly, without a doubt. But on the other hand . . .

If Juan Castro was no match for this *condenado* angel of death who'd stalked and harried them like dogs through an entire day and a night, what could he hope to accomplish with his own slender frame? It would be madness even to attempt it. What help could his own death be to his rapidly weakening partner?

The pangs of guilt were merely temporary. Juan Castro, after all, was not the most desirable of companions. His only true assets were his enormous size and his bull-like strength. And if these were not sufficient to protect himself and those with him from one solitary and determined enemy . . .

With a shrug of resignation and another furtive glance at the two sweating bodies locked in deadly combat on the ground, Miguel took a cautious step backward, and then another. Suddenly he turned and darted quickly away between the trees.

An instant before he'd left the sounds of the struggle behind, he thought he heard Chekita Joe say quietly: "You 'member what I said 'bout makin' me a shirt? Where you think I ought to start? Here . . . ?

If there were tortured screams of agony that followed, Miguel was running too fast to pay them any heed.

❖ ❖ ❖

Peek's head dropped forward and he jerked it up with a start. He'd let himself doze off while seated on the middle thwart of the skiff. How long had he slept? Had their pursuers managed to locate their hiding place while he was wool-gathering?

In sudden panic, he peered all around him while listening intently to the nearby sounds among the mangroves. Nothing could be heard but birds and insects. Momentarily relieved, he glanced at the sun through the ragged canopy of leaves a few inches overhead.

He'd only slept a few minutes, apparently. He uttered a long and grateful sigh. With Miranda still recovering from her hurts and exhaustion, one of them had to stay awake in case Cabell's men should see this inlet and come investigating.

He could feel his shirt clinging to his back from the midday heat, even in the partial shade of this stagnant backwater among the saltbush and mangroves. There was no breeze, and everything was very still. The only movement was the flicker of gnats and no-see-ums, with an occasional water bug skimming the glassy surface or hovering above it.

The silence and forced inactivity made Peek restless. He was tempted to rise to his feet or shift the boat's position in order to improve his seriously limited range of vision. But any such move would disturb the tight-knit lattice of branches that now enclosed them. And even a faint stirring of leaves in the calm estuary would be a dead giveaway to anyone who happened to be close enough to notice it.

Instead he reached for his canteen and took a long, slow drink. Then he gently replaced the container beside the sleeping young woman at his feet. From time to time he'd seen her rise up on her elbows to take a swallow from it, without ever opening her eyes or becoming fully awake.

She'd had a mighty rough time the past couple of days. And probably for longer than that. But he'd yet to hear her complain. Quint had told the truth to his outlaw friends: This here was a woman with steel inside of her.

He sat for a few minutes longer, watching the rise and fall of her breathing under the thin fabric of her blouse and reflecting what a lucky man Doc Westfield was—even in the short time he'd been on this earth—to have such a woman for his wife. Peek didn't count himself in the Doc's class as a man. Not yet anyway, and maybe not ever. But Miranda was his responsibility now, and he meant to see that her husband hadn't died in vain. He'd get her to safety or give his own life in the trying.

All the while he was thinking this he was listening—not to the familiar woodland sounds, which he'd managed to push to the back of his consciousness, but for any slight plash of oars or murmur of voices from the bay a hundred yards distant. If Cabell's search did bring him in range of their hiding place, Peek had a mind to be the first one who knew it.

An hour crept slowly by, and then another, with nothing to see or hear but the flicker and buzz of insects, the watery plop of fish jumping in the shallows to landward, and the occasional long, lazy swoop of a heron between the mangroves. Peek could feel his eyelids growing heavy from lack of sleep, and more than once he caught himself dozing again, only to blink awake and frantically try to shake off the cobwebs before resuming his watchfulness.

When the warning finally came he almost didn't heed it.

The many kinds of birds in the neighborhood, from jeering gulls and grackles to high-voiced ospreys, were so much a part of their surroundings that he'd all but shut his mind to them. At first the harsh *gaw-gaw-gaw* of two tiny black-faced balls of feathers that skittered from the mangroves a little way off scarcely earned a casual glance.

But then some unknown impulse made Peek take a second look. He felt the hair rise on the back of his neck as he realized what he'd seen. The mangrove cuckoo was one of the shyest birds around. But something—or someone—had upset these two so badly that they'd fled the safety of their hidden nesting place.

He held his breath and narrowed his eyes, trying to guess the distance to the thicket from which he'd seen the birds emerge. Too close. Too close to be out at the edge of the bay; and there was only one route through this maze of plant life that was liable to invite a nearer approach. Someone or something was on the estuary behind them!

It could be a gator or some other native predator. But Peek wasn't willing to bet his and Miranda's lives on it. If the intruders were human, that almost surely meant Cabell and his men. The likelihood of other visitors in this thinly settled wilderness was too remote to consider.

He looked down at his companion, unsure for a moment whether to rouse her or not. But she had already pushed herself up on one elbow with her dark eyes wide open, watching him alertly.

"Somebody comin'." He barely mouthed the words. Miranda nodded, then lifted herself up to put her head next to his. Her hair brushed his cheek. "'Pears they're in the channel yonder, and there ain't any other way out."

"What do we do?" Her own voice was a scarcely audible whisper. But there was no fear in it, and Peek saw that she held her husband's pistol ready. "Can we fight them?"

"I'd as soon not try it," he said soberly. "They's prob'ly three or four of 'em, and with us all in boats in this here li'l channel, somebody's goin' to get hurt bad or kilt. Might be us." He glanced past her at the reed-choked marsh and the distant trees of the mainland. Then he swallowed hard.

"I got a mind to try somethin' else, if you figure you're game for it. It ain't goin' to be no Sunday school social, though." Without mincing words, he explained his thoughts about wading to the mainland and making their escape into the forest.

Miranda's eyes were studying the marsh as he talked. Suddenly she interrupted him: "All right. Turn around for a second."

Puzzled, Peek did as he was asked, shifting his position on the thwart so his back was toward her. "I ain't sure how much time we got," he went on in a half-whisper, "maybe just a couple minutes. We'll need to try an' hold our guns up out of the water, so's . . ."

"Shh. I understand." The next sound he heard was a faint sloshing and gurgling. He glanced around and saw the blond-haired young woman in water up to her armpits, balancing the pistol and her hastily bundled dress on top of her head.

"Come on," she whispered, turning away while suppressing a grin at the cow hunter's expression. "The last one ashore is a rotten egg!"

20

PEEK WASTED NO more time on talk, pausing only long enough to sling the canteen over his shoulder and unbuckle his cartridge belt, wrapping it tightly so he could carry it in one hand. Then he swung his feet around and slipped noiselessly into the dark water on the far side of the boat.

He'd kept his boots on, though they were a considerable nuisance as he slogged clumsily forward, treading gingerly on the springlike roots and sinking ankle-deep into the soft muck of the bottom. He hoped Miranda was still wearing hers also. Everywhere about them there were root tips and other sharp objects that could rip open the flesh and cripple a person in seconds. He could see nothing like footwear in her carefully balanced bundle of clothing, so he had a notion she had kept hers on.

They advanced single-file, moving their legs slowly and evenly so as to make no unnecessary waves or splashing sounds. Peek was content to let Miranda keep the lead for now. She showed no hesitation as she traced a serpentine path of least resistance among the close-growing mangroves toward the open salt marsh and the forest beyond.

He'd heard and seen nothing of the men he believed were behind them since that first fluttering disturbance of the cuckoos. Yet all of Peek's instincts told him they were there, and were likely coming closer.

It could be that they'd turn back and make for open water without ever finding the skiff. In that case, or if he'd been wrong about what upset the cuckoos, all of this here was an exercise in futility. Still worse, they were leaving behind their fastest and most comfortable means of travel to some eventual place of safety.

But the alternative was a risk Peek wasn't prepared to take. There was nowhere else to go except out the way they'd come, and even with the skiff partly hidden as it was, a person could hardly miss their hiding place once he rounded that final bend in the waterway. The distance from there to the skiff would be less than thirty feet. And as he'd told Miranda, a gunfight between two open boats in such tight quarters would be mighty close to suicide.

Still, he reminded himself, the course they were taking now was a chancy thing too. Before long they'd be crossing an open salt marsh, perhaps seventy yards wide, toward what he could only hope and pray was solid ground. Peek knew from his own experience that a good part of that area was clearly visible to a man standing on the thwart of a boat. And if that man was any kind of a pistol shot . . .

There'd be few places for concealment once they got

that far—just some taller bunches of reeds that followed a winding channel through the marsh, and more high reeds on the landward side. The rest of the sedgelike growth wasn't over two or three feet high. As for protection from bullets, there would be none at all until they reached the safety of the distant trees.

Even without the possibility of being shot at, there were still the dangers of sawgrass, quicksand, and underwater drop-offs, along with the crabs, rays, snakes, gators, and who knew what else hiding beneath the surface of these murky waters.

They arrived at the edge of the marsh without incident, and after a hurried but careful survey of the mangrove thickets behind them, Peek took the lead and they started across the reed-choked expanse. Spurning the narrow channel that twisted and buttonhooked its way among thick clumps of peat and marsh grass, he chose the most direct route while still trying to take advantage of any available cover.

Their progress was slower and more exhausting than it would have been along the channel's sandy bottom, though the distance was two or three times shorter. More than once they had to take hold of the grass with their hands and pull themselves bodily through clinging masses of underwater roots. Several times they narrowly missed plunging into stands of razor-sharp sawgrass.

At Peek's whispered instruction, Miranda remained close to his elbow, so they'd always be within arm's reach if one or the other should accidentally blunder into quicksand or a sudden deep hole. More from luck than design, they avoided these hazards. But neither could avoid being snared and tripped repeatedly by the submerged tangles of wirelike roots.

By the time they'd made it halfway across they were caked with mud and gasping for breath. Yet Peek forged ahead grimly with no pause for rest. He felt an urgent need to get them past this exposed place of danger as quickly as it could be done. Once they'd left it, and were safely out of view behind a screening wall of trees, there would be time enough for more leisurely travel.

The marsh had grown shallower as they neared the forest, and despite their exhaustion, he gritted his teeth and started picking up the pace. They were calf-deep in water and twenty yards from shore when they heard the shout behind them.

Without wasting precious time on a backward look, the cow hunter plunged forward with Miranda at his side. Suddenly they felt the angry whip of a bullet over their heads, followed a second later by the flat report of a pistol. Peek stopped and unholstered his six-gun.

"Start runnin'!" His voice was a hoarse bark as he turned to face their attackers. "Head for the trees! I'll try an' hold 'em off till you get there!"

"No! Come with me!" Miranda seized him by the arm and started pulling him toward the cover of the forest. "They want me alive!" she gasped as Peek took a reluctant step backward. "That first was only a warning! Stay close, and they won't risk hitting me!"

It was no time for questions, even if he'd had the breath for them. Peek snapped one well-placed shot at the stand of mangroves where he thought the boats were hidden and heard a startled yelp in confirmation. Then he turned, and with arms around each other's waists they plashed and stumbled through the shallows to the high wall of reeds along the far shore.

When they were out of sight behind these it was just a few more shambling steps to the wooded cover of pines and laurel oaks.

After another dozen yards they came to a small clearing blanketed over with pine needles, and Miranda dropped to her knees. Her thin shoulders rose and fell with deep, racking sobs as she fought to recover her breath.

Peek accepted the unplanned halt without comment, for he was close to being used up himself. He turned and kept a wary eye on their backtrail, resting his weight against the thick bole of a pine to ease a painful stitch in his side. While his own breathing grew more regular, he replaced the empty cartridge in his revolver with a fresh one from the belt in his fist.

He'd little doubt Cabell and his men would come after them. But they'd face the same obstacles of water and marsh that the lady and he had just left, and their progress could scarcely be faster. It should at least give them time for a brief rest.

As he rebuckled the cartridge belt around his hips and bent to tie the thongs, the thought came to him that he could hide nearby and try to pick them off one by one as they crossed the open marsh. But shooting men from ambush still went against the grain. And—what was more important—he might not be able to finish the job before one or another got lead into him. And where would that leave Miranda?

After several minutes he spoke over his shoulder in a half whisper, taking care not to look in the young woman's direction:

"You best be gettin' dressed if you ain't done it already. We got to be movin', 'fore them others has a chance to . . ."

As if to lend urgency to his words, a faint splash came to them from beyond the mangroves, followed in quick succession by two or three more.

"I'm almost ready," she answered from the ground behind him. "Just one more second while I unlace these boots. . . ."

"Leave 'em on." The stress of the situation had brought an unintended harshness to Peek's voice. He turned and went on more gently: "I know the wet is liable to cause blisters. But they's prickly pears an' saw palmettos an' all manner of hurtful things in these woods hereabouts. Not to mention snakes. We'll be better off takin' a chance on the blisters."

Miranda nodded. "Yes, of course," she said with a weary sigh. "I wasn't thinking." When she'd retied the boots, Peek held out a hand to help her to her feet.

He took the lead at a brisk walk, choosing a winding course among the vine-draped trees and thickets of dahoon holly, with the idea of putting distance behind them while saving some energy for a later burst of speed if necessary. Miranda kept pace gamely, uttering no words of complaint, even when she tripped over a root or lost her footing briefly on a slick carpet of pine needles.

Peek noticed that she'd hiked up her skirts for easier movement in the forest. But it was her pale face and flushed cheeks that he kept glancing at while they trudged steadily forward.

"You doin' all right?" he asked after some ten minutes of walking in silence. He knew the question might be taken as idle conversation, but he seriously wanted to know. There was something about the rigid set of the lady's finely chiseled jaw and her uncommon quietness that was starting to worry him.

"I mean," he said, dropping back beside her, "you reckon you'll be able to keep on like this till dark? Or do we need to make some diff'rent plans?"

"What else can we do?" she replied dully without looking up. Then her voice grew more deliberate: "You just lead, and I will stay with you."

"All right," Peek agreed mildly. "But anytime you need to hold up an' take a breather, you let me know." He paused to glance at her out of the corner of his eye. "You hear?"

Miranda nodded but said nothing further.

❖   ❖   ❖

Miguel had no idea where he was at the moment, or

how far he'd come. But he had a definite direction of travel in mind: south. He meant to keep going south until he reached a port like Fort Myers or Punta Rassa. There he'd find a berth on a ship—any ship at all that would take him farther south and would sooner or later put into some harbor in his native Cuba.

For six generations his family had farmed a small acreage near the eastern tip of the island: a poor place that he'd sneered at with contempt when he left it to seek his fortune on the sea. Now the serenity and simplicity of that life held an irresistible attraction. There had been yucca and plantains, and fish for the taking; and a thatched roof over the head, with cool afternoon breezes. In all honesty, what else did a man need to pass his days in contentment?

The only *indios* in that region were poor farmers like Miguel and his kind. And what was more important, they were all lovers of peace!

It had not been difficult to find his way south, even among Florida's pine barrens and junglelike hammocks. He'd only to keep the sun on his right through the afternoon, and in the morning it would rise on his left. Nor was he far from the coast. Sometimes, when the wind was just right, he could taste salt in the air.

Another day, perhaps two, should be all that was needed. He'd been moving swiftly with few stops to rest; for he had no way of knowing whether or not he was still followed. There had been no obvious sign of pursuit since he'd left the scene of the two big men fighting. But it was always safest to anticipate the worst.

When night came he'd have little choice but to stop until morning. The risk of losing his way was simply too great. He'd rest then. But he would not sleep—not even for a few precious seconds.

If that merciless dog of the devil was behind him, the hours of dark would be a time of deadly peril.

For more than an hour, Peek and Miranda had been hearing the sounds of Cabell's men behind them. At first it was from a distance, and only when someone raised his voice to announce the discovery of a footprint or other sign of their passing. But the sounds had gotten steadily louder, and by now there could be no doubt that the bad men were gaining on them.

Alone, Peek might have outrun them—though he couldn't be sure of that. Someone in their crowd was a skilled tracker, and all of them moved easily in the forest.

But Miranda, despite her grit and determination, was practically fainting from exhaustion. It showed in every line of her youthful face and body. The cow hunter thought it a wonder that she still managed to keep putting one foot before the other.

Without being asked, he'd stopped several times to let her rest and catch her breath. But it was never enough, for the longer they stayed in one place the closer their pursuers came.

To make matters worse, he'd grown painfully aware of the blisters inside his own wet boots, and when his companion started to limp and lean heavily on his arm, he knew the game was almost up. At their present shambling pace it would be just a matter of minutes before Cabell and his henchmen ran them to ground. And there wasn't a thing in the world they could do to prevent it.

He set his jaw and kept plodding grimly ahead, until they came at last to a clearing among the trees, divided in two by the bole of a huge pine that had been brought down to earth by some long-ago storm. He stopped to consider the layout while Miranda stood clutching his elbow, breathing in ragged gasps and trembling with fatigue.

"Reckon this here's as far as we go," he said, turning his head to glance at the forest behind them. "We ain't about to outrun them men back yonder. And them an' us both know it." Miranda looked up at him and he gazed into her flushed and perspiring face. "This openin' in the woods is where we make our stand."

He put a supporting arm around her waist and escorted her quickly to the fallen tree. Then, after another wary glance over his shoulder, he lifted her up so she could scramble to the shelter of its opposite side. A minute later he was kneeling beside her.

"You just set still an' catch up on your breathin'," he said quietly. "I don't 'spect we got long to wait." He unholstered his Colt and laid its barrel across the rough bark of the tree, keeping his eyes on the woods at the far edge of the clearing.

After a minute he added under his breath, "But whilst you're at it you might lay hands on that six-shooter of your husband's. 'Case anything happens to me . . ."

"Nothing will happen to you."

There was something so firm and certain about her whispered declaration that it startled him into lowering his eyes to look at her.

"It's just a feeling." She lifted one shoulder in what could have been a self-conscious shrug. "But I do feel very safe in your company, Peek. I've felt that way ever since you found me this morning."

He realized he was blushing and could think of nothing to say. Miranda shifted position so she could reach a hand into her skirt pocket. "But you needn't worry. I have James' revolver right here. And I haven't the slightest reservation about using it."

"Good girl," he muttered, a little too casually. Then he returned his gaze to the trees.

"This time I'll take more careful aim," she went on with icy deliberateness, "than I did the last time I saw them."

Peek kept his eyes on the forest. He needed no look to tell him of the bitter hatred that now darkened his companion's delicate features. The cold in her voice said it all. It almost made him shiver in the afternoon heat.

"You keep yourself down out of sight back of this tree," he said firmly after a moment of silence. "And don't you go to shootin' 'less they bring it to you. If it's a all-out war they want, I'll do my dangdest to see can I oblige 'em!"

Miranda made no reply, and he had an uncomfortable suspicion that his words hadn't impressed her. Yet in spite of his worry for her safety, he couldn't help but feel a stir of admiration. This here was a woman to ride the river with!

A few minutes later he heard the faint rustle of fabric against branches, and then they could make out stealthy movements among the shadowed woods before them. Soon Peek was able to identify Ethan Cabell's dark-suited bulk, standing partly concealed behind the jagged bole of a cabbage palm. Beyond and on either side of him were other stirrings that told of several men advancing, though it wasn't yet possible to guess who or how many.

"You-all just hold it up right there!" The cow hunter's voice rang out sharply above the background chatter of birds and insects. He saw the man in black freeze for an instant, then drop quickly to his knees behind the base of the palm.

"If y'all light a shuck right this second," Peek continued, his words now sounding unnaturally loud in the suddenly quiet forest, "you might just make it out of this country ahead of a rope an' a posse!" He paused for breath with his Colt aimed at where Cabell had gone to ground, his eyes probing the woods that extended to right and left of him.

There was no reply from the outlaws.

"Or come on ahead," Peek shouted with a long-suppressed fury, "an' take your chances if you're a mind to! I'm wore to a frazzle, my feet hurt, and I feel 'bout as mean as a ole she-bear with young'uns. So it don't make a heap of nevermind to me which one you choose!"

Those were bold words, but he meant every one of them. In the past couple of days he'd been beaten, shot, chased through the woods, and a man he'd known briefly but considered a friend had been brutally murdered. The fur on Peek's back was up now, and he was mad clean through.

If they wanted to turn tail and run, he'd leave 'em to a posse like he'd said. At least till he could get Miranda to some place of safety. But he had an idea they wouldn't do it. And if that was the way they wanted it, he'd be every bit as pleased to meet them in the smoke.

21 🌿

THERE WAS A long minute of silence. Then Cabell's voice rose from a clump of palmettos a few yards to the left of the tree where he'd first gone to cover. Peek's gun muzzle swung in this new direction almost of its own accord.

"Who the hell are you?" There was frustration and anger in the gambler's voice, and he sounded a little winded as well. Peek allowed himself a cold smile.

"Peek Tillman's the name! We met out yonder on the prairie a couple weeks back. I told your boys to remember me, 'cause I figured it wasn't the last time we'd meet!"

Suddenly, a stirring in the branches caught his eye, a dozen yards to the right of Cabell and farther back among the trees. "You tell that man to stay put if he wants to keep his hide in one piece!"

The stealthy movement continued and Peek snapped a shot into the midst of the trembling leaves, low down and close to the ground. There was a muttered curse and the motion stopped abruptly.

"Whenever I tell y'all somethin', I ain't a mind to repeat

it! Now you can either back off an' light a shuck by the time I count to three, or we can open the ball. We got us a big ole tree trunk for cover here, and alls I can see that y'all got is some branches an' leaves!"

He was running a bluff, and a dangerous one at that. So far he could guess the location of only two of their pursuers, and even they might have moved. But Peek wanted each man out there to believe he'd been seen, and that he could be the next target.

He'd quietly replaced the empty cartridge in his Colt while he was talking, and now it was once more aimed at what he thought was Cabell's hiding place.

"One! . . ."

"All right!" It seemed Cabell had shifted position only slightly, perhaps to some hidden depression in the ground. There were no trees of any size in his immediate vicinity. "All right, have it your way! You just hold your fire an' we'll head back the way we came!" There was a brief pause. "But you got to give me your word that you won't do no more shootin' whilst we're leaving!"

"I ain't the one here what goes in for back-shootin'!" Peek responded testily. Miranda put a hand on his arm.

"Do you really think they'll do it?" she whispered, close to his ear.

Peek didn't look at her; his eyes were scanning the wooded brakes in front of them. "You ever know him to tell the truth up till now?" he asked in a low tone.

"No," the young woman answered coldly.

"What I figured." Peek raised his voice again: "But just so's I won't get all flustered an' worry whichaway ever'body's headed, you just holster your six-shooter an' stand up there in the open till the others has left!"

He thought he could hear Cabell curse softly. Then after a couple of seconds: "How do I know I can trust you?"

"You don't. But somebody told me you're a gambler, Mister Cabell. So you just lay your bet down an' pick up a card!"

There was another long silence. Then the man in black broadcloth rose slowly behind the palmettos, holding his empty hands away from his body. The dense thicket that had concealed him came almost to his waist as he stood up and his gaze came to rest on the downed tree and the cow hunter behind it.

"All right boys!" he called as his eyes met Peek's. "You-all heard the feller. I reckon he ain't given us no other choice!"

The faint rustling of fabric against branches could be heard again, and several dark figures started to move. Peek kept watching Cabell, but his attention was on either side of the black-clad man, alert for other telltale motions he might spot from the corners of his eyes.

He didn't expect the outlaws to leave without a fight— not when they'd got their quarry pinned down and outnumbered to boot. So it came as no surprise when he saw someone approaching stealthily on his left, in a clear attempt to outflank their covered position.

"Keep a sharp lookout on the right," he whispered to Miranda, while his own attention stayed on the advancing man. "I got a notion they'll try comin' at us from both sides now."

He waited his chance with the calm patience of a hunter. And sure enough, before many seconds had passed the man broke into the open, making a quick dash from one stand of trees to another.

Almost without thinking, Peek led him slightly and squeezed off his shot. The Colt bucked in his fist and he saw the man take two more plodding steps before sprawling head-long among the low-growing branches of a wax myrtle.

Suddenly the entire forest seemed filled with smoke and the jarring explosions of pistol fire.

In the same instant the cow hunter fired, Ethan Cabell's hand swept down like lightning for his pearl-handled revolver. Peek saw the movement and desperately brought his Colt's muzzle back to the right. Too slow! Cabell's six-shooter was blossoming flame before his own could be got into line!

He heard an angry *thunk!* as the heavy bullet slammed into the tree bark in front of him, and somewhere in the back of his mind was an awed realization that the gunfighter had missed! He took one more scant instant to make sure of his own aim, then put a hole through the top button of Cabell's dark vest.

The big man staggered, and his next shot went wild. With a guttural snarl of pain and rage he stepped from behind the palmettos, gripping his revolver in both hands.

When it started to lift, Peek shot him again.

The pistol seemed to grow heavy in the other man's fingers. Yet he spread his legs apart and tried tenaciously to bring it in line. Peek fired into him a third time and Cabell dropped to his knees.

"Let go the six-shooter!" the cow hunter shouted, "an' I'll leave you be! It ain't been no help to you so far!"

"God damn you!" Cabell's black suit was smeared with blood and his face was a twisted mask as he glared at his foe across the clearing. "I'll see you in hell bef—!"

Again his pistol lifted, and again the Colt bucked against Peek's sweating palm. This time he saw the gambler's eyes roll back in his head, and he toppled slowly forward to lie face down in the sand.

Somewhere on the fringes of his consciousness during the desperate shootout, he'd been aware that Miranda was firing too. Quickly now, he turned in her direction.

"You okay?" He felt a wave of relief even before the question left his lips. The young woman who knelt beside him with a smoking six-shooter in her dainty fist was clearly unharmed. And there was a faint smile of triumph on her pale features as she kept a wary eye on the woods to their right.

"Yes." After a moment she sat back and lowered the revolver to her lap. "I'm perfectly fine. And it gives me a certain satisfaction to report that the little man who once planned to 'have his way' with me, is not."

Peek's eyes flicked curiously to the edge of the clearing while he dug into his pocket for cartridges to reload his Colt. He could make out the sprawled form of a body there but could not see its face.

"Butch." Miranda spat the word. "A short, brutal name for a brutal mindless beast!" Her shoulders slumped and she sighed heavily. "There was a time," she went on in a dull and muted voice, "not so very long ago, when I'd not have believed any man's death could be a source of satisfaction. But the way that . . . creature . . . leered at me, and reached for me with his filthy paws . . ."

Peek put an arm around her shoulders, for he had a feeling that in spite of her angry words she was mighty close to tears. She leaned over and buried her head in his chest. Then after a moment she pushed herself away and turned to look about them. "Are the rest of them . . . ? I mean, did you . . . ?"

"Ethan Cabell won't go chasin' no more women through the Florida woods. I reckon I got lead into another one too, some feller I never seen before." He spun the cylinder on his reloaded pistol and shrugged.

"There could be others, but I ain't seen hide nor hair of 'em so far. I figure the safest thing is for us to just sit tight for the time bein', and keep a sharp lookout. Feller once told me that when they's wild Injuns in the neighborhood, the first one to move's usually the first one to die."

"That's good advice," a familiar voice said from the shadows of a laurel oak a dozen yards away. "'Long as you figure the Injuns ain't friendly!"

255

Peek hurriedly reached out a hand and laid it over Miranda's, gently forcing her revolver's barrel down. She had been ready to shoot almost as soon as she heard the unknown speaker. When she turned to meet the cow hunter's eyes, he was grinning from ear to ear.

"Now, where in the dickens did you come from?" he asked, keeping his own voice low so it wouldn't carry past the edge of the clearing.

"Followed the sounds of shootin'. 'Pears you didn't need my help, though."

"I sure wouldn't of turned up my nose at it if you'd got here a mite sooner!"

"You reckon it's all right for me to show myself? That friend of yours seems kind of quick on the shoot."

"She'll do when they's trouble shapin' up, and that's a fact. But I reckon she's figured out by now that you're one of the friendly Injuns. So come on in and have a set."

As the tall newcomer crossed the clearing to hunker down beside them, Peek smilingly met Miranda's eyes. "Miranda Westfield," he said formally, "Say hello to my good friend an' saddle pardner, Chekita Joe!"

Quint had deliberately hung back when the others started their advance on the Yankee woman and her companion. He did recall Peek's unusual name, and he'd guessed at their first meeting the young man with the tied-down six-shooter wouldn't be any bargain in a fight. As for the lady's ability and readiness to shoot, he had first-hand experience.

After he saw Billy go down he started drifting slowly back into the deeper cover of the trees. When Ethan Cabell took the first bullet from the cow hunter's Peacemaker, he simply turned tail and lit out running. He'd seen more than a few shootings in his day, and he knew at a glance that the gambler was finished.

By the time the echoes had stopped racketing through the forest he was five hundred yards away and still moving fast. With a mite of luck he'd cross that salt marsh to where they'd left their boats before anybody behind him took a notion to come looking.

And there should be just enough daylight left to row himself back to camp, pick up a few things, and take to the saddle.

He'd had a bad feeling about all this ever since Cabell let the woman escape after the death of her husband. Feelings ran strong in this part of the country toward men who mistreated women, and every hour she was loose increased the chance she'd find somebody to tell her story to.

Which is just what had happened.

If she and the cow hunter survived—which seemed more than a little likely now—the young man's talk of a rope and a posse was no idle bluff. Most men on this frontier would see no reason to involve judges and juries over such a clear-cut offense.

And it didn't matter how much buried gold there might

be on these islands hereabouts. A fellow couldn't spend any of it with his feet dangling three feet off the ground!

The only thing left now was to get clean out of the country, and to do it just as fast as his big sorrel horse would carry him. With a night and part of a day to lose himself out on that big trackless prairie, he might just make it . . . if he didn't waste around gathering daisies on the way!

There hadn't been any sounds of movement or voices from the silent forest for the better part of an hour. Finally, Cheeky Joe slipped off to scout the vicinity.

"Three men dead," he reported on his return. "Nobody else here." He hunkered down on the grass across from Peek and Miranda, who exchanged tired but heartfelt smiles of relief.

"Was another," the big man added with a shrug. "But he took off runnin', back the way they came."

"He'll be headed for the boats," Miranda said, looking at Peek.

The cow hunter nodded and got stiffly to his feet. "An' right about now he's welcome to 'em." He made a weary move to stretch his sore muscles. "Next time I catch myself hot-footin' it through these here woods without no horse underneath me, I hope somebody shoots me to put me out of my misery!"

"Reminds me," Cheeky Joe said, pushing his wide hat

brim away from his forehead, "I come acrost your pony a few miles back. Figured from how the reins was tied that you'd set him loose."

"No foolin'?" Peek grinned broadly. "Well, now that's a piece of luck! 'Least Miz Miranda here'll be able to give her blisters a rest till we reach some kind of a settlement."

"We'll take turns," the young woman said firmly while she grasped Peek's arm to pull herself up beside him. "It's been a long, hard journey for both of us!"

Cheeky Joe glanced at the sky and then got to his feet also. "Might's well wait till morning 'fore startin'," he said. "Day's almost over, and we got some graves to dig."

Miranda's grip on Peek's arm tightened and she lifted her eyes toward him. "Speaking of graves . . ." she said haltingly, her voice scarcely more than a whisper, "could you, or someone . . ." When he looked down, Peek saw her dark eyes had filled with tears. "—I mean, James is still back there. . . ."

Peek laid a gentle hand on top of hers. "I'll see to the matter personal," he said, "whatever you want done." Then he told her of the shallow grave he'd stumbled on near the couple's last campsite. "You . . . you figure on takin' him back up north with you?"

She hesitated only briefly. "No." Her voice was firm now, and she even managed a faint smile through her tears. "No, I think he would want to be buried here in Florida, near the place where he fell. He always had a great feeling of kinship toward those ancient peoples we studied, especially the warriors. I think it would please him to remain here with their spirits. He has certainly proved himself worthy of them."

"Then that's what we'll do," Peek agreed with a nod. "And we'll do it proper too, with a stone marker an' a preacher to read words over him an' ever'thing. Like you said, he's sure enough earned 'em."

He was aware of her warmth and softness as they stood there together in the late afternoon sun. To his surprise, the feeling didn't make him the least bit uncomfortable.

Later that evening, over a small fire after supper, Peek finally asked Cheeky Joe about the two sailors who'd ambushed them.

The Calusa's face was unreadable, his eyes veiled by the dark shadow of his hat brim. "Big one didn't make it," he said simply. "Wasn't up to the job. The little one . . ." He shrugged a calico-clad shoulder. "He ran. I let him."

"An' that first one, the one with all the tattoos . . . ?" Peek remembered vividly his companion's threat back at Punta Rassa, about skinning the big sailor alive. He wasn't sure he wanted to know any details if it really had happened. But his curiosity wouldn't let him drop the matter.

"Had me some plans," the native confirmed seriously, "to make a war shirt from his hide." Peek glanced at Miranda, sitting wide-eyed at his elbow, and wished with all his heart that he'd let sleeping dogs lie. He could feel the hairs on the back of his neck starting to tingle.

"But then I got to thinkin' 'bout all the hard work an' trouble a job like that would take—the skinnin' out, the stretchin' and scrapin', the curin', the sewin'. . . ." If Cheeky Joe was anything less than serious, there wasn't a hint of it in his manner. Peek grew aware that Miranda had turned to look at him. He avoided her eyes. ". . . An' finally I made up my mind that it just wasn't worth the effort." He put a hand to his neck and drew a rawhide cord from under his shirt. "So I took these instead. Lot handier to carry, an' prob'ly worth more in the long run."

At the end of the cord two heavy gold earrings clinked musically together as they glittered in the fire's light.

22 ✺

MIGUEL KNEW IT was time he should stop. The cobalt patches of sky beyond the limbs overhead were rapidly growing darker, and the shadows under the nearby clusters of vines and Spanish moss had turned an inky black.

But *where* to stop? That was the question. What sort of resting place could he find where he'd enjoy even modest safety with that dog of the Devil *indio* haunting his backtrail?

Every minute that passed, every wary step he took on his lonely trek through this dim wilderness, only served to deepen Miguel's conviction that the bloodthirsty savage was practically on his heels—the same merciless fiend who'd sworn to skin Juan Castro alive, and then appeared from nowhere to do it! Even now, hours later and miles from the scene, his former partner's fate aroused visions of terror in his overtaxed imagination.

He moved more slowly in the gathering dusk, scanning each unfamiliar shadow with care for hints of another's presence, pausing in midstride to swing his head nervously about at every strange and unexpected sound. It was like their journey the previous night—except then Juan Castro had been with him, and he wasn't so completely alone.

Tonight there were only his badly frayed senses to warn him—and the five bullets in his pistol to guard him.

He reached back to take hold of the weapon's comforting weight and shift it to the front of his waistband, where it would come more readily to hand in case of need. He'd keep on just a little farther before halting. There seemed to be some kind of a clearing among the trees ahead. . . .

He heard a horse blow and the faint jingle of harness before his eyes could pick out any shapes in the all-pervading darkness. As he froze in place, his fingers made their way to the pistol with scarcely a thought. He was standing just outside the clearing now. And something—someone—was less than a dozen feet in front of him.

A tall man, it appeared, though possibly not as large as the one he expected. But who could tell for certain in the near total absence of light?

Miguel did not wait for certainty. The pistol leapt in his hand almost the instant it came level. There was an orange stab of flame, a low-voiced moan of hurt and surprise, and the shadowy figure went down on its knees.

Miguel fired again and heard another gurgling cry over the echo of the gunshots. He watched while the dark figure seemed to melt into a shapeless mass on the ground. Then he shot into it a third time. After that he stood very still for many long seconds. Unable to detect any further signs of life from the motionless shadow before him, he finally stepped from the trees with his pistol cocked and ready.

He had no particular need or wish to approach the fallen body, and he gave it a wide berth as he crossed with slow and easy strides to where the man's horse stood with its head raised warily at the far edge of the clearing. The animal had retreated instinctively from the sounds and smell of death. But its reins still trailed the ground, and it had not gone far.

Miguel's gentle words managed to calm it, and after a few minutes he was able to get hold of the reins and put a foot in the stirrup. It was a big, muscular animal, one that might take him far from here by morning if there was a moon to offer guidance. And Miguel was prepared to let it do just that, once it occurred to him that the moon would rise in another few hours. Until then it would be enough just to feel those powerful muscles beneath him, steadily putting distance between himself and this accursed place of danger.

He'd already suspected it was some stranger that he'd killed, and this creature confirmed it. He'd seen the other's shaggy mount, and the two were not to be compared. On such a horse as this, he might outdistance even *el Diablo* himself!

When the moon at last peeked over the horizon they were in view of the prairie's western extension. Miguel guided the big sorrel through the trees and into the open, then swung its head south and cheerfully endured the unaccustomed jolting of a fast-moving canter. Already he could taste the salt spray of the Gulf on his lips. And Cuba itself was but a day's sail away!

❖   ❖   ❖

It was two hours longer before the moon rose above the trees to bathe the still figure in the clearing with its brilliant rays.

But Quint didn't mind the wait. He was past minding anything at all now. His bullet-riddled body lay sprawled face up on the grass, gazing at the sky with unseeing eyes.

It no longer even mattered that he'd never learn the identity of the stranger in the dark who'd so calmly and impersonally shot him to doll rags.

❖   ❖   ❖

"Heighdy, young'un!" Cooter grinned up at Peek from where he squatted nursing his coffee by the campfire. "Seems like I ain't put eyes on you in near a coon's age!" He rose to his feet and gripped the younger man's hand warmly. "Reckon it ain't been but nine or ten months. But without no news or nothin', I'd started thinkin' maybe you took off for Californy or some such heathen place!"

"Pert' near as bad," Peek answered with a grin of his own. He bent to fill his cup from the pot on the coals. The sky in the east was streaked with salmon at the start of a new day. "I been livin' the last couple months up to Princeton, New Jersey!"

"No foolin'?" The older man's eyes narrowed under his slouch hat and he took his friend's elbow to walk him a short distance from the fire, where the other Rocking JG cow hunters were exchanging furtive glances. A couple of them had knowing smiles on their faces.

Cooter lowered his voice. "You mean you an' that Westfield woman . . . ?"

Peek shifted his feet self-consciously and tasted his coffee in silence. It looked to his partner like he'd filled out a tad around the chest and shoulders since last he'd seen him. Or maybe it was just something different about how the younger man carried himself.

"I done heard about her husband's killin' an' ever'thing," Cooter went on softly when Peek seemed to hesitate. "Got it firsthand from Cheeky Joe a week or two after, though by now I reckon the story's traveled all the way up to Georgia an' back. You made quite a name for yourself, son, the way you took on Ethan Cabell an' his outfit almost single-handed, and wiped 'em out. . . ." He paused to spit tobacco juice. "Still, I wouldn't of thought you an' that lady . . . I mean, so soon after . . ."

"Aw, Cooter!" Peek felt himself blush in spite of everything he could do. And it came close to making him mad. "It wasn't nothin' like that. Miranda—Miz Westfield—was grateful for my help, is all. And it happened she'd got these rich friends up yonder with this big ole house an' a heap of spare rooms. . . ." He suddenly realized his voice had grown louder in response to Cooter's questioning. When he glanced toward the fire he saw the others were now openly staring at him.

"Anyway," he went on more quietly, turning his back on the unwanted audience, "after the lady'd had a couple months to get herself situated an' settled back in, she wrote askin' me to come up for a visit. I was cuttin' ties for the railroad up to Wildwood right then, with the dog days of summer a-starin' me in the face. So a li'l stay in the North sounded mighty appealin'." He paused for a swallow of coffee.

"'Sides, I figured I might never have another chance to get a look at that part of the country, or to see the kind of a life them university folks live. So I told myself, "What the heck? An' used what I'd got left from my cow-huntin' an' tie-cuttin' wages to buy me a ticket on the steam cars." Peek grinned broadly. "An' the way them rich folks all looked after me an' fussed over me, it had swingin' that ol' two-sided ax down in the swamps beat all hollow!"

He fell silent for a moment, and his face grew more serious.

"Like you said, I'd started gettin' a name for myself hereabouts. And it weren't just exactly a name I much wanted. I figured if I could sort of drop out of the picture for a while, it'd give ever'body time to forget. An' maybe pin that gun artist title on some other young buck."

Cooter nodded. "I think you done a wise thing thataway. They's a heap more important 'complishments for a man to be knowed for, than just bein' good with a gun."

"That was my thinkin'." Peek finished his coffee and flipped out the grounds. "You know, some of them rich folks up yonder didn't have no more'n I got when they started. But if a man's willin' to work hard, save his money, and use his noggin to in-vest it careful—say, in land or orange groves or cattle—there ain't no tellin' where he might wind up. I plan to hang on to my wages from this year's cow hunt, an' that'll make a start. Then who knows? One of these days Peek Tillman could be a name to reckon with, right alongside men like Judge Ziba King!"

Cooter hooked his thumbs in his suspenders, cocked his head to one side and studied his friend's face for a long minute. "I got me a notion," he said finally, "that you're just the feller to do her!" He clapped Peek on the shoulder and the younger man started to turn away.

But Cooter's curiosity still wouldn't let him drop the subject of Miranda Westfield. He pulled his companion to him and whispered in his ear:

"So you an' that Yankee lady didn't never . . . ? I mean, you ain't . . . ?"

"Cooter," Peek drew himself up to his full height and met his friend's eyes. "Miz Miranda Westfield is one of the finest ladies I ever known, or will ever hope to know. And I believe I'd flat shoot any man that said any diff'rent." He paused to take a breath.

"But all her roots an' her friends an' family is away up the country yonder, together with the work she was doin' with her husband. She means to go back to college now for some kind of a higher de-gree, maybe even be a Doc of Philosophy her ownself. That there's her world, and it suits her real fine. . . ."

He shrugged and his eyes lifted toward the brightening horizon studded with palm trees and the gray domes of cypress. "And this here ol' Florida backcountry is mine. There ain't a awful lot the two has in common. And I reckon that's just as true of me an' Miranda.

"Will we stay in touch an' swap letters time to time? I'd surely like to think so. And maybe we'll even see each other in our travels here an' there. We'll always have some warm friendly feelin's for one another, no matter what. But that there's the sum total of it. And for me it's a-plenty."

Despite all of Cooter's stern-voiced moralizing, Peek could see from the sorrowful expression on his face that the old cuss was a romantic at heart. He looked so down in the mouth right then that Peek couldn't keep from laughing.

"What's more," he said, jabbing a friendly elbow into his saddle partner's ribs, "I found out that that lady is just a ace shy of her twenty-sixth birthday! Why, she's almost ready for the rockin' chair an' the liniment! Now, me, I'd sooner throw my rope over some partly broke filly that can still kick up her heels!"

Cooter favored him with a long sideways glance. Then he grinned and shook his head. "You best pray to your Maker you don't never latch onto such a female as that. She's liable to clamp a ring in your nose an' turn you ever which way but loose!"

"Might be. But it could be a heap of fun learnin' the ropes!" He paused, smiling at a memory. "Come to think on it, there was this gal on the train from Savannah to

Gainesville—pretty as a button and kind of pert along with it. We talked a mite. An' maybe after this drive is over . . ."

"Mount up!" Ed Porter's bellowed command sliced through the brisk morning air like a hatchet. Peek and Cooter interrupted their conversation to go fetch their horses.

The Cracker pony tossed his head and did a little sideways dance when Peek put a foot in the stirrup, just to show he was ready to travel with no wasting around. Peek grinned as he swung a leg over and turned his mount. He felt the same way himself.

"You're right, boy." He put both hands on the pommel and inhaled deeply. "It's a fine day for a ride, and a great day to be alive!" Then he lifted the pony into a canter and they loped out onto the prairie.

"Head 'em up!" the trail boss hollered from the point some sixty yards away. "And move 'em out!"

THE END

ACKNOWLEDGMENTS

No work of historical fiction would ever be completed by me without the input from various experts of whom I unabashedly take advantage to fill gaps in my knowledge. Unfortunately, by the time a novel is finished I've often forgotten where and from whom I gleaned this or that tidbit of information. I've made a partial effort to remedy this oversight in the present case and would like to publicly extend my thanks to Dr. William Marquart of the University of Florida, for his definitive debunking of Old John Gomez and Gasparilla the Pirate; Carlos and Dr. Maria Santa Maria, and fellow teachers Juan Cordova and Larry Lyall, for their invaluable Spanish language assistance; Mr. Lynn Bingham of Idaho Falls, Idaho, who shared firsthand insight into the fearsome experience of cattle stampedes; Allen Waggener, Florida cattleman and sometime "gator wrangler," and Dr. Andy Nichols, parapsychologist and one-time gator wrestler, for their knowledge of Florida's most notable reptile; and J. T. Glisson, for his unparalleled knowledge of all things Floridian. Last but not least, I would like to thank Henry James Butler, Regina Stahl Brisky, David Brisky, and the folks at Pineapple Press for their ongoing support and encouragement.

HISTORICAL NOTES

Alligator calling: A highly developed art still practiced by a few native Crackers. There are many accounts of the fierce reptiles being lured out of the water and onto solid ground by skilled callers. It was only one of several methods used by south Florida cow hunters to rid the "gator holes" of their inhabitants and obtain water for their herds, however. A more prosaic approach involved the use of a specially designed hook and ropes.

Alligator wrestling: This dangerous pursuit is rendered slightly less so by the fact that while the muscles alligators use to clamp their jaws shut are enormously powerful, those used to open them are relatively weak—allowing the "wrestler" to hold the mouth closed with the grip of one hand. Still, there remains a definite risk of losing one's fingers or other body parts in the process—even for former Seminole chiefs!

Brevard County: At the time of the story, it encompassed all or part of six present-day Florida counties, extending south from Orange County to Lake Okeechobee along the Atlantic Coast—with a total population of some 500 humans and 6,000 cattle.

Calusa Indians: A fierce warrior people who dominated southwest Florida from the time of the early Spanish explorations until at least the eighteenth century. Many believe the tribe to have disappeared completely prior to the arrival of the Seminoles, but I have my doubts about this theory, especially in view of the tenacious survival of similar aborigines in Europe (such as the Picts and the Basques). It is *just possible* that Chekita Joe (whose Second Seminole War namesake, incidentally, was reported to be unusually tall for a Seminole) either elaborated upon or was honestly mistaken about his ancestry. In any case, it's not likely that anyone who knew him would be tempted to call him a liar.

Cattle drives in Florida: Even from as far east as the Indian River, cattle were customarily driven west across the peninsula in the nineteenth century, to Punta Rassa or ports on the Manatee River, from where they could be shipped to the lucrative Cuban market. There were no deep-water ports on the Atlantic south of St. Augustine at the time.

Circle O Ranch: See *Ziba King*.

"Coon rack": See *Cracker horse*.

Cow hunter: Florida's name for those hardy individuals whose challenging livelihood it was to hunt wild long-horned cattle out of the state's swamps, hammocks, and palmetto prairies, and then bring them to market. (Florida remained an open-range state until 1947; until then, the stock roamed freely.) "Cowboy" is strictly a Western term, and many an old-timer still insists that it was a man's job in these parts: No "boys" need apply!

Cracker horse: A distinct, registered breed native to Florida. The unimpressive-looking Cracker horse was legendary for its stamina and endurance on this hostile frontier. Descended from sturdy Spanish stock, it is shaggy-maned, small (typically about fourteen hands), highly intelligent, and sure-footed among the treacherous bogs and palmetto prairies of Florida's backcountry. Many have a natural running walk, and some a single-foot gait known as a "coon rack." Long strings of remounts, or "remudas," were unknown on Florida cattle drives; both the cow hunter and his horse worked "from can't see to can't see."

Cypress dome: The pond cypress is one of two ancient species native to Florida and related to California's redwoods and giant sequoias. These trees frequently congregate in "domes," or circular stands, in which the trees grow progressively taller as they approach the center. The ground underneath may range from marshy to completely submerged, and is generally studded with a profusion of low-growing woody "cypress knees." Such domes are easily recognized from a distance in open country and may still be seen in parts of the "real Florida" south of Disney World.

Hamilton Disston: A nineteenth-century entrepreneur and visionary who purchased four million acres of "public lands" from the cash-strapped Florida Legislature (at 25 cents an acre!), then plunged his considerable energies and fortune into a long-term scheme to drain most of it (including Florida's largest lake). Although his assault on Lake Okeechobee was not ultimately successful, he did manage to destroy vast areas of irreplaceable wetlands and to change the natural course of the Caloosahatchee River forever. Confronted in the end by the dual specters of bankruptcy and failure, Disston shot himself to death in 1893.

Florida's Spanish Heritage: Although many do not realize it, Florida was a Spanish colony for 236 years—half again as long as it's been part of the U.S. The ties with Cuba, just 90 miles away, have remained close ever since. With this in mind, Peek Tillman's informal knowledge of Spanish is as common as it would be for an "uneducated" cowpuncher from Texas or California.

Fort Basinger: Originally constructed during the Second Seminole War (on December 21, 1837) by Colonel Zachary Taylor's troops for use as a base while they proceeded south down the Kissimmee River, this fort was named for an officer killed three years earlier in the Dade Massacre. As with many such military posts, both here and in the West, a civilian settlement developed nearby.

Fort Ogden: Established as Camp Ogden on July 11, 1841, about 20 miles north of the Peace River's outlet into Charlotte Harbor, its tenure as a military post only lasted three months. Following the Third Seminole War (1856–58) it became known as Fort Ogden and was a popular destination for newly arrived settlers, especially cattlemen. A wharf was built there in 1859 for the transshipment of beef to Cuba, but this enterprise was curtailed by the War Between the States and was later abandoned in favor of more desirable ports at Punta Rassa and along the Manatee River. In 1880 Fort Ogden had a population of 500, which dwindled after Arcadia was named the seat of DeSoto County eight years later.

Gasparilla the Pirate: See Juan Gomez.

Juan ("Old John") Gomez: A historical figure—fisherman, charter boat captain, and *raconteur*—who was well-known along Florida's southwest coast before his death in 1900. It was Gomez who almost single-handedly perpetrated one of the most enduring frauds in our state's too-often fictionalized history. There is absolutely no record whatever in any contemporary document to support the existence of a pirate known as José Gaspar or Gasparilla. The character evidently grew full-blown from Gomez' fertile imagination, based in part on the names of islands that appear on maps several hundred years older than the supposed nineteenth century freebooter. The old storyteller's fanciful lies were reported in print by various writers who should have known better, and even today there are many who stoutly insist that Gaspar was a real person. He wasn't. And one tragic legacy of Gomez' innocent prevarications is the wanton destruction of dozens of important pre-Columbian archaeological sites by the greedy and gullible, in search of "buried pirate treasure" that never existed!

Hammock: A local term that is best understood from its Indian origin, which means "shaded area." Typically, these are dense thickets of hardwoods that either occupy the flood plains of rivers ("low hammocks") or rise slightly above surrounding prairies, swamps, or pine-studded flatlands ("high hammocks").

Hijo de cabrón: Literally, "son of a goat." But the implication, based on the common association of that species with sexual amorality, is highly insulting in Spanish. The only thing worse than being called the *son* of a goat, of course, is . . .

Ziba King: A historical figure who was a preeminent Florida cattleman, businessman, and civic leader of the late nineteenth century. He moved from Tampa to Fort Ogden in the 1870s, where he opened and operated a mercantile store; later he became involved in cattle ranching, orange grove ownership, and banking. At the time of the story, his Circle O brand was well-known all over southwest Florida, and it was one of the largest cattle operations in the state. Though frequently referred to as "Judge King," he was in fact a justice of the peace. But on Florida's frontier this tended to amount to the same thing in practice; the nearest district court was in

Key West, and it only met four weeks out of the year.

Mangroves: Most often (as in this book) the term refers to a community of salt-tolerant plants of several different species that inhabit tropical or subtropical coastlines such as south-west Florida's. In addition to saltbush, buttonwood, *et al.*, there are three distinct varieties of mangroves found in these communities: **red mangroves**, which grow in or immediately adjacent to the water and are characterized by a dense network of aerial prop roots spreading downward from the trunks and lower branches; **black mangroves**, which inhabit sandy shorelines and have stubby vertical root extensions that project several inches up from the ground; and **white mangroves**, the most landward-growing of the three. At the time of the story, virtually the entire Gulf Coast south of Tampa Bay was lined with these dense thickets. Nowadays they've given way to development and are relatively rare north of the Ten Thousand Islands.

Marshtackie: Of the same general descent as the Cracker horse, this stocky, short-gaited, and durable breed was especially prized by the Seminole Indians in south Florida's swampy terrain.

Ninety-Mile Prairie: A vast area of grassland and palmetto prairie that at one time extended west from the Kissimmee River nearly to the shores of Charlotte Harbor. Parts of it still remain much as they were in the nineteenth century, although old-timers report there are more trees nowadays. And of course there were no fences, highways, canals, or encroaching subdivisions at the time of the story.

Pease River: Now known as the Peace River, this major waterway of the south Florida cattle frontier was originally called Pease Creek or the Pease (or Peas) River because of the wild peas that had grown along its banks since prehistoric times.

Punta Rassa: Located southwest of Fort Myers and adjacent to San Carlos Bay, it served as a major port for the shipment of cattle to Cuba during the late nineteenth century. Its facilities and their appearance at the time were essentially the same as described in the story. Today the ramshackle buildings and cattle pens have been replaced by high-rise condominiums.

Rocking JG: The date and the Brevard County location of this outfit are fictional, but the brand itself is real. It belonged to my uncle, Joe Gramling, who raised cattle in eastern Hillsborough County during the 1950s and 1960s.

If you enjoyed reading this book, here are some other fiction titles from Pineapple Press. To request a catalog or to place an order, write to Pineapple Press, P.O. Box 3889, Sarasota, Florida 34230, or call 1-800-PINEAPL (746-3275). Or visit our website at www.pineapplepress.com.

CRACKER WESTERNS

Bridger's Run by Jon Wilson. Tom Bridger has come to Florida in 1885 to find his long-lost uncle and a hidden treasure. It all comes down to a boxing match between Tom and the Key West Slasher. ISBN 1-56164-170-7 (hb); ISBN 1-56164-174-X (pb)

Ghosts of the Green Swamp by Lee Gramling. Saddle up your easy chair and kick back for a Cracker Western featuring that rough-and-ready but soft-hearted Florida cowboy, Tate Barkley, introduced in *Riders of the Suwannee*. ISBN 1-56164-120-0 (hb); 1-56164-126-X (pb)

Guns of the Palmetto Plains by Rick Tonyan. As the Civil War explodes over Florida, Tree Hooker dodges Union soldiers and Florida outlaws to drive cattle to feed the starving Confederacy. ISBN 1-56164-061-1 (hb); 1-56164-070-0 (pb)

Riders of the Suwannee by Lee Gramling. Tate Barkley returns to 1870s' Florida just in time to come to the aid of a young widow and her children as they fight to save their homestead from outlaws. ISBN 1-56164-046-8 (hb); 1-56164-043-3 (pb)

Thunder on the St. Johns by Lee Gramling. Riverboat gambler Chance Ramsay teams up with the family of young Josh Carpenter and the trapper's daughter Abby Macklin to combat a slew of greedy outlaws seeking to destroy the dreams of honest homesteaders. ISBN 1-56164-064-6 (hb); 1-56164-080-8 (pb)

Trail from St. Augustine by Lee Gramling. A young trapper, a crusty ex-sailor, and an indentured servant girl fleeing a cruel master join forces to cross the Florida wilderness in search of buried treasure and a new life. ISBN 1-56164-047-6 (hb); 1-56164-042-5 (pb)